A Dark and
Twisting Path

Julia Buckley

BERKLEY PRIME CRIME
New York

BERKLEY PRIME CRIME
Published by Berkley
An imprint of Penguin Random House LLC
375 Hudson Street, New York, New York 10014

ISBN: 9780425282625

First Edition: August 2018

Printed in the United States of America
1   3   5   7   9   10   8   6   4   2

Cover design by Alana Colucci

For Victoria Holt

Acknowledgments

I am grateful to the many people who made this series possible, especially Kim Lionetti and Michelle Vega, and to my public library, where I spent many hours of my childhood poring over book-flap descriptions to find the most alluring tales. Thanks to booksellers everywhere for maintaining a noble and important profession. And a final thank-you to the readers of this series who have told me that this story holds something compelling for them. We must keep telling and reading stories if our world is to retain its imagination—a crucial component of humanity.

Bestselling Books by Camilla Graham

The Lost Child (1972)
Castle of Disquiet (1973)
Snow in Eden (1974)
Winds of Treachery (1975)
They Came from Calais (1976)
In Spite of Thunder (1978)
Whispers of The Wicked (1979)
Twilight in Daventry (1980)
Stars, Hide Your Fires (1981)
The Torches Burn Bright (1982)
For the Love of Jane (1983)
River of Silence (1985)
A Fine Deceit (1987)
Fall of a Sparrow (1988)
Absent Thee From Felicity (1989)
The Thorny Path (1990)
Betraying Eve (1991)
On London Bridge (1992)
The Silver Birch (1994)
The Tide Rises (1995)
What Dreams May Come (1996)
The Villainous Smile (1998)
Gone by Midnight (1999)
Sapphire Sea (2000)
Beautiful Mankind (2001)
Frost and Fire (2002)
Savage Storm (2003)
The Pen and the Sword (2005)
The Tenth Muse (2006)
Death at Seaside (2008)
Mist of Time (2009)
He Kindly Stopped for Me (2010)

(a four year hiatus)

Bereft (2015)
The Salzburg Train (2016)
Death on the Danube (2017)
Death at Delphi (in progress)

AUTHORITIES JOIN FORCES TO
SEARCH FOR MISSING CHILD

Jake Elliott, Associated Press

NEW YORK—Authorities in Greece have joined forces with American agencies to aid in the search for Athena Lazos, the infant who was stolen from her mother, Victoria West, in early February. West had previously made headlines when she disappeared from her New York home more than a year ago. Her ex-husband, Sam West, had been a suspect in her disappearance, and for a full year the New York police and DA had waged a public war against Mr. West, painting him as a murderer before any body was found.

Sam West, who had relocated to Blue Lake, Indiana, was about to face trial for his ex-wife's murder when evidence came to light that Victoria West was still alive. Days later Victoria West was found, safe, on a yacht belonging to billionaire business tycoon Nikon Leandros Lazos, the father of Athena Lazos. Nikon Lazos is the prime suspect in the disappearance of his daughter, and authorities fear he will use his vast wealth to prevent anyone from finding little Athena, whose mother has made several distraught appeals for her return.

Despite an initial romantic relationship between Lazos and Victoria West, the latter has claimed that he held her against her will for many months, preventing her from contacting anyone in the outside world and confining her on the yacht, which served as their home. Mrs. West has made very few public statements about her time with Lazos, but in a recent interview with the New York Times, *she admitted that "Nikon Lazos has a powerful charisma that is difficult to resist, and if he enlists the aid of others to help him conceal the whereabouts of my daughter, I am quite certain he will be able to persuade those people that he is the injured party. Have no doubt, though, that he is cruel and manipulative, and that once I understood I was essentially his prisoner, I was able to see him more clearly and to realize I did not want my daughter to grow up with him. I am grateful to the people who worked so hard to find me, and I hope that they will work even harder to find and rescue my innocent child."*

As of yet, neither the police in Blue Lake—where Athena was abducted—nor the CIA, nor Interpol has indicated that they have any leads in Athena's disappearance. While they did locate the getaway car in an Indiana field, the driver, Leonard Wilson, was not with the vehicle, and it is believed that he and the child were picked up by another car. Blue Lake police detective Douglas Heller suggested that Lazos will make a mistake and police will find him soon. "Lazos should know that we are on this. We are confident that we will reunite Victoria West with her daughter," he said in a recent press conference. Heller is credited with finding Mrs. West, although he suggests that two Blue Lake women—neither of whom are members of law enforcement—were instrumental in the recovery.

As has been previously reported, Victoria West herself has offered a reward of a hundred thousand dollars to anyone who has information that leads to the discovery of Baby Athena.

Delia had come to Greece to face her demons, what-ever form they might take. She was frightened, yet also relieved, that the showdown was at hand, and that, one way or another, she would find resolution.

—From *Death at Delphi*, a work in progress

VICTORIA WEST, TRAGIC and beautiful, spoke into the camera. Her expression revealed her pain, as it had on every news broadcast on every channel for the last two months. It also conveyed her determination. In a firm yet vulnerable voice, she said, "I know that my daughter is in this country, and I know that people are being paid handsomely to keep her hidden. The authorities have assured me that Nikon, or whoever acted on his behalf, did not leave the United States with my Athena. I appeal to everyone watching to please help me find my daughter and bring her home." She paused, and I had the sense that the whole world hung on her words. "I am not the only one who has been affected by Nikon Lazos's selfish actions. My husband, Sam, suffered terribly, accused of taking my life. My friend Taylor died in her quest to find me. These are terrible, irreparable losses, and I do not wish to add my baby girl to the roster of things that cannot be reclaimed." She dabbed at her eyes, and her parents rushed forward to put their arms around her. Her lawyers, too, wore faces of the utmost concern.

My friend Allison put down her slice of pizza and turned to me. "Lena, I know she's been through a great deal, but she's *so* melodramatic. And Sam isn't her *husband*. He's *your* man."

This is why Allison is my best friend. I would never have dared to say that Victoria West hadn't gone through terrible things, nor would I have ventured to criticize her frequent press conferences. Of course she wanted her child back, as we all did. I worried about the baby that Nikon Lazos had stolen in broad daylight, and like everyone I was shocked that the police and the government agencies had been unable to locate the child. She had been taken at the end of February, and tomorrow would be the first of May. Yet, like Allison, I couldn't help but feel that Victoria had almost come to enjoy her time in front of the camera, as she had come to depend, once again, on the company and support of her ex-husband, Sam West.

Victoria stepped away from the podium, and one of her lawyers began taking questions from the crowd assembled in New York. She had flown out for the event, which had been combined with the DA's public—and extremely belated—apology to Sam West. Sam had declined to attend, and I supported his choice. Why should he take part in the pageant that Camilla now called "The Victoria West Show"?

Allison sniffed and turned the television off with her remote control. Immediately the peace of her large and sunny living room comforted me and soothed my frayed nerves. It was Monday, her day off, and she was letting me decompress at her house. "Thank you for saying that about Victoria. I have to admit I am getting a little tired of sharing Sam with her. He's trying to be noble, offering support because her therapist says she needs to feel the permanence of her former relationships. I get that. But to rent a house in Blue Lake? And it's walking distance from Sam's place. Camilla made such a face when I told her."

"Camilla's right," Allison said. "I mean, you won him fair and square. She and her lawyers can wait things out in Indianapolis if she's so convinced that Nikon is in Indiana."

"That's only one theory, of course. That he's hiding in plain sight. To me that seems like paranoia. The man had a yacht—although that's been seized temporarily. But he has so much money he could have bought another one, under someone else's name, like he did last time, and he and his daughter could be in Kamchatka by now."

"Kamchatka," Allison said appreciatively. Then, brightening, she said, "We should play Risk! Wouldn't that be fun? With Sam and John? And maybe Doug and Belinda, if they're still a thing."

"I don't know. I should visit Belinda at the library and put out some feelers. I haven't seen her since Camilla and I returned from our tour."

"Yeah, tell me more about that. Was England beautiful?"

A rush of happy memories flooded through me. "So amazing! The scenery, the landscapes of those little towns—just wonderful. Well, you saw the pictures on Facebook."

"Yes. Gorgeous!"

"I saw the village where Camilla grew up. There's a pub there with all her book covers framed on the wall. God, I took so many pictures, Allie! I could have stayed there forever."

"Did you get to make speeches and stuff?"

"Camilla always spoke first, and then when she was finished she would introduce me and talk about working with me, and then people would ask me questions. I felt very important, but that was all due to Camilla's generosity. You know how she is."

"It sounds amazing."

"And at the end of our tour we were right on the sea, and we visited her mother in her little cottage. She was delightful. So much like Camilla, but her own distinct person. She made us tea and called Camilla "pet," and I was in love with her instantly."

Allison put another slice of pizza on my plate and handed it to me where I sat lazily on her couch. I took it absently and said, "We met one of her sisters, too. Philippa. She was nice, although a bit distant. Camilla said she's always been like that, and singularly unimpressed with any of Camilla's books. Philippa is a barrister. We had lunch in London."

Allison clapped gleefully. "Listen to what you just said! Oh, Lee, this is the life you always daydreamed about. You're living it. A published book, and a house with Camilla, and a dreamy, mysterious boyfriend."

"Whom I haven't seen since I came back. He told me he'd be gone when we returned and he was sorry about it. He and his lawyer were following a lead about the baby. It's déjà vu, Allie. First he was following leads about Victoria, now they're about poor Athena. Although why that's Sam's job I cannot even imagine."

Allison shrugged. "You said he promised to use his resources on her behalf."

"Sam is supportive and kind, which are both things I love about him, but this has gone on long enough. He needs to delegate these jobs and get on with his life."

"With you," Allison said brightly.

"Yes. With me." I sounded smug, and I suppose I felt it, too.

The phone rang, and Allison sprang up to get it. She came back a moment later. "That was John. He'll be home by four. Can you stay for dinner?"

I sighed. "I love your house, and I would actually like to stay for the whole week, but I still have unpacking to do, and I want to make sure Camilla isn't doing too much too soon. Adam is more worried about that than I am, actually. That man is protective, and he can barely stand to be away from her."

"That's sweet. He must have missed her. You guys seemed to have been gone forever."

"It was so great. But I missed Blue Lake, and you and John, and Doug, and Bick's Hardware, and Schuler's ice cream . . ."

"And Sam."

"And Sam." I *still* missed Sam. I had texted him several times, asking when he would be back. He had responded briefly but passionately, telling me I could never leave again, which I thought was a bit hypocritical, and yet was satisfying to my lover's ears.

"Anyway," I said, getting up and stretching, my eyes on the alluring woods in her backyard—the reward of a corner lot that merged with a small forest preserve. "I have to go. We'll get together soon, I'm sure." I gave Allison a hug, and she walked me to the door, which stood open to admit the warm breeze.

Outside, we paused on her porch and inhaled the spring

air. Allison bent to get her mail, then frowned. "Oh boy. There's no mail in here, and it's usually delivered by now. I hope our mailman isn't getting revenge."

"Why would your mailman want revenge?" I said, almost laughing.

"Because yesterday we got a magazine that was mangled. I can't even tell John about us not getting mail today, because he already got into a fight with Eddie about that magazine." She was distressed, but she also looked sort of proud of her husband.

"Even in paradise there are problems," I said, admiring her lovely neighborhood, green and fragrant and full of nature sounds.

She brightened. "Do you hear those birds, Lena? Blue Lake has gifts for me in every season, but those birds singing might be the best of all. So many different calls, and John and I are starting to learn them. You hear that one? It's a blue jay. John says that he yells "thief," but I think it's a lonelier word. Maybe he's saying 'speak.'" She looked up at the leaves, smiling. "He's beautiful, but I only see him once in a while. He likes to stay in the tops of the trees."

"You've become a naturalist," I said, my tone accusing.

"You will, too. Join us next time we go bird-watching. It sounds boring, but it's so fun."

"Everything is fun with you," I admitted. "Enjoy your birds, and I'll call soon."

"I'm glad you're home," she said.

"I am, too."

I walked down her driveway, waving briefly to the woman who knelt in her garden directly across the street. She was dark haired and pretty, somehow reminding me of a woman from an old movie. She waved back and returned to her petunias.

I breathed deeply, soaking in the Blue Lake air. Despite my wonderful trip to England, despite the beautiful places I had seen, not one of the picturesque villages had replaced Blue Lake in my affection.

Blue Lake was my life's paradox: it represented both the worst and the best things that had ever happened to me.

I climbed into my car and drove slowly down the flower-scented lanes, eventually speeding up on Green Glass Highway, then turning down Sabre Street and making my way toward the water. I drove up the gravel road that ascended the big bluff overlooking Blue Lake, enjoying the satisfying crunch of pebbles beneath my tires. Camilla's place was at the top of the ridge. I left the car idling at the bottom of the driveway, appreciating the vista of Camilla's big house, the cloudy sky above it, and the trace of Blue Lake sparkling below.

My phone beeped; I picked it up and slid my finger over the screen. "Hello?"

"Hey, honey." It was my father. I had not seen him since I had come to Blue Lake in October, and in a rush I realized how much I missed him.

"Dad! How are you? How's Tabitha?"

"Fine, fine." He was moving something around, papers or files. He always kept his hands busy while he talked on the phone. "I haven't heard about your big trip, and I figured I'd just give you a call."

"Oh, Dad, I'm so sorry. We actually just got back, but I was going to call you, I swear!"

"I know, I know. I just got impatient."

"Dad. Now that things have calmed down here a bit— why don't you and Tabitha come out? There's a lovely guesthouse in town where you could stay, and you can have all your meals with Camilla and me. The weather is getting nice, and I can show you all my favorite places. Now we know that Sam isn't a murderer and that Victoria West is alive—you can meet him! Oh, I'm getting excited about this now! What do you say?"

"I would love to. But I don't want to get Tabitha's hopes up unless you're sure."

"I'm sure! I miss you. Let me just clear it with Camilla, and then I'll call you tonight with some calendar options."

"That sounds great, honey. Maybe Tab and I will be there in time for your birthday. We'd love to celebrate it with you."

"Me, too," I said. My eyes had grown slightly moist, and I wiped at them with one hand. I promised my father again that I would contact him that night, and I ended the call, feeling energized.

I drove up the rest of the driveway and parked against Camilla's long front porch. I got out and darted up the stairs, inhaling the scent of a nearby lilac bush.

Inside I was greeted by Camilla's German shepherds, Heathcliff and Rochester. I bent down to pat their heads. "Hey! You know, I really missed you guys. Did you miss me?"

They snuffled against me, enjoying my caresses, and I laughed. Rustling sounds came from Camilla's study, and I called, "Are you still unpacking, tour buddy?"

Adam Rayburn appeared in the doorway. His glasses were missing; Camilla told me that he had bought contact lenses. He looked handsome, like an aging James Bond. "Hello, Lena."

"Oh—hi, Adam. Are you helping Camilla unpack?"

He frowned slightly. "I was. She told me she wanted to take a walk. Without me."

I straightened, walked over, and patted his arm. "Were you hovering, Adam?"

"She says so. I just wanted to be sure she wasn't over-tiring herself. She looked rather frail when you returned from England."

Camilla didn't look frail; we had eaten heartily on our trip, and we had both gained a few pounds in the process. "Adam, she's fine."

He sighed. "I know. I can't help it. I tend to be—smothery—when I care about someone."

"It's very sweet. But you have to pull back a little. You know that Camilla is independent."

"God, yes," he said, but he was smiling a little now. We moved into Camilla's office, where Adam had clearly been helping to sort through some of her suitcases. He sat on the edge of her desk and sighed. "I've loved her for a very long time. Longer than she knows. And she only loved me back for a very short time and then she left."

I sat down, too, in my favorite purple chair. "She had to go on the tour, Adam. It's part of her job."

"I know that. It just felt—sad."

"I know exactly what you mean. I don't even know where my boyfriend is right now."

Adam gave me a surprisingly charming smile. "Perhaps you and I should start a Lonely Hearts club."

"Perhaps we should," I said, laughing.

"Perhaps you should what?" asked Camilla, walking in. She wore a pair of blue jeans and a purple sweater, along with some sturdy brown walking shoes. She clutched a small bouquet of wildflowers.

"Adam and I are going to keep each other company when our love interests wander off," I said lightly.

Camilla pursed her lips and sent a look to Adam, who lifted his chin. "Adam Rayburn, you are quite impossible," she said. Her voice was indulgent rather than angry.

"You've always liked a challenge," Adam said.

Camilla sniffed, then laughed. "Lena, my dear, Adam has asked that I not unpack any more today, since he fears it will drain me of precious energy."

"It is pretty exhausting. I gave up, too, and spent the morning flopped on Allison's couch."

"Did you have lunch?"

"Yes. She fed me pizza. I'm full as can be."

"Good, good. I gave Rhonda the day off, and Adam is taking me out for a late lunch. Will you be fine on your own?"

"Of course."

I watched, admiring, as Camilla left the room to put her flowers in water, then returned, affectionately patted Adam's cheek, and picked up her small purse from a nearby chair.

"I'm ready, dear," she said to Adam, who beamed at her. Despite his talk of her frailty, I thought Camilla had never looked better. Her silver hair had been recently cut into a shorter, bouncier style; her face had grown slightly fuller since our trip, making her look years younger; and there was an energetic spring in her step that suggested she was happy.

I smiled. "You two have fun. I will either unpack or lie on my bed with Lestrade, who has not yet fully forgiven me."

Camilla smiled. "I happen to know he was spoiled by Rhonda. Who wouldn't want to have a chef as a babysitter? I'm thinking she gave him some special meals, despite his nonhuman status."

"True," I said. "I'm sure he'll get over it soon."

Adam slid an arm around Camilla's waist. "I have reservations," he said.

"About feeding cats?" I joked.

Camilla giggled and Adam smirked, and then he led her to the door. She turned to say, "This is a rest day, Lena. We'll talk about getting back to work tomorrow, all right?"

"Yes, that's great."

I waved and they went off into the spring day.

I sighed and spun around where I stood, feeling happy. It had never ceased to amaze me that I lived in Camilla Graham's house—Camilla Graham! She, who had been my idol for more than ten years before we met. Since my arrival just about all of my dreams had come true: I had published a book with Camilla, I had traveled with her on a book tour, and I had met a man and fallen in love with him.

I strolled to Camilla's desk, where the dogs lounged and snored against the wooden legs and where the newspaper sat on her blotter. She had already read the whole thing, I was sure, while she had her early-morning coffee. The top headline was something about the world financial market, but under the fold the headline read "Lazos Continues to Evade Authorities." The world couldn't get enough of the story of Victoria West, her errant lover, and her missing baby. *Poor little Athena*, I thought. I had seen the child only once, just before she was abducted. She was a beautiful baby, with dark eyes and dark hair, and she had looked right at me, studying me with her child's gaze before she was whisked away by Victoria's driver—a man that she had thought she could trust. I had been standing nearby— spying, really—and I had not realized that I was watching a kidnapping.

I dreamed about her sometimes, the lost Athena, and in every dream I was at fault, failing to understand that she needed my help, failing to protect her from the man who led her away.

They were all looking for her now—international agencies along with American authorities. Surely it would only be a matter of time before they found Nikon Lazos? And yet the man had eluded them for a year with the missing Victoria, and we had found him only by sheer accident. This is what worried me—that he had the money and resources to stay underground indefinitely, keeping Victoria's daughter from her as a punishment for what he probably saw as her betrayal.

No matter how I felt about Victoria's relationship with Sam, my heart always went out to her when I thought of her sweet daughter.

With a sigh I left the study and climbed the stairs to enter my own beloved room—a sunny, blue and white space, brightened now by a large glass bowl of white roses, which Rhonda had put in my bedroom and Camilla's to welcome us home.

I touched the roses, still firm and lovely, and inhaled their fragrance while I studied Lestrade, who glared at me from the bed. I had interrupted his bath, and now half of the fur on his head was matted down, making him look comical. "Are you still mad at me?" I asked him. We had never been separated for more than a day since I'd gotten him as a kitten, and ever since I'd returned from England he had been distant in that special way that cats have perfected.

He turned his back on me and continued his bath.

I sat on the bed and touched the tip of his tail. "I missed

you, Lestrade. Every time I saw a little cat wandering down a lane in some pretty English village, I thought of my own little buddy in Blue Lake."

His tail twitched under my hand.

"I thought of how funny he was, and how beautiful, and how much I loved him."

He flicked his tail away from me, but some sputtering purrs escaped him. I took this as encouragement and scratched his fuzzy ears. "You know you're my special boy," I said.

The purring grew louder, but he continued to face away from me, giving me a view of what Allison called "your gross cat's big butt."

"Lestrade, my sweet pea, you can't stay mad at me. Who will keep me company at night?"

My cat licked a paw with delicate attention, then turned to honor me with a glimpse of his face, which was slightly less angry now. It held, in fact, some benevolence—a king granting amnesty.

"You're my little bundle of fur," I said, pouncing on him and kissing his ears while my hand mussed the soft fuzz of his belly.

Lestrade turned on the full purr machine and let me assault him with love and apology.

I lay back on my pillows and Lestrade walked up to join me. "Want to take a nap with me?" I asked him.

He did. As he snuggled against me, I grabbed my phone from a side table and typed a text message to Sam. *Where are you? So lonely.*

I set the phone down, only to have it beep almost instantly. *Back in the morning. No luck on Athena clue. Already kissing you in my dreams.*

That was an acceptable response, and, despite Sam's wild-goose chase, I was smiling as I drifted off to sleep, though it wasn't Sam's eyes I saw behind my closed lids, but the dark and watchful eyes of Athena Lazos, trusting me to know she was in danger.

2

In ancient days, the Oracle at Delphi told people their fates, and Delia wondered, as she contemplated the ruined temple, if she would have been brave enough to find out her own.

—From *Death at Delphi*

I WAS SITTING on Camilla's front porch the next morning, enjoying the warmth of the first May sun. Camilla was on the phone with one of her relatives in England; she had told me we could start our work around noon.

May. I sipped my tea and contemplated the fact that I had now lived in Blue Lake for nearly seven months. It was a place I never would have visited on my own, much less have chosen as a residence. Now, though, it was home. I leaned against a banister of the porch and stretched out my legs on the top step, a vantage point from which I could see the road leading partway down the bluff. I couldn't see Sam's house, but I hoped I might see Sam himself walking up the rocky path. His text had said he'd be back sometime this morning, and I was getting restless.

The sound of a car crunching over the gravel made me sit up, alert. Camilla's dogs appeared at the screen door, their ears up straight. "Who is it, guys?" I asked them.

A moment later a Blue Lake police car pulled up to the driveway and parked next to Camilla's—an honorary spot for Doug Heller, our friend and protector.

Doug emerged from the driver's side, looking handsome as always, his blond hair mussed slightly by the wind. He wore a blue oxford shirt that said "Blue Lake PD" on the pocket and a pair of khaki pants. Another man, wearing a similar getup, got out on the passenger side. He looked somehow familiar to me, but as far as I knew I had never seen him before.

Doug came around the car and approached the steps. "Hey, Lena," he said.

"Hey, Doug. You want to come in for some breakfast?"

"No, I'm on duty. I wanted to introduce you to Clifford Blake. He's joined us from Saint Louis, and he's going to be my partner."

"Your partner?" I said, automatically shaking the hand that Clifford Blake offered me. He was tall and thin with a stubbly face and brown hair going gray at the temples. I couldn't picture Doug with a partner; Doug worked alone. Doug was like a superhero in Blue Lake. Then again, I had rarely seen Doug off duty. Maybe he needed some relief. "Nice to meet you," I said.

Clifford Blake offered me a charming smile. "You, too. I didn't know the girls were so pretty in this town."

Doug jabbed him in the ribs. "You're barking up the wrong tree, Cliff. This is the one and only Lena London."

Blake's smile disappeared as he studied my face. "I've heard about you, Lena. I followed the Sam West case very carefully, and Doug told me how instrumental you were in sparing him from prison."

I wasn't sure what I thought of Clifford Blake. Something about him had my inner voice murmuring, but not in a way that I could hear. "So is that why you came to work in this little town?"

Doug sent me a surprised look. "We're lucky to get Cliff; he's a decorated officer with an impeccable record. He happens to have family in Indiana, so it was a good time for him to make a move."

Cliff nodded. "Sometimes obligation dictates geography."

"I would invite you in to meet Camilla, but she's on the phone with her English relatives right now," I said.

Doug shook his head. "We've got things to do, but I just wanted you to meet Cliff. Next time you call it just might be him showing up instead of me. Allows us to be in lots of places at once."

I nodded, then changed the subject. "Doug, I wanted to tell you that my dad is coming to town. Camilla and I worked it out last night, and he'll be here in a couple of days. I want you to meet him."

"Sure," Doug said, shading his eyes from the sun. "Be happy to."

"And also he's going to be throwing me a birthday party. You're invited, of course." And then, because Clifford Blake was standing right there, I said, "You, too, Cliff."

"Why, thanks," Cliff said with his easy smile. "How nice to have a social invitation on my first day in town. I'm thinking if Doug's at the party, I'll probably be on duty, but I appreciate the thought."

The radio in Doug's car squawked. Doug pointed. "Can you check that out, Cliff?"

Cliff nodded and jogged back to the car, climbing in to hear the message.

Doug moved closer to me and lowered his voice. "Two things: one, there's a rumor going around that there are still reporters in town, pretending to be something else. Presumably they're still looking for anything they can get on Sam West, Victoria West, Nikon Lazos, whatever. So don't confide in any strangers."

"Got it."

"Also, can you do me a favor? I know you just got back and everything, and I want to hear all about the trip. But— I wonder if you could talk to Belinda for me?"

"Belinda? Why?"

He shook his head, looking bemused. "I don't know. You thought there was something there, right? With me and her."

"Of course. You're dating, aren't you?"

He sighed and kicked at the bottom stair. "It feels like history is repeating itself, you know? I thought things were heating up with you and me, and you ended up with Sam. Then I thought things were going well with Belinda, and suddenly they aren't. I don't know if I said something, or did something, or she just lost interest, you know?"

I stared at Doug Heller's handsome face and found it hard to believe that Belinda had lost interest. She had been downright smitten with Doug. "Listen, this is none of my business . . ."

"Except that I'm asking you to make it your business. Just get a sense of things, okay? And then tell me what you think. See what you can find out."

"You really like her, right?"

He sighed, impatient. "Yes. I really like her. Will you do this for me, Lena?"

Camilla had told me, months earlier, that she saw Doug's and my relationship as similar to a brother-and-sister bond. I had come to see it that way, as well. "Yes, of course. You would do it for me, so I will gladly do it for you. Give me a day or two and I'll find a reason to meet with her. Okay?"

His face creased into a smile. "And put in a good word for me while you're at it."

"Will do." I grinned at him.

My phone buzzed in my pocket and I pulled it out quickly, hoping it was Sam. I held up a finger, asking Doug to wait. "Hello?"

"Lena." It was Allison's voice, but it lacked all the bright happiness that it usually held. A chill ran down my spine.

"Allison? What's wrong?"

"Lena, you have to come here now."

"Come to your house? Why? What happened?" Doug stiffened, on the alert.

"Something terrible. I don't know what to do. It's terrible. I—you have to come."

"Allison. Doug is right here. Should I have him come, too?"

"Oh God," she whispered. Now I was really afraid. "I don't know. No. Just come."

"Allison?"

Now Doug was leaning forward, trying to take the phone. I moved backward. "Allison? Tell me what happened. Are you okay?"

"Lena, just come here. I need you. I won't touch anything until you get here." She ended the call.

I turned to Doug. Cliff had emerged from the car and was loping back.

I took a deep breath to calm my suddenly jittery nerves. "That was Allison. I have to get going."

Doug was wearing his cop face. "What's going on?"

"I don't know. Nothing. I mean, something. I'll let you know."

He narrowed his eyes at me, but Cliff arrived and tapped him on the shoulder. "Paula said, come pick up your messages at the office. And the mayor called."

He shrugged and pointed at me. "Keep in touch."

"I will." They went back to their car, and I ran inside to get my keys.

Camilla appeared in the kitchen doorway. "What's happening?" she asked.

"It's Allison—there's an emergency at her place."

"Go," she said. "Call later to fill me in."

I waved and ran down the steps. Doug and Cliff's vehicle had already driven off, shooting up gravel in its wake. I paused a moment, watching the retreating car. It was strange seeing Doug with a partner. And why did Doug suddenly need more help in little Blue Lake?

I shook my head and ran to my car. Allison was my priority now.

 · 3 ·

*The body lay at the foot of the hill, and for a moment,
in the disconcerting timelessness of the temple ruins,
Delia had the odd thought that someone had left a
sacrifice for Apollo.*

Then the thought faded, and she was left contemplating a dead man.

—From *Death at Delphi*

I DON'T REMEMBER the drive to Allison's place—just the
way I lurched into her driveway and stumbled out of the
car, half-fearful that she would be murdered by some unknown assailant. This was not rational, since she had called
me herself, but her tone had left me chilled and frightened.
I ran to the door, which was open, and Allison stood inside,
trembling.

"What's going on? You scared me," I said.

Allison grabbed my hand and squeezed it tightly. She
was dressed for work in pink hospital scrubs, her hair tied
neatly back, her St. Andrew's ID clipped to her pocket: her
smiling face over the name "Allison Branch, Emergency."

"I don't know what to do. Remember I said John had a
fight? A fight with the mailman. His name is Eddie Stack."

"Okay, slow down. What about Eddie? Did he come
back?"

She nodded, and two fat tears rolled down her face. "He's in my backyard."

"What? What do you mean?"

"He's dead."

"Allison! Call the police! Call an ambulance. Here, give me your phone."

Her hand tightened on mine. "He's dead, and I think someone killed him. Lena, everyone will think it was John!"

"What? Of course they won't. John's an *accountant*," I said nonsensically. "He's a pacifist. Why would anyone—"

"Because they had a fight yesterday, about the mail. Eddie started yelling, so John yelled, too. People came out of their houses to see what was happening. They saw, and now Eddie is dead in *our yard*."

"Allison. Take a deep breath. Do it! Okay, now think. First of all, are you sure he's dead?"

"I'm a nurse," she said. "I went out and examined him."

"And how do you know he didn't die of natural causes?"

She turned pale. "I didn't turn him over, but there's blood on the leaves around him. He—there's blood." She grabbed my wrist and led me to her living room window, where I saw nothing at all. I turned to her.

"Allie? There's no one out there."

She pointed. "Look beyond my backyard, to where the forest preserve begins."

I peered out and saw, in the shadow of the tall trees, something on the ground. Some*one*.

"How did you find him?"

She sighed. "I like to take a walk in the woods before I go to work. It centers me. This morning I went for a walk, and there he was. I couldn't believe—I just—this seems like a bad dream. Now I know how you and Sam feel."

I put a calming hand on her arm. "Okay. Now think about this. Doug Heller is the one who will investigate this. Doug is one of John's best friends. Doug *hated* Sam, and even for Sam, Doug was willing to suspend his dislike to look at the case rationally. And in January, when a body appeared near Sam's house, Doug didn't immediately assume that Sam was a murderer. He won't make a crazy assumption, Allison. Not to mention—when did this body appear? John's at work, right?"

"Yes. But I don't know how long Eddie has been lying there. I just happened to walk that way . . ."

"We need to call Doug," I said, looking into her eyes. "Unless you're telling me you think your husband actually did this."

Her eyes grew huge with indignation. "Of course not! I just—oh God, I know you're right. I might not—I haven't been thinking straight."

I gave her a big hug. "You've had a terrible shock."

"And now I wonder—I think I've been really irrational, Lena—I wonder if I could have made a mistake. Maybe he's not dead. But I—I can't bring myself—"

"I'll go," I said, acting brave for Allison but feeling cowardly. I had seen my share of dead bodies in Blue Lake, and a part of me was really having trouble believing I was about to see another one. I let go of her hand and made my way to the sliding glass door, out into the yard, and toward the shaded wood beyond. As I approached, serenaded by birds and caressed by a lighthearted breeze that did not seem to acknowledge the seriousness of death, I saw that the man under the tree was lying disturbingly still, and I felt certain that Allison had been right. Still, I moved cautiously toward him. He was almost entirely facedown, but just slightly tilted to one side. I peered at him long enough to see the stiffness of his features and then, feeling sick, I pulled back, ready to retreat, but something underneath him glinted in a beam of sun. I leaned back in, looking at the small part of his chest that was visible. There, protruding from his shirt, was a silver handle embedded with blue twinkling gems.

I stood quickly and staggered backward, not sure whether I wanted to retch or cry.

There was no mistaking the little knifelike object. It was a letter opener; a sterling silver replica of the sword that King Arthur pulled from a stone. I had learned that Sam liked Arthurian legend, and I had purchased the little knife for him on Valentine's Day.

Now Sam's distinctive letter opener was stuck in the chest of a dead man. Once again, Sam's name would be linked to a murder. Once more he would be in the headlines, where he had never wanted to be again. I wondered briefly what would happen if I put my hands on the hilt and pulled the knife out. Was it all right to tamper with evidence to protect an innocent man?

Allison called me from the door. "Lena? I did what you said. I called Doug. This is all just a bad dream, right?"

"A nightmare." I spared one last glance at the body on the ground, then walked toward her without looking back, depressed and worried. The poor man remained behind me, frozen, just the way that someone had left him there. Despite my feelings of sympathy for the dead man, I couldn't stop thinking about the living.

How had my present to Sam ended up in Eddie Stack's chest? What could he possibly say to Doug to avoid suspicion?

It couldn't be happening—and yet it was.

* * *

DOUG AND CLIFF arrived five minutes later, looking official. They marched into Allison's backyard and came back in almost immediately. "Did you touch anything?" Cliff asked, his face stern.

Allison lifted her chin. "I touched him to find out if he was in distress. If he needed help. I'm pretty sure he was already dead. I mean, I could be wrong, but—"

"He's been dead for hours," Doug said, covering her hand with his own and sending her a reassuring glance. It was generous of him, I thought, to care about her feelings in a moment when all his thoughts had to be focused on crime.

Allison looked relieved. "Do you have a minute to talk alone?" she said to Doug.

Cliff looked surprised; he scratched at some stubble on his jaw, then pointed to the back door. "I'll call the team from out there," he said.

Doug nodded, then turned to Allison, his brows raised. "What's up?"

"That's Eddie Stack. Our mailman. *Your* mailman." Doug lived just a block away from Allison and John.

"Oh wow. Eddie! I thought I recognized the face. Poor guy."

"The thing is—he and John had a fight yesterday."

Doug's face remained impassive. "What about?"

"He was always giving us the mail in terrible condition." Allison looked near tears. "Mangled magazines and envelopes that were torn. John confronted him, and Eddie got defensive and started yelling, so John yelled back. All the neighbors saw."

"So?" Doug asked.

"So—he's right behind our house, in our yard. I don't want you to think John had anything to do with it."

"I don't," Doug said. "But thanks for telling me. I'll make a note of it. Maybe a lot of customers had a problem with Eddie."

Now the tears were flowing out of Allison's eyes. "Other than that, he was an okay guy. We didn't even get mail today, though. That must mean—I—oh, God. I'm sorry this happened to him. But John—this wasn't—"

Doug pulled her into a quick hug. "You're dressed for work. Are you able to call in for today? Maybe call John to come and be with you?"

She nodded tearfully and went to find her phone. Doug turned to me. His blond hair was once again slightly mussed from being outside in the gentle wind. "You okay?" he asked.

"Not exactly. We need to talk, before Cliff comes back in."

He almost looked amused. "Are you going to tell me that your boyfriend also had a fight with Eddie Stack?"

"No. I'm going to tell you that my boyfriend's knife is in his chest."

Doug was normally unflappable, but now his mouth dropped open. "What?"

"I gave Sam a letter opener last month. A replica of Arthur's sword; it's silver with blue stones in the handle. I saw part of it—sticking out of that guy out there."

"What—do you have any idea—?"

"No. Sam didn't say that he lost it or anything, but then again I haven't seen him since I got back from England. It's a moot point, because he's not even in town, but—"

Doug's eyes flicked away from me.

"What?" I said. "What do you know?"

His eyes flicked back. "Sam's in town. I saw him this morning."

This news hurt more than the knowledge that my gift to Sam had killed someone. Sam was in Blue Lake and hadn't told me so. Hadn't called, hadn't texted. Almost as if he hadn't wanted me to know . . . "Are you sure it was Sam?"

"I talked to him," Doug said. "He was at the gas station, filling up his car. He said he was headed home to wash up. He'd had a long ride."

I tried to be casual. "When was this?"

He shrugged. "It's eleven now, so maybe around eight?"

"Huh." Some terrible emotion was boiling in me, but I hadn't yet determined what it was.

Doug nodded. "Call him up. Tell him to head out here. I'll want to ask him some questions."

We'll both want to ask him some questions.

I looked out the window and briefly made eye contact with Cliff Blake, who was on the phone. His expression was something between sympathetic and suspicious, and for some reason it made me feel guilty.

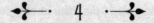

4

*The man who had led Delia to the temple reappeared
when she was ready to leave; he seemed to sense her
every need, and his eyes, bright and blue even in the
sun, seemed to her exactly the way Apollo's eyes must
have looked when he appeared in mortal form.*

— From *Death at Delphi*

I DIALED SAM'S home number on my cell and waited while
it rang, and until he answered I hadn't believed that Doug
was right. "Sam West."

"Sam," I said. "You *are* home. Doug told me he saw you."

"Lena." His tone was warm, as always. "God, it's good
to hear your voice."

"*Sam*. I had to hear from *Doug* that you were back in
town. Because he happened to run into you at the *gas station*."

"Babe, don't be mad. I went straight from there to bed,
for a couple hours of shut-eye, and then I took a shower. I
didn't want to see you with bloodshot eyes and sour clothes.
We debriefed in Indianapolis, and then I drove straight
through to get back. I was wiped out."

"Still. You could have texted me."

"Lena, if only you knew how much I wanted to see you.
What dangerous speeds I was doing on the expressway just

so I could get back to my own house and then walk up the bluff to meet my beautiful girl."

"Don't call me a girl."

"Sorry." His voice held the hint of a smile. "How long are you going to be mad at me?"

I sighed. "I don't have the luxury of being mad at you. Get to Allison's house right now."

"What?"

"Sam. I don't know how to say this. There's another dead body."

"What?"

"It's in the woods behind Allison's house. It's her mailman—a guy named Eddie Stack."

"I don't know him," said Sam, clearly mystified. "Why do I need to come to Allison's?"

"Because Doug is here, and he has questions."

A pause. "I'm still not clear, Lena. Why does this have to involve me—or you—in any way? What kind of questions does Doug need to ask me?"

I sighed. "He needs to ask you how your Arthurian letter opener ended up in the man's chest."

A longer pause this time, and again I heard the tactless birds singing their merry songs. "That is a good question," Sam finally said. "I'll be there in ten minutes."

WHEN HE ARRIVED I was waiting at the foot of Allison's driveway. He parked his car across the street, which was now clogged with emergency vehicles, and jogged toward me. I flung myself into his arms. "I'm very mad at you," I said, clinging to him. He did smell nice, as though he had just emerged from the shower—not that I had doubted his story.

"I know. I'm sorry. I'll make it up to you." He kissed my hair, and then my cheek, and then my lips. After that I felt significantly less angry. Sam smiled, seeing this. "Let's get this out of the way so we can go home," he said.

We moved up the driveway. Allison's neighbors—the ones who weren't very welcoming—were out in their yards, staring at Allison's place and talking amongst themselves. The dark-haired gardening woman from across the street was standing in her front yard and clutching her gardening gloves against her chest. Next door to her a middle-aged couple peered over their hedge, and on Allison's side of the street several neighbors had gathered, their faces concerned as they contemplated the police cars and emergency vehicles. One man in particular wore a highly scandalized expression as he stared at the yellow police tape that an officer had just finished wrapping around Allison's property. The man walked up to Sam and me. "What's going on here?" he asked.

"We're not sure," I said. It was part lie and part truth.

He narrowed his eyes. He was tall and thin, with a white mustache and some sparse white hair. "I know you. Aren't you Sam West?" he said to Sam. "I've seen your picture in the papers."

Sam nodded briefly. He hated being accosted by strangers.

"Does this have something to do with you?" the man asked, jutting out his chin.

I stepped in front of Sam. "In case you don't recall from the newspapers, Sam wasn't guilty of anything. It was everyone else who was guilty of believing things that weren't true." I stared him down and he moved away, shaking his head.

Sam's mouth curled up on one side. "You don't have to be my bodyguard, Lena."

"Yes, I do. You've dealt with enough nonsense from these people."

He slung an arm around me. "You would think. Let's go face the authorities." We walked in the house, where Allison was being comforted by a newly arrived John, and Doug was deep in conversation with someone from the coroner's office.

Cliff Blake approached us. "You can't go beyond this point. Allison and John will be staying in a hotel after they answer our questions, and you'll need to leave after Doug talks to you."

I nodded. "Cliff, this is Sam West." Cliff turned stiffly toward Sam, as though just noticing him there, and said, "Mr. West." They shook hands. I thought Cliff's eyes held suspicion now, too, but maybe that was just the way his face looked. "Sam, this is Cliff Blake. He's Doug's new partner, from Saint Louis."

Sam said, "Lena tells me I have once again been involved in a crime against my will."

Cliff looked solemn. "I hope that is not true. Do you possess a silver letter opener with blue stones in the handle, Mr. West?"

Sam sighed. "You can call me Sam. Yes, I do. Lena gave it to me last month."

Doug had finished his conversation, and now he approached us. "Sam," he said.

Sam held up a hand in greeting. "Do you have a photograph of the knife in question?"

"It's not a knife," I said.

Doug tapped his phone a few times and then held a close-up photo of the thing that I presumed was still in the dead man's chest. "Here it is."

"It looks a lot like mine," Sam said.

Doug scratched his head with his phone. "Might you have dropped it somewhere, maybe in a place where someone else could have picked it up?"

"I wish I could say yes," Sam said. He sent me a helpless look, then switched his attention back to Doug and Cliff. "But it was a gift from Lena which I valued highly, so I kept it in a place of honor on the desk in my office. You've seen my desk."

Yes, Doug and I had seen it. It was a big, beautiful antique in a lovely room with a view of the woods on the bluff. The weapon had been safely inside Sam's house.

"This must be a replica," I said. "It's not one of a kind. Someone else could have ordered one."

Doug nodded. "We'll need you to go home and see if yours is there. If not, we have some more questions to ask."

Sam shook his head. "I don't have to go home. Lena mentioned it on the phone, and I went to check in my office. I kept it in a special holder. The holder is still there, but the letter opener is gone."

Doug and Cliff exchanged a glance—one of those inscrutable cop things. Then Cliff looked at us. "You have security? An alarm? A camera?"

Sam brightened slightly. "I did install security, very soon after I got to Blue Lake. I got some—interesting calls and letters back then."

I squeezed his arm.

Cliff persisted. "Any sign that the alarm went off while you were out of town?"

Sam looked regretful. "I can usually check in with the system on my phone, but it malfunctioned about two days ago. To be honest, I didn't think much of it. Foolishly I believed that life had quieted down here and I was looking at nothing more than a dead battery. I might have been wrong about that."

"What about cameras?" Doug asked.

"We can check those. As far as I know they were working."

"I'll come later today, if that's all right," Doug said.

"Of course."

Doug puffed out his cheeks and consulted something on the screen of his phone before he said, "And just for the record—you didn't know Eddie Stack?"

"Is that the guy who's dead? I've never heard the name. I assume I wouldn't recognize the face, but it's a small town, so I can't guarantee that one. He's not our mail carrier—Lena and I both have a very chatty fellow named Harvey who delivers our mail." I nodded. This was true. "I'm sorry to hear about this Eddie's death. I'm even sorrier that someone wanted to link me to it."

Cliff was studying Sam closely. Was he assessing the veracity of Sam's words?

It looked as though they were finished questioning him for the time being, so I said, "In any case, I'm going to invite Sam to Graham House for now. He can get away from the madness here, and we can talk about it in a safe and friendly environment."

"Fine," Doug said. "We'll be in touch."

"Don't tell me," Sam said with a hint of bitterness. "I shouldn't leave town, right?"

Doug's eyes wouldn't meet ours. "It was my understanding that you just got back."

The saddest part of the whole exchange was the sudden look of resignation on Sam's face.

* * *

ALLISON AND JOHN joined us on the front porch. John touched my arm, his expression concerned. "Lena, I want to take Allie away from all this, but I have to go back in to work for a couple of hours. I have to make a presentation today."

Allison looked proud. "John is next in line to be promoted, and this presentation is important for him."

John sent me a beseeching look. "I know this is terrible timing, but—"

"She can come back to Graham House with us. Camilla needs to hear what happened, and she'll want to comfort Sam and Allison with some of Rhonda's cooking. No problem—take as long as you need at work."

"Thanks, Lena," John said. "Sam, I'll see you later."

"John." Sam nodded.

John hugged his wife, then jogged off to his car. Allison sighed.

"You're still madly in love, aren't you?" I asked her.

"Yup. And thanks for saying I can come over. Shall we all ride together?"

Sam pointed. "I have my car. I'll meet you there."

"Don't stop off at your house yet," I said. "If someone's been lurking around there, I don't want you going in alone."

Sam looked amused, but he nodded. "All right, Lena." He kissed my forehead gently and a few butterflies began to fly around in my midsection. "My protector."

"Yes, I am. And apparently you need one."

He gave me a wry look. "Meet you there." He turned and headed for his car. Allison's rude neighbor was staring at Sam while pretending to trim his perfectly trimmed hedges. I glared at him, but he refused to notice me.

"What's going on?" Allison said. "Why are you looking at Mr. Hendricks like you want to murder him?"

"I'll tell you in the car," I said, grabbing her hand. For a moment I felt transported back to high school, when Allison and I had experienced many things hand in hand: walking through the doors of our first all-school dance; braving our first haunted house; moving on trembling legs toward the dreaded gym class balance beam.

I squeezed her hand more tightly, and she sent me a grateful glance. "I'm glad you're my friend, and I'm even gladder that you moved to Blue Lake," she said. "I can't imagine dealing with this without you."

"I'm glad I'm here, too," I said. As we walked down the cobbled street to my car, I looked back at Allison's house and saw Cliff's face in the doorway, watching us as we left the scene of the crime.

CAMILLA'S FACE WAS grim as we sat at her kitchen table and told her, over coffee and apple pie, about the body at Allison's, the tiny sword, and the probable break-in at Sam's.

Her eyes were compassionate. "I'm so sorry, my dear. Lena and I know just how you feel, since we have seen a body in our backyard, as well. I can tell you that the memory doesn't leave, but it does become bearable."

It was true; I could sometimes look at that particular stretch of sand at the foot of the bluff and not remember the dead man who had lain there.

"I just can't imagine who would kill Eddie, of all people," Allison said. "I mean, he could be obnoxious sometimes, and gossipy, and he was really a terrible mailman . . ." Her eyes filled with tears and Sam patted her arm. "But he was just a regular person. We all have our flaws. And sometimes

Eddie was really nice. When I was sick once he gave me some cough drops out of his bag because I didn't have the energy to go to Bick's and get my own. It was sweet. Oh, what his poor wife must be going through. They just married last year, did you know? One of those later-in-life marriages."

This silenced us all for a moment.

I poured some more coffee into her cup, then Sam's. "We need to put this out of our minds for a while," I said.

Sam clearly wasn't ready to do that. "We seem to be overlooking the very obvious fact that this is the third murder this town has seen within a few months. Would it be so very unlikely to assume that this death could have something to do with one or both of the previous ones?"

Camilla frowned down at her plate, but said nothing.

Allison, wide-eyed, said, "But what possible link could there be? There were two separate murderers for two separate murders. There were individual motives. This seems like—something new."

"I'm not so sure," Sam said, his brow wrinkled with thought.

"What bothers me even more than the dead body is Sam's knife at the scene," Camilla said. "That speaks of intention. Of premeditation."

"Doug will get to the bottom of this," I said. "For sure. We need to let him and Cliff go after this psycho and put him in jail, and then we'll all feel safer and happier."

This did not affect the generally morose mood around the table, so I changed the subject. "Listen, everyone. My dad is coming to town."

Allison brightened, and Sam came out of his reverie.

"Your dad? Oh my gosh, I haven't seen him in years!" Allison cried. "When is he coming?"

"In a couple of days. He wants to see you, Allie, and he

wants to meet Camilla and Sam. And he's going to throw a birthday party for me. That hasn't happened since I was a girl, but I don't care. It will be nice to have something happy to celebrate. Between poor Baby Athena and this murder, Blue Lake is under a terrible dark cloud. I want to see the sun again."

Sam studied me in surprise. "When is your birthday? I never even asked. I didn't miss it, did I?"

"No. It's on May thirteenth. I share a birthday with Daphne du Maurier—one of Camilla's heroes."

Camilla clapped. "Oh, Lena, that is perfect!! You have Gothic fiction in your blood."

"I take it this Daphne woman is a writer?" Sam asked.

I stared at him. "She wrote *Rebecca*? *The House on the Strand*? *Jamaica Inn*?"

Sam and Allison exchanged a wry glance, and Sam said, "Clearly I am a philistine. But I am very glad I haven't missed your special day."

I slid my hand into his. "I know your birthday, because you have a Wikipedia entry that I happened to read when I first met you and became obsessed with your story."

"You and the whole world."

I turned to Allison and Camilla. "Sam is a summer boy. He was born on June twenty-first."

"I share a birthday with a famous writer, too," Sam said, sipping his coffee.

"Oh? Who?"

"Sartre." Sam grinned at me.

Allison looked disappointed. "You mean that French guy that always wrote about life being meaningless and stuff?"

"Yes. Lena and I discussed Sartre on the day I met her." Sam's eyes held affection and something more.

"We did," I agreed. "And at the time I thought Sam was just about the rudest man I had ever met."

Camilla laughed. "You two were destined to fall in love. It's as predictable as the novels that we read."

The doorbell rang just as Sam's phone buzzed on the table.

Allison said, "That will be John," and she got up to answer the door. I studied Sam's face as he glanced at his phone; his brow furrowed, and then he looked at me and said, "I have to take this."

He slipped out of the room and walked down Camilla's long hallway.

I pursed my lips at Camilla. "Ten bucks says that's Victoria on the phone. I know she calls him all the time."

Camilla's eyes were sympathetic. "He wants to be supportive. He's in a difficult position."

"I know." I sighed noisily. "He's always in a difficult position."

She leaned in. "Listen. Before Allison comes back, we need to talk about this dead man."

I shook my head. "Doug is on it. For all we know, it's some drug deal gone wrong."

"A drug deal in which a random criminal decided to frame Sam West?"

That silenced me.

Camilla's expression was hard. "We know who this is, don't we, Lena?"

"What?" I could feel my eyes bulging with surprise. Allison was coming back, chatting with her husband, so I leaned in and hissed, "You think this is *Nikon*?"

Then Allison and John were with us, and Allison was talking brightly. She was visibly happier than when she had left her house and the terrible scene there. "Camilla, thank you so much for hosting me. Let me help to clear away some of this coffee stuff." She gathered some empty mugs and brought them to the sink.

"You and John are welcome to spend the night," Camilla said. "Sometimes a bit of distance helps."

Allison returned to the table and gave her a spontaneous hug. "You are so sweet! But John's mom and dad have a house here in town that they rent out to summer visitors. It's not open for the season yet, so we're welcome to use it whenever. We'll stay there until things are . . . resolved."

John put a protective arm around her. "It will be nice, like a little vacation. We haven't had one of those since our honeymoon."

"You must come again," Camilla said, rising and extending her hand. "I still get to see Allison at our monthly knitting group, but John, I rarely get to talk to you."

"We'll be back for sure," John said, clasping her hand in his. "When things settle down."

Camilla looked at me. "Poor Lena. We've been telling her that since she got here last October. *As soon as things settle down.* And then something else happens."

Allison's smile dimmed. "I guess that's what life is. Just one thing after another."

I forced a smile of my own. "Good things, too, Allie. Put the bad out of your mind. Go have a nice dinner with your husband and stay in your resort home. That doesn't sound terrible at all."

Allison's expression was vulnerable; she was still in her pink nurse's scrubs, and her blonde ponytail was looking a bit scruffy. "No, I guess not," she said.

John kissed the top of his wife's head and said, "Thanks again, Camilla and Lena. We'll see you soon."

We went to the door with them and waved as they moved

down the steps. Then I turned back to Camilla. "Why do you think it's Nikon?"

Sam appeared at the end of the hallway; he reached us in a few long strides. "Why do you think *what* is Nikon?"

Camilla waved us back into her office, where we took our familiar spots: Camilla behind her desk, I in my purple chair, and Sam in a green armchair that he pulled over from its place under the window. Camilla folded her hands and looked at us both in turn. "Sam, you must have noticed the particular personality of this crime. It's almost— petulant. Taking something of yours and shoving it into a dead body. Yes, I am assuming the body was already dead, because I saw that letter opener when Lena bought it for you; it would be a very small and imprecise murder weapon. Look at the crime, either way: it's horrible, it's cruel, but it's also petty."

"And his motive would be . . . ?"

"In his mind, you've taken his wife away."

Sam's eyes widened. "How could anyone, even an insane man, think that I did anything to Nikon? I am the *victim* and always have been."

I shook my head. "Camilla's right. That's not how he thinks. Sam, the man tried once before to frame you for murder! Why? Because he didn't want anyone looking for Victoria. He traveled here, planted evidence, went to a whole lot of trouble—just to make sure you were put behind bars."

"Doesn't this look similar?" Camilla said. "Nikon is at large. He could be anywhere, including here. He could also have someone in Blue Lake who is willing to do his bidding. He has a whole lot of money."

Sam shook his head. "I guess I was harboring an illusion, despite Vic's sufferings. I just didn't think he was my problem anymore."

"Maybe he's not," I said. "Maybe it isn't him." But now that Camilla had said it out loud, I couldn't imagine anyone but Nikon Leandros Lazos being behind this murder.

"It's him," said Camilla, studying her desk blotter with a thoughtful expression.

Sam thought about it for a moment. "Why the mailman, then? Why that poor guy?"

"Maybe he just needed a body to put the knife in," I said, horrifying myself.

"You need to tell Doug," Camilla said. "He may already be thinking these thoughts, but we need to compare notes."

I thought about Doug Heller and the crime scene and Cliff Blake. "Cliff seemed suspicious," I said. "I don't know why. At first he seemed very sympathetic about your whole story."

"I'm used to suspicion," Sam said. "I've learned not to take it personally."

I opened my mouth to protest, but he held up a hand. "I have to go back to my place and look at my security footage. Will you come along?"

I looked at Camilla, who waved me on. "Go. We're not going to get any writing done while we're worrying over this new death. Let me know what you find."

Sam and I stood, and Camilla said, "Do tell Doug our suspicions. And if Cliff is there—well, just tell Doug. We don't know Cliff. He'll have to earn his way into our inner circle."

I nodded my agreement. Cliff was a cop, but he was new to Blue Lake, and he didn't understand the dynamic of this town, or the histories of the people within it.

I had never been one to ostracize, but I felt it very strongly now as I accompanied Sam down the stairs: Cliff Blake was an outsider, and I didn't trust him.

* * *

AT SAM'S HOUSE, in his office lit by Tiffany lamps, we sat on chairs behind his desk to watch him pull up security footage.

Doug pointed at the computer. "Let's see what you've got," he said, taking a sip of some coffee that Sam had provided. Sam nodded, but did nothing.

"Sam?" I said.

He turned to us with some reluctance. "Before we view this, I need to fill you in. There's been an added complication."

"What?" Doug asked, leaning forward. He set his coffee down on the desk and put his hands on his knees.

"I just checked my messages, which I admit I haven't done for a day or so. Lena and I usually text, and she's the only one I expected to hear from . . ."

"What is it, Sam?" I said.

With a sigh he reached out and pressed a button on his answering machine. We heard an unfamiliar voice say, "Sam West? My name is Eddie Stack." I gasped, but Doug held up a silencing hand. "I live in Pine Haven, and I followed all the stuff about you in the news. There's something you should know. Something about that little missing girl. And I'll be happy to tell you, but I need money. Meet me at the park on Wentworth Street on Monday night, around eight o'clock. You can tell me how much it's worth to get that guy once and for all."

That was the end. Doug whistled. Sam shook his head. "You can check the machine, or my message service, or whatever you check. I didn't listen to this until about half an hour ago."

"How do we know it's Eddie?" I said.

"It's Eddie. Or someone doing a really good impression," Doug said. "He had a distinctive lisp."

"So he's saying—what? He knew something about Athena?" I asked, shocked. "What can that mean? Could he have intercepted a letter, or . . . ?"

Doug said, "Let's not get ahead of ourselves. This is valuable. He makes a direct reference to Nikon Lazos."

"He didn't say the name," Sam said. "He just said 'that guy.'"

"But it has to be Nikon. He mentioned the baby," I said.

Doug poked Sam's blotter with a pencil. "Sam's right. We can't assume. But now the case is different. He knew something. He wanted money for that something. And now he's dead; it could be that someone wanted to silence him."

We thought about that for a moment in the dark, quiet room. Then Doug stood up and looked into Sam's forested backyard. He was in thinking mode. "No one can know about this. Lena? Don't even tell Allison, or Camilla. Not anyone. This is privileged information."

"Okay," I said, reluctant. How could I keep it from Camilla? "But then you don't tell Cliff." I said it without thinking, and both men turned sharply toward me.

"What?" Doug said. "Why not?"

"I don't know. He's—new. An outsider."

"He's a *cop*," Doug said. "A good cop. And he's helping with this investigation. You're starting to get paranoid, Lena."

My eyes moved to Sam, who wore a quizzical expression. "Fine. I guess I am. Phone messages from dead men tend to freak me out."

Doug nodded. "Meanwhile, we need to watch the tapes."

Despite the fact that Doug vouched for Cliff, I was glad he had given him the evening off, so it was just the three of us who watched the fast-forwarded footage of Sam's front stoop. It was not exciting viewing.

"You were gone how long?" Doug asked before taking a sip of his coffee. I wondered if he needed it to stay awake. He'd been working a lot of hours, it seemed to me.

"Eight days," Sam said. "This is footage from the first day, which was April twenty-second."

"Looks like this one is a no-go," Doug said. "And does that front porch light stay on all the time?"

"It's on a timer. It switches on at seven o'clock every night and goes off at six in the morning."

"Okay. So if someone shows up, we'll see them."

We finished April 22nd and started on April 23rd.

"Shakespeare's birthday," I said with a smile.

Both men looked at me as though I had sprouted antlers. I pointed at the date. "The twenty-third. It was the day he was born and also the day he died."

"Fascinating," Doug said, although his face said otherwise.

The 23rd had nothing to offer except a wayward raccoon who tried to open Sam's mailbox and a deer who briefly wandered past the camera.

Sam clicked on the file for the 24th, and Doug started telling us a story about a deer who made it into the lobby of the police station.

"What the hell?" Sam interrupted. He paused the image and leaned forward. "Do you see that?"

At first I saw nothing but Sam's front stoop. The time stamp was two a.m. Then, at the edge of the screen, I saw a figure in black. "Oh my God," I said.

Doug leaned in, his eyes bright with cop excitement. "Can you slow it down?"

"I think so. Hang on." Sam fiddled with some things on

his keyboard and then we watched the video in slow motion as a figure in black—complete with a hood that was weirdly sinister despite the fact that it was connected to a coat—stood in front of his door. For a moment the person—man? woman? it was hard to tell, except that they seemed fit—blocked the view of the door, and in the next moment the door swung open and the person went inside.

"I'll be damned," said Sam.

"This is unbelievable." Doug was staring hard at the screen, but the door closed. "Do you have other angles? Other rooms?"

"I do. I'm guessing we should check this room, right? That's where the knife was."

"Set it up." Doug put his coffee cup on the desk, then leaned back and stared at the ceiling. "What is happening in this town?" he said.

"Yeah," I said, trying to be lighten the mood. "Before Sam came here, all you had to worry about was that deer in the lobby."

Neither man bothered to laugh at this. They were both tense, alert, waiting to see what Sam's computer would reveal. Finally Sam said, "Okay. Here's the twenty-fourth, and this is the office camera. I'll forward to two o'clock."

On the tape the room was dark, but there was a security light outside the window that illuminated just enough for us to see movement. Thirty seconds in we saw a door open and a figure move into the room. He or she held a small flashlight, which they used to study the room in a disturbingly methodical way. They looked at the desk last.

"Can you make out a face?" Doug asked.

"No. I can barely see the figure. Maybe your guys can have a go at this footage? Enlarge it or something?"

"I'll see what we can do."

"They're at the desk now, can you see?"

"I can." Doug's mouth was a thin line. He took exception to crime, but he especially took exception to a frame-up, and Sam had been the victim of more than one.

The figure was opening drawers in the desk. They seemed to take something out of one of them; a flash of white paper in the darkness. "That's weird," Sam said. "I don't know what—there! He's touching the holder where I kept the knife. Do you see it? It's like he's contemplating whether or not to take it—and he just did! Did you see that little flash of metal?"

"Yes! I saw it!" I yelled. "Doug, look!"

"I see it. Sam, I'm sorry. You know I didn't suspect you, but it probably looked as though I did."

Sam froze the image on the screen and made a note about its location for Doug's tech people. "I get it," Sam said. "Whoever's doing this is trying to make it inevitable that you would suspect me. It's not your fault."

"This is a puzzle," Doug said, tilting back his chair. "This is not Eddie Stack in the picture. The person isn't the right height. Stack was quite tall, and this visitor is only medium height."

"Could it be Nikon?" I asked.

He shook his head. "Lazos is tall, too. So far we've got nothing linking this to Nikon. Even the message is vague."

"Except for the mention of the child. He used her name, didn't he?"

Sam shook his head. "He said 'that little missing girl.' There are plenty of missing girls in the world."

Doug nodded. "It's almost like he was purposely unclear—as though he feared someone was listening. We've got to take some steps before we work on that message. We have to find out who our little ninja visitor is, for starters. I can try to fingerprint the doorknobs, but your hand has been on all of them . . ."

"No." Sam pointed at the screen with a pencil. "He's wearing gloves," he said. "See? Look where he's clutching the knife."

"Shoot," Doug said. "I might need to share this info with our FBI friends."

"Oh yeah, because they've been really helpful in the past," I said with some bitterness.

Sam smiled at me. He was always surprised by my loyalty; I wondered why.

"The timing of this is strange," Doug said, not registering my response. He pointed a finger at Sam. "This break-in happened more than a week ago. But Stack was only killed this morning. And the only reason he didn't meet with you was apparently that you didn't get his message." He paused, thinking.

Sam took up the idea. "So this break-in was about something else. Right? And they took some souvenirs, but maybe didn't know they'd use them on Stack. The break-in and the murder have to be related because we have that letter opener linking them. But what if the letter opener was just an afterthought?"

I raised my hand. "If Eddie Stack knew something, and they knew he knew, they would have killed him last week. They couldn't have known that he called you, or they would have killed him to prevent your meeting, right? So he must have given himself away somehow. He must have done something to draw their attention. And maybe that's when they decided to use their surveillance of Sam to their advantage."

"But why the surveillance?" Sam asked, still mystified.

"Camilla had it pegged. Only Nikon is this weird," I told him.

Doug sighed. "Nikon? I'm going to need some more coffee. I have a whole bunch of questions for you, Sam."

I suddenly felt exhausted. "You won't need me for those, right? Sam, I think I'm going to head back to Camilla's."

Doug stood up, looking weary. "Not alone, you're not. Sam, if you'll make another pot of coffee, I'll walk Lena home."

"Deal. But I get to walk her to the door," Sam said, which meant he wanted to kiss me. Doug inclined his head and bent over the computer, typing some notes into his phone.

Sam followed me to the front entrance. "Sorry about all this. I was hoping to snuggle up with you tonight."

"First we'll focus on catching your mortal enemy. But yes, snuggling sounds good." I put my arms around his neck and kissed his warm mouth. "It's hard to believe you were once notorious," I said softly.

"Don't kid yourself. I'm still notorious to a whole lot of people. I am living proof that you don't need any evidence to decide you hate a person."

"Shush. You have to think positively. Look at all the friends you have and how determined we are to help you."

"You're right." He smoothed my hair off my forehead.

"Hey. What did Victoria want?"

He sighed. "You guessed, huh? I didn't want to tell you because I thought you'd be upset."

"I was, sort of. But I get why she wants to talk to you."

"She wants consolation. Not just about poor little Athena, but about me. She wants to know there are no hard feelings. That I believe her when she says she knew nothing about Nikon's attempts to frame me."

"And do you?"

"Yes. He seems just crazy enough to have done it all on his own."

"So could this—ninja visitor have anything to do with Athena?"

He shook his head. "I just can't imagine how. Or why. But the reality is that Eddie Stack is dead. A man I never met, but who connected himself to me. None of it makes sense."

"It will. Doug likes puzzles. He'll sort this out."

"Or maybe you and Camilla will. My mystery-solving friends."

Doug came around the corner, zipping up his jacket. "Finish making out and then let's go, Lena."

I grinned and gave Sam one last kiss, which was meant to be quick, but Sam's mouth lingered on mine, longingly.

Doug opened the door with an impatient sound, Sam let me go, and I went out into the chilly evening with Doug Heller, fearful that a hooded figure in black might be standing in the trees, watching our departure.

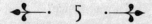

5

> *As they hiked the southern slopes of Mount Parnassus, they encountered a young woman from the hostel who introduced herself as Ariadne, and for the rest of the day she dogged their steps, determined to become one of their party. Delia couldn't help but feel suspicious of her enthusiasm—what would make her want to spend time with strangers?*
>
> —From *Death at Delphi*

ON MAY 2ND I awoke to sunbeams that illuminated my room and warmed the fur of the cat who slept beside me. Something buzzed on my bedside table; I checked my phone and found I had two texts: one from Sam West (*Good morning. I love you*), and one from Doug Heller (*Looking into our ninja visitor. Don't forget Belinda*).

I sighed and stretched, then texted back to Sam (*I love you, too. Don't worry, we'll figure this out*) and Doug (*I'm making arrangements now*) and then Belinda: *Can we meet sometime today? Maybe during your lunch hour?*

I set the phone aside and slid out of bed. Even the carpet was warm, and it gave me a good feeling. I showered and dressed in record time so that I could be at breakfast with Camilla, who was an early riser. As I descended the creaking stairs, clad in blue jean shorts and a Blue Lake sweatshirt, I pondered the latest act of malice against Sam West.

Why wouldn't the world just leave him alone? What had he ever done to anyone? Why had Eddie Stack selected Sam, even if he had information about the missing Athena? Why didn't he just call the police?

But I knew the answer to that question. He had wanted money, and Sam was wealthy. Had Eddie's greed cost him his life?

Camilla sat at her dining room table, drinking coffee and crunching cinnamon toast. She greeted me warmly, although she seemed distracted. I had told her the night before what we had found on Sam's recording, but not about Eddie Stack's call. I felt traitorous not sharing that information with her, but Doug had insisted.

"Lena," she said, pouring coffee for me. "I'm thinking about Sam's night visitor." I nodded and took a piece of cinnamon toast from the tray in the middle of the table.

"Yes. It's hard to think of anything else."

"Doesn't this merely confirm my idea that somehow Nikon Lazos is behind this?"

I shrugged. "I don't know. Doug doesn't want to rule anything out. We did mention Nikon to him last night. Unfortunately, Sam is such a public figure that any number of people could have formed grudges."

"Yes, *grudges*. But who is so vengeful that they would steal a knife from Sam's house in order to plunge it into the chest of another man? How is anyone that angry?" Her face was distressed.

"It's terrible to contemplate. I've been refusing to do it."

She sighed. "I won't make you think about the crime, then. But we do need to think about the perpetrator."

"But I can't imagine how Nikon could blame anything on Sam. Nikon is the one who ran off with Sam's wife, not vice versa. Nikon is the one who essentially held her prisoner. And Nikon is the one who stole a baby. How is any of this Sam's fault? I can't imagine that Nikon is involved, and yet there is the reality of—"

Her expression was quizzical. "Yes?"

I studied her noble face. "This is ridiculous. I'm not doing it."

"What are you talking about, Lena?"

"Doug told me to keep something to myself. To not tell anyone, even you. As if you would somehow blab it around town! You have to know, because you and I work things out together."

"You're telling me there's more? Beyond the night visitor?"

I sighed. "Sam had a message on his phone from Eddie Stack."

For the first time since I'd known her, Camilla Graham looked truly surprised—almost dumbfounded. "From the dead mailman?"

"Yes." I told her about the call, relaying it to the best of my memory.

"Oh my," she said. There was a gleam in her eye, despite her generally solemn demeanor, that suggested a part of her was enjoying this information. Camilla was, at heart, a solver of mysteries.

Now she looked thoughtful. "But he didn't mention Nikon by name? Or the child? So Doug doesn't want us jumping to conclusions. All right. Who else would be a likely candidate for framing Sam? Possibility one is that some random person built up anger against Sam after reading about him in the paper for a year. When Sam was exonerated, that person needed for him to be guilty, so he created another crime."

I nodded slowly, not convinced. "Sounds strange, but real life is stranger than fiction. What's another option?"

She tapped her fingers on the tablecloth, brows furrowed. "Just a couple of months ago Doug caught another murderer in this town. Perhaps someone is angry about that. And linked as that story was to Sam West, this person who is angry about the arrest—a family member, perhaps?—might have somehow conflated that with Sam."

"Yes . . . but that seems weirdly similar to theory one."

"But not quite, because it's linked to a particular person. Theory three is that this is a motive unrelated to anything we know about. But that's not likely, is it? Because after a year in the spotlight, it's unlikely that Sam West has any secrets. And Eddie Stack mentioned a child. Would we be leaping to conclusions if we decided that the phone call and the ninja visitor were related?"

I pointed at her. "It seems hugely coincidental that one man would call Sam, demanding money for information, and that a separate person, for separate reasons, stole a knife out of his house and plunged it into the very same man who had left the message. But as Doug pointed out, the timing is wrong. Eddie was killed a week after the ninja invasion. So perhaps there was a different motive for the break-in, and Eddie managed to get himself in trouble later. He got careless, perhaps. Somehow let them see that he had suspicions."

She put her hands on the sides of her face. "I need to wrap my head around this, preferably while taking my walk around the lake. I'll do that later." She stood up. "Let me just take some dishes to the kitchen. Rhonda won't be here until noon today. Now perhaps we can distract ourselves with some work?"

"Of course. I'll meet you in the office." Camilla walked out of the room, and I briefly consulted my phone. Belinda was indeed available for lunch. "Camilla, if it's all right

I'll be going out for lunch. I asked Belinda if she would dine with me."

Camilla reappeared in the doorway. "Oh, Belinda! We haven't seen much of her lately."

"No. That's partly why I want to talk to her—to find out if something is going on."

"Fine, fine. I'll tell Rhonda that it's just Adam and me for lunch. He likes to come here on his way to Wheat Grass each day."

"Great. I'll give you lovebirds a chance to be alone. And if you ever need me to just vacate the premises, you can let me know."

Camilla smiled. "We're not twenty-five years old, but thank you. Adam is very fond of you, you know. You remind him of his daughter."

"He has a daughter?"

"And a son. Unfortunately they both live far away—one on the West Coast, one on the East. So they rarely see each other, which is a regret for him. He has toyed with the idea of moving one place or another, but he fears he would relocate and then his gypsy children would just decide to wander again. Besides, you know the effect of Blue Lake . . ."

I did. It was the sort of place one couldn't imagine leaving.

"He should invite them over more often. Make up an occasion."

"I'll tell him that." She smiled. "See you in a minute. Bring your notes."

WE MET, AS we always did, at Camilla's desk. She sat behind it in her customary spot, and I sat in a plump purple armchair that had become my special seat. We worked in the middle, looking at proofs, considering notes, sharing ideas. It was our established way of collaborating.

Today we were looking over the final pages of Camilla's novel *Death on the Danube*. It would hit the shelves in just under two months, and we needed to be sure everything was perfect.

"You and I found many of the same typos," Camilla said. "The comma error on page forty-nine was particularly glaring."

"Yes. And I found another one last night—look at page two hundred fifty-three. On line twelve, the word 'bridge' is repeated, and then there are no final quotation marks."

Camilla frowned, looking at the error. "Goodness—let's be sure we jot that down for the proofreader." She made some notes on the page in her elegant handwriting, then looked up at me.

"I'll mail these out today. But the big question is: what's our next project? I'd like to hear your ideas."

"Mine?" I stared at her for a moment. "You don't have something in mind?"

She shrugged. "Oh, ideas are always floating in there. But you must have some, too."

"I do, I always do, but—well, let me think." My pulse had increased suddenly, and I tried to calm myself while I considered her question. "Well—you always start with a place, don't you? A setting?"

"Often I do, yes. Did you have a setting in mind?"

"Just the other day I was thinking that even though so many terrible things happened in the last year, and even though Victoria went through a great deal in the Greek islands—I did extensive research about Greece, and looked at many images. I sort of fell in love with the place, independent of Victoria's dilemma."

"Greece is beautiful. I've set a book there, as you recall."

"Yes! But it was set on Corfu, and I was thinking more about Delphi. The place of the oracle, with such antiquity and solemnity. It would be a great backdrop for a mystery."

"I agree!"

"We could call it *Death at Delphi*."

Her eyes glittered with interest. "You have been thinking about this."

"A little, yes."

She took out a file folder and set it in front of her. She wrote "Death at Delphi" on the file tab, then set down her pen. "We'll keep our preliminary notes in here. Sound good?"

"Camilla—yes—if you're sure—"

She touched my hand. "Oh, your sweet little face. You take such joy in everything. It's really beginning to rub off on me, I must tell you."

"I'm just excited!"

"Yes. I am, as well. Now, let's jot down some ideas. Who is our heroine, and what brings her to Delphi?"

BY THE TIME I left Graham House for my lunch with Belinda, Camilla and I had accumulated three pages of notes for our new project, and we were both pleased with our progress and with our expanding idea. Camilla and I had agreed, for the sake of our sanity, to try to put the whole Nikon thing out of our minds for the present. We would reconvene to discuss it after we'd both spent some time focusing on other things. The theory, she assured me, was that by relaxing and thinking other thoughts, we would allow our minds to come to a solution, or at least a hypothesis, in an unconscious, non-stressed state. I had agreed; I was happy, on this sunny day, to leave it all behind me for a while. Doug and Cliff were on it.

I was still glowing when I got to the Blue Lake Public Library, an ivy-covered building located about a mile north of Camilla's house. The parking lot was surprisingly crowded, but I found a spot near the fire door and walked back through the lot to the entrance.

Someone had erected an archway over the main doors, filled with springlike artificial flowers and greenery. It looked almost real, and it was quite lovely. Attached to this arbor were various books that were meant to appear as though they had sprouted from the leaves—paperbacks, hardbacks, graphic novels, children's books. Someone had put a lot of work into it, and it had a powerful effect on those strolling in. At the base of the arbor was a sign that said, "Welcome to the Secret Garden."

I scanned the room and saw only an unfamiliar woman checking out books for a family at the main counter. I walked toward her, waiting until the three little children and their mother had claimed all the items they were borrowing. "Hi. I'm looking for Belinda?"

"Oh, sure. Is she expecting you?" she said, studying me with a surprising amount of interest.

"Yes. I'm stealing her away for lunch. Are you new here?"

She stuck out her hand. "Yes—I started last month. I'm Darla." She had dark hair and blue eyes, and she wore black-rimmed glasses that looked attractive on her. She was perhaps in her early forties.

"Oh—nice to meet you, Darla. I'm Lena."

"Oh wow, I thought so!! I recognized you from the newspaper. I've been catching up with some back issues. I mean, I'm new in town, but even in Wisconsin we had heard of Sam West!"

She smiled, but I didn't smile back. "Yes," I said. I could barely grind out the word.

Her smile faded. "Oh, don't think I'm one of those psycho stalker types. I had to study Sam West because he was the topic of my final paper in my graduate class last year. I was researching the way that public perception influences legal proceedings."

"Ah," I said. I still didn't want to talk about it.

"I was defending Mr. West," she tried, her expression hopeful. "I think it's just terrible, the way he was treated."

I saw Belinda coming from her back room, and I waved. "Oh, here's my lunch companion," I said.

"It was nice meeting you, Lena. You're even prettier than your pictures. Does Sam ever come in here?" she asked, still with a hopeful expression.

"No, not really," I said. I sounded unfriendly, but I couldn't help it. When would people just leave Sam alone? Why did they treat him as some kind of celebrity?

She was undeterred. "Well, I know you'll see him. Tell him I'd love for him to read my paper sometime. It exonerates him in a way that might surprise you. And him. I got an A on it."

I forced a smile. "That's great, Darla. I'll be sure to mention that to him."

"Thanks!" Her smile was bright with hero worship.

"Nice meeting you," I lied, and moved toward Belinda, who looked as lovely as ever in a pale yellow spring dress and a white cardigan sweater. The pastels brought out the golden color of her hair, and she sported a new pair of glasses that made her look attractive in an intelligent way.

"Hey, pal," I said to Belinda. "Long time, no see."

Her pale brows shot up. "Has it been that long? Well, it's good that we're meeting, because I have been compiling little bits of information."

"Ever on the job," I said, giving her a quick hug.

"It's true. Where are we going for lunch? I'm craving a Caesar salad with lots of grilled chicken."

"Wheat Grass?"

"Sounds perfect. Let me just tell Darla." She moved to the desk and spoke to the clerk in a low voice, but Darla's eyes kept darting back to me.

We went outside, and I offered to drive. As we tucked into my car, I said, "What's up with Darla?"

Belinda giggled. "She's just enthusiastic. She had terrific references, and a degree in library science. Now she's working on a law degree, as well. A very ambitious person, and she does a good job. Is this the first time you've seen her? She's been here a month."

"I guess I haven't been to the library in a while, but I still expected to see you. Where have you been hiding out?"

"Nowhere. Just working a lot. Diving into research. I have some stuff for you . . ."

"Have you been spending time with Doug?" I asked, turning on the ignition.

"Now and then. Not so much lately. We're both busy."

"That's not what he tells me," I said, keeping my voice light.

She turned stiffly in her seat. "Oh God. Is this some kind of love intervention?"

I sent her a regretful smile. "Doug asked me to talk to you. He really likes you, Belinda. And he feels—forlorn."

"Forlorn?" She thought about this word for a while. "I don't know. I think he'll bounce back nicely."

Now I was confused. "I thought you had a huge crush on him. You called him Inspector Wonderful before you even met him, and then you two seemed to be going strong."

"Yes." She sighed. "It was beautiful, while it lasted."

"Belinda, come on. We're friends, aren't we? You can tell me."

She stared out the front window, her blonde hair glinting in the sun. "It was really great, until I started to feel like he was still thinking a lot about someone else."

"You mean a former girlfriend? Granted, I think Doug has a few of those, but nobody that I've ever—"

"You're going to make me say this, and then I'm going to feel weird. Okay: it was *you*, Lena. I had the feeling he was still hung up on *you*."

"I—why? Doug and I talked it over and agreed that whatever little five-minute attraction we had was in the past. I love Sam, and Doug knows it. Besides, we're like brother and sister."

She looked uncertain. "I don't know. Every conversation we had, it reminded him of something you said, something you did. That's not normal, is it?"

"Do you have a brother?"

"Two of them."

"Do their names come up a lot when you're talking?"

She shrugged. "Sometimes."

We drove for a while in silence. When we got to Wheat Grass, I turned to her and said, "I won't bother you about this anymore except to say: Give Doug another chance. Tell him he can lay off on all the Lena stories and focus a little more on building some Belinda memories. He'll be happy to do it."

She looked at her hands. "I miss him," she almost whispered.

"He misses you. So much so that he interrupted an investigation to ask me to talk with you. Okay?"

"I'll think about it."

I pulled up next to the entrance. "That's all I ask. Would you run in and snag us a table by the window, if you can? I'll try to find a spot."

She did as I said, and I parked quickly and pulled out my phone, then sent Doug a text:

Talked to Belinda—she says she misses you. Told me that she felt you were pining for someone else, namely me. I told her this was not true, and that she should give you another chance. Time to bowl her over with a romantic gesture.

Pleased with my efforts, I tucked away my phone, locked up my car, and went to join my friend for lunch.

Belinda had found us a seat near the south window, where the sun shone on a vase of the roses that Adam always had fresh on his tables. Today's flowers were pale pink, a pastel as delicate as the color of Belinda's dress. "I've missed seeing you," I said as I sat down. A waiter appeared instantly, and I ordered an iced tea. Belinda wanted lemon water.

"Me, too," she said. "I've been working on our file, just as background. I have some good stuff to show you."

"The London File?" I said, grinning at her. She had called it this when we first met, saying that it sounded like the name of one of Camilla's novels.

"Yes. Some articles and pictures relating to Nikon Lazos. I'm not sure how helpful they might be, but you can look."

"I will. Anything to help. I know Victoria is going crazy,

and I feel terrible for her. If there's anything you can look into—to help find the baby. I know that sounds impossible, but any little clue at all would be helpful." I wanted to tell her about Sam, the knife, the phone call—but I had already broken my promise with Camilla. If Doug wanted Belinda to know, he would have to tell her.

"Of course. I'm working on it a bit every day."

"I wonder—if there's something else I can ask you for." This had been on my mind, but I didn't really have Sam's permission to discuss it. He had confided in me, over the winter, that before his family died they had contacted him about some "good news" that his mother had received in a letter. They wanted to talk to him about it in person, but they had died before Sam could learn what it was. It had remained a mystery for almost thirteen years.

"Sure." Her green eyes grew brighter behind her glasses. Belinda genuinely loved research, and new projects got her excited.

"The thing is—Sam told me something a few months ago that I'm not at liberty to discuss, at least not yet. It had to do with his family. I don't know if you are aware, but Sam's family—"

"Died in a plane crash," she said, her eyes sympathetic. "I know. I came across that information while I was working on the London File. Poor Sam. When I think about what he's been through. First being orphaned, and losing his sibling when he was just a teenager, or what—twenty years old? And then all this stuff with Victoria, and more than a year of persecution. I don't know how he managed not to jump out a window."

"I know. Anyway, I can't go into it right now, but I wonder—if you could just start some general research about his family—mom, dad, sister. I doubt you'd find that much, but whatever. Just as a sort of background file. That way, if he ever did want to research this particular thing, you would have some material for him."

"That's mysterious! But yes, of course. Articles about the crash will be easy to find, so I'll use them as a starting point and work my way backward."

"Thank you. And just so you know—this is confidential. Between you and me."

"Of course." The waiter appeared with our drinks and took our orders. Belinda sipped her tea and said, "I saw something on the news about a murder. Another murder in this tiny town. I don't suppose you know anything about that?"

I sighed. "I know more than I want to. You've met my friend Allison?"

"Yes—at Camilla's party for Sam, last winter."

"It was in her backyard. Her mailman, as a matter of fact."

"Someone killed a mailman?" she asked, her face blank.

"Yes. It's hard to believe. Not just the victim, who seems kind of random, but the number of murders. I feel like I've cursed Blue Lake. Someone was murdered the day I got here, and people have been getting killed ever since."

Belinda nodded. "That is a weird coincidence, but that's what coincidence *means*. A random intersection. Nothing to worry over."

"You would think." I toyed with the napkin on my place mat.

"Something else is going on? What do you know?"

"Nothing yet. Let's just say it seems to involve Sam once

again, just when the poor guy was starting to feel free of all the public scrutiny."

"They didn't mention him on the news."

"Good." I thought about this. "I think that will make someone out there really angry."

"Why?"

I sent her an apologetic glance. "I probably can't talk about it—not yet. But soon I'll give you the whole sordid story."

"Okay." She sent me a mischievous glance. "Or maybe I'll get it from Doug."

"I have a feeling he'll be showing up at your door sometime soon."

"And I have a feeling you texted him while I got our table."

"We both have good instincts," I joked, clinking my glass against hers.

She sighed and leaned back against her chair. "I do like him so much, Lena."

"I know. And he likes you. *Believe* me. He reminded me about ten times to talk to you."

A little smile played at the edges of her lips. "Yeah?"

"Just know that he's going to be pretty busy. There's a lot of weird stuff happening."

She leaned forward, interested. The waiter appeared with her salad and my sandwich, and we paused while he set them on the table. "Thanks," Belinda said, and then leaned in again. "Does this have anything to do with all that stuff that happened in the winter? The Victoria West stuff?"

"I don't know. I—it looks that way. I do know that whoever is involved is crazy."

"Oh my." She forked up some of her salad and then

looked at her watch. "Shoot. I'm probably going to be a little late. I'd better call Darla."

She made a quick call to the library, talking in low tones. "Thanks, Dar," she said.

I rolled my eyes at her, and she laughed. "Darla's great. She works hard, and she basically showed up out of nowhere just when we needed her. I'm not sure why she applied in Blue Lake when she has all this big-city experience, but she was really eager to get this job."

I thought of Doug's warning about disguised reporters, embedding themselves into Blue Lake daily life. "Listen, Belinda—I don't want Darla to know about the London File. Or anything about Sam or Doug or Victoria. Nothing, okay?"

Her eyes widened. "I wouldn't anyway, but why not? She's also a good research librarian."

"She's an outsider. I know I'm officially an outsider, too, but—I just don't trust them right now."

She nodded. "Understood. Everyone's a little paranoid these days, and with good reason. First Camilla's house is exposed as some kind of drug tunnel, and then—well—the murders."

"And don't forget what the press did to Sam and me not too long ago. I learned my lesson: I trust no one."

"I will be discreet. Now I'm going to talk about my food. This salad is amazingly good. How's your sandwich?"

"Great. Adam really found his calling. He chooses the best of everything, including his chefs."

She leaned forward. "Are things getting serious between him and Camilla?"

"I think so. But I don't know how much Camilla feels like changing. I mean, I suppose she could end up marrying Adam, but I can't imagine her leaving the house, or changing her lifestyle, or altering anything. Maybe that's just my selfish view."

"Plus, no offense to Adam, but Camilla Rayburn is not as cool a name as Camilla Graham."

I stared; I had not thought of this. "No. She *has* to remain Camilla Graham!"

"Just as you have to remain Lena London. 'Lena London West' sounds like a location in England."

My face grew hot. "Well, I don't think that's a danger. I mean, we've never talked about—things are still in the early stages."

Belinda grinned. "Okay." She took her last bite of salad and said, "Mmmm, that was good. And now you have to drive me back to work before I get fired."

"They wouldn't dare fire you. You're one of a kind."

"Thank you, Lena," Belinda said. She seemed genuinely flattered.

We paid our bill and left a nice tip for our waiter, then made our way out of the restaurant. A bearded man in a booth by the entrance seemed to be staring at us. I suppose it wasn't unusual for a man to stare at women, although it was rude. There was something in his expression, though, that made me nervous, and when I made direct eye contact with him, he didn't flinch or look away.

In the parking lot I said, "Did you know that man who was looking at us? The man with the beard?"

"Hmmm? Sorry, I didn't notice anyone. Maybe he just thought we were cute."

I didn't think so. His expression had bordered on hostile, and there had been something vaguely familiar about him.

When we left the parking lot, Belinda's mood seemed to have lifted, while mine was descending into paranoia.

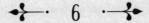

6

Delia had never realized the depth of her feeling for her parents until she traveled far away from them. Now everything reminded her of something her mother had done, something her father had said. It was painful to discover this deep love from such a distance, especially because she had no idea when she could return.

—From *Death at Delphi*

THE FOLLOWING MORNING I skipped down the stairs. My father was coming today; the visit was long overdue, and I was suddenly overwhelmed with a feeling of homesickness. I went into the kitchen to get coffee and found an envelope on the table with just the word "Lena" on the front. It wasn't Camilla's handwriting. Intrigued, I picked it up, opened it, and pulled out a sheet of thick cream-colored stationery that I recognized. At the top it said "Sam West, Investment Counselor," and at the bottom was Sam's contact information. It was spare and elegant—typical of something Sam would use. Scrawled across the middle of the paper, in black ink, was the message "Hello, Sweetheart! I have a surprise for you!"

I stared at it. Why would Sam leave me a cryptic note when all he had to do was text me? And why would he put it on his professional stationery? Sam had never called me "sweetheart." The whole thing was odd.

I moved into the hall and peered into Camilla's office, where I found her behind her desk, drinking a cup of tea. "Camilla? Where did this note come from?"

She looked up. "Oh, you found it? Good. It was sitting on the front steps this morning when I got the paper."

"It's very strange," I said. I walked into the room and handed it to her. Her smile disappeared and her brows creased.

"Sam didn't send this," she said. "Call him."

She gestured to the phone on her desk; I picked it up and dialed Sam's number. "Sam West," he said. Even in a stressful situation I was always able to appreciate the low and sexy timbre of Sam's voice.

"Sam."

"What's wrong?"

"I got a note from you, on your stationery. Did you—"

"No, I didn't send anything. It's on my stationery? The stuff from my desk? The ninja took something out of my desk, remember? Lena, call Doug right now."

"Okay." I hung up and dialed Doug Heller, who said he would be right over. Sam came over, too, and half an hour later the four of us studied the letter.

Doug was grim. "We can fingerprint it, but we got nothing from Sam's house. The ninja wore gloves; the letter writer might have worn them, too. My concern is that they've brought Lena into this. Why? Is this meant as a threat?"

I sighed, my eyes spiked with tears. "I don't know what's going on, but I do know my dad is getting here in an hour, and I don't want him to know anything about this. So we will all pretend that everything is fine."

Sam and Doug exchanged a glance, then nodded. "Okay,

yeah," Doug said. "You just enjoy the time with your dad." He had sealed the note in an evidence bag. "But if you get any more of these, don't touch them. Okay? Just leave them alone, and I'll get them to the lab."

Doug left soon afterward, warning us to be vigilant and promising that patrol cars would pass Graham House throughout the day. "I'll canvas the area, see if anyone saw someone delivering your note," he said.

Sam spoke briefly with Camilla and me, but he wore a determined expression that told me he was going to want to investigate some things on his own. Sam, like me, needed to take action to feel that he was in control. He pulled me against him in an almost savage hug, then left with a promise that he'd return later to meet my father.

When everyone had left, I tried to put the letter out of my mind. I looked out the window and focused on Blue Lake, breathing deeply. In the back of my mind, though, there was a small voice, mocking me: "Hello, Sweetheart!" What did it mean? Why was it addressed to me? Was it as sinister as it seemed, or would we find it was all a big misunderstanding?

But of course we wouldn't find that, because it wasn't a random note on random stationery; it was stationery stolen from Sam West. I stared harder at the lake, then closed my eyes and concentrated only on breathing in and breathing out.

An hour later I paced back and forth in the driveway of Graham House. Heathcliff and Rochester seemed to share my excitement and occasionally milled past, nearly tripping me with their big bodies. "Settle down, boys," I said, but I could barely calm myself, much less the spirited dogs.

The day was not quite as sunny as the one before, but occasional beams of sun made it through the layered clouds and warmed the gravel under my feet. When I had first come out a light drizzle was falling, but that had gone away, and the weather seemed to be contemplating its next move.

I walked to the edge of the driveway and squinted down the road to see the edge of Sam West's drive. I halfway hoped to see him there, since he had said he would be returning. I saw nothing, no one, and I started pacing back toward the porch. Then I heard the car. It came up the bluff at a sedate pace, and I moved to the porch, calling the dogs to safety on the steps. We stood there and watched as the gray rental car pulled up parallel to the house and a driver leaped out to get luggage out of the back hatch. Soon after that my father emerged, his gray familiar head bent over his wallet. Tabitha, his wife, climbed out gingerly, adjusting her blouse over her blue jeans. She made eye contact with me first, and I waved. "Lena!" she called, and then my father looked up. His warm brown eyes were just the same, and full of love when he jogged around the car and opened up his arms.

I dove into them and hugged him tightly. He smelled like spearmint and Magno soap. The latter was something my mother had once gotten him for Christmas and that he had continued to buy as his signature scent: "Dad," I said. "I've missed you so much."

He kissed my hair and stepped back to look at me. "You are just beautiful. I guess this little town agrees with you, despite all the drama. From what we've seen, it's a scenic place."

Tabitha approached then, and I hugged her, too. "You look great," she said.

"You, too, Tabitha. You two must have found the Fountain of Youth in Florida."

She giggled. "You're so funny, Lena." Tabitha continued to labor under the delusion that I was hilarious, which I accepted since it was flattering.

I clapped my hands. "I want to show you guys everything! But first you have to sit down, have something to eat or drink. I know Camilla has put together a little spread for you in there. And of course you have to meet her, and some other people. These insistent creatures at our feet are Heathcliff and Rochester. They're the guardians of the house, but also my walking friends. We've been through some stuff together."

Tabitha bent to scratch Heathcliff while my father patted Rochester on his big head. "They're gorgeous," Tabitha enthused.

"Come on up. There are people inside who want to say hello."

My father paid his driver; I grabbed a couple of their bags, and he and Tabitha each picked up one. We moved up the stairs and into the hallway, where Camilla stood, smiling at us. "Mr. London. How nice to meet you," she said, holding out her hand.

My father ignored it and gave her a hug. This was typical of him, and Camilla looked only briefly surprised before she laughed. "Oh my. All of the Londons are affectionate."

"We are. And you can call me Eric," my father said. "This is my wife, Tabitha."

Tabitha held out her hand and shook Camilla's, and the women exchanged some pleasantries. Adam wandered in, holding a bottle of champagne. "Hello, hello," he said.

Camilla touched his arm. "Adam Rayburn, this is Lena's father, Eric London, and his wife, Tabitha London."

"Lovely to meet you," Adam said. "We're just preparing a little champagne brunch in your honor."

"How sweet," Tabitha said. "And what a lovely house you have, Camilla."

"Thank you. I'm sure Lena will give you a tour when the time is right. Would you like to go up to your room and set down your things? Adam can help you carry those, perhaps?"

"Of course, of course. Hold this, dear." Adam gave Camilla the champagne and lifted a heavy-looking bag, then instructed my father and Tabitha to follow him up the stairs. Camilla had chosen the only other lake-facing room for them; it was wide, airy, and attractive, decorated in shades of white and pale yellow, and adorned today with a vase of roses from Wheat Grass.

I heard my father and Adam booming at each other upstairs in those loud voices men use in social situations. I turned to Camilla. "I'm already exhausted," I joked.

She laughed. "Would you like to come into the dining—"

"Lena?" Tabitha called from upstairs. "Could you come here for a moment?"

"Excuse me," I said to Camilla, and darted up the stairs. Adam and my father were standing in the hallway, inspecting the wood trim for some unknown reason. Tabitha was in their bedroom, beckoning me.

"Come here just for a moment, hon," she said.

I walked into the room, which was just as Camilla and I had left it, aside from the bags that now sat on the floor. "Do you like the view?" I asked.

"Oh, it's lovely! We might just have to make this a regular visit," she said. Her brown curls bobbed slightly with her enthusiasm. Tabitha was a pretty woman—perhaps in her mid-fifties—and she was proud of her looks. She maintained them scrupulously with regular trips to the hairdresser to dye out her gray and carefully sculpt her brows. Her face was kind, which had been a relief to me when she first started dating my father. I knew when I saw compassion in her eyes that their relationship would work.

"That would be terrific. Camilla says that you're always welcome here at the house. I had been planning to put you up at the Red Cottage, but Camilla wouldn't hear of it."

"That's very generous. And I know they're expecting us downstairs, but I just wanted to give you a little something."

She opened a garment bag and took out a tall cardboard package. "That's not a little something," I said.

"No—well—I just had this idea, after we heard about your publication. Your father was just so proud, and of course I was, too."

She pushed it toward me and said, "I'm sorry it isn't wrapped very well, but I was mostly worried about protecting it."

Curious, I pulled off some duct tape and carefully tore at the top of the cardboard. I pulled out what looked like a framed picture. Moments later I saw that it was—a poster-sized enlargement of the book cover for *The Salzburg Train*—my first collaboration with Camilla. She had written the book, but she had included some passages written by me, and then very generously included my name on the cover.

I looked at it now, large and lovely, and felt the same burst of joy that I had upon first seeing it. "Tabitha—this is just so thoughtful. I can't believe you did this."

She was pleased with my response, but held up a hand to indicate that it was nothing. "We were just so excited when you told us—and then when we saw it online and in our bookstore—it was just amazing. The ladies at my salon are all Camilla Graham fans, so they are just fascinated by these stories you tell us, and which I tell them, you know."

I leaned the poster against the large bed and pulled Tabitha into a hug. "This is a lovely gift. Thank you so much. I'm going to hang it up today in my room, in a spot where I can see it every morning when I wake up."

She nodded. "I thought you could do that—a way of celebrating your success, you know. Can I see your room? You described it, and you sent your dad that one picture, but—"

"Of course. It's right next door. And then we have to go down and be sociable."

I led her to my room, where we found a dozing Lestrade. He woke up and glared at us, but soon went back to sleep. Tabitha murmured about the view and the wood floor and the carpet and the bedspread until I took her hand and led her back to the stairs. "Did you have a nice trip?" I asked.

"It was fine. Not as long a flight as I thought, which is good. I'm not much of a flyer."

"Well, I'm so glad you made the journey. Now let's get you something to eat."

We went into Camilla's dining room, and Camilla ushered us into seats. Rhonda came in with a breakfast casserole, and Adam followed her with a large fruit salad. On the table already were a variety of coffee cakes and cheeses. Tabitha enthused over this and Camilla made a toast to our visitors, and we all imbibed some morning champagne.

As we ate our brunch, Adam and my father enjoyed a lively conversation about Adam's restaurant, and about my father's favorite eatery in Florida, about which Adam had many questions. Camilla and Tabitha had started talking about the dogs, and Tabitha revealed that she'd had a much-loved German shepherd as a child. What followed were some delightful canine tales about the eccentricities of pets.

I ate and watched, at one point exchanging a smile with Rhonda, who had come in to replenish the fruit salad.

When everyone was finished eating and in fine spirits, my father said, "Adam, Camilla, I will want to consult you about a special project I'd like to undertake while I'm visiting Blue Lake. But for that I will need a certain daughter to be out of the room."

They all looked at me, their faces indulgent, and I saw an opportunity. "You know what, Dad? I wanted to introduce you to Sam, and I'm surprised he hasn't shown up yet. I'm going to run over to his place to find out what's happening, and you can talk to your heart's delight."

"That sounds like a plan," said my father, who had grown rather loud with his champagne. "Bring him back in half an hour or so."

"Sure. See you then," I said, ducking out of the room with a smile, but also a sense of relief. Why had I not realized how draining family visits could be? And surely it was even more exhausting for Tabitha and my father, who had made a journey and now had to meet strangers in a new place.

I left the house and breathed in the May air. The drizzle had still not returned, but now some humidity had replaced it. Behind me Heathcliff and Rochester snuffled at the door; I informed them, with an apologetic tone, that this time I wouldn't bring them along. "Later today, okay, guys?" I thought I saw a bit of reproach in their eyes.

I jogged down the driveway and onto the dirt road that led down the bluff. Then I walked a bit more sedately to Sam's drive. I turned in with a feeling of bemusement—so many things had happened right here under the large pines that flanked Sam's driveway, starting with our first meeting—and I walked up to Sam's door. I tried the handle and found it unlocked; Sam often left it this way for me during the day, but I frowned at it now. While this hooded ninja was on the loose, he needed to lock his door.

I went inside, down Sam's handsome, masculine entry hall, and to the back of the house, where his gorgeous kitchen provided a view of the woods on the bluff. At the end of the hallway I turned right, into the big space of his kitchen, and saw Victoria West in Sam's arms.

She was crying, and her lovely titian hair flowed down her back in some disarray while she sobbed against his chest. Sam looked at me with a helpless expression; he knew in an instant how I felt about seeing his ex-wife in his embrace.

"Oh," I said. "I'm interrupting. I'll come back."

Victoria looked up, surprised, and I was annoyed to find that, even with tear-smudged makeup, she looked attractive. She wiped at her eyes. "Oh, hello, Lena. I'm just pouring out my troubles on poor Sam."

Victoria and I hadn't met very many times; the most memorable of our meetings had occurred on the day her baby was stolen, when she found me standing in Sam's front yard, looking dumbly after the retreating car. She had claimed to be grateful, because I supplied the license number that had allowed the police to find the vehicle and formulate a theory about who had paid off the driver. Now I wondered if she didn't resent me for not somehow warning them, or preventing the theft that I hadn't realized was happening. It had looked normal, initially, as though she had merely told her driver to put the baby in the car. It was only later that I realized Victoria never would have entrusted her baby to someone else . . . .

"It must be very hard, waiting to hear news of Athena."

She sighed. "Yes, it is. I know the police are doing the best they can, but it's just so frustrating, wanting to hold my little girl again, worrying that she misses me, that she's lonely."

She looked directly at me, and her genuine love caused tears of empathy to form in my eyes. "I wish I had done something differently that day," I said. "I wish I had known. In my memory it all seems to happen in slow motion, and it's so very cold . . ."

"No, none of that," she said, waving my concerns away with an elegant hand. "If you had intervened that man might have hurt you, or Athena. And as you said, you didn't know."

One of her arms was still wrapped around Sam, who stood in silence, looking uncomfortable. How strange for him to be in a room with his former wife and his current lover and to have to pretend it wasn't awkward.

"Well, I have to run," I said. "I just stopped in to say hello, but I'm interrupting. I need to check on Allison." I was talking rapidly and backing away.

Sam looked miserable now. "Lena, you don't have to go—"

"Yes, I actually do. I promised I'd look in on her today. I'll see you later, Sam. Victoria, I hope you hear some good news soon."

I rounded the corner and moved swiftly back down Sam's hall and out the door, where I saw a large man, dressed in blue jeans and a dark shirt, leaning against a nearby tree. Had I seen him before I went in, I would have guessed that Victoria was inside, since she went everywhere with a bodyguard these days. I looked away from him—I couldn't help but feel that he was smirking at me—and moved back down Sam's driveway. I wasn't able to pinpoint one feeling in the strange cocktail of emotions that I would have to sort out later. Instead I turned on the path and walked all the way down to Wentworth Street, where the potted flowers glistened with the recent rain and the road glimmered in the humid air. I turned right and made my way past several residences with brightly painted doors (a Blue Lake custom) until I came to one with a lavender door and the number 180.

The door was wide open, and I could hear Allison's laughter inside, so I knocked once and then entered, saying, "Allie? I'm here to check up on you." I moved down a main hallway of the unfamiliar house, with bright white walls that reflected the sun, and found Allison leaning on her kitchen island while John kissed her neck.

She looked past him and, as was always the case, her face brightened when she saw me. "Lena!" she cried, her smile wide.

"Oh gosh. This is my day of interrupting embraces."

"What does that mean? Is something wrong?" She moved away from John and said, "John just came home to keep me company at lunchtime."

"Well, I'll leave you to it," I said.

John held up a hand. "No, fun as it was, I have to get back to work. You two talk and I'll continue kissing my wife at a later time."

Allison laughed and kissed his cheek, and he picked up a briefcase from the floor. "See you, Lena."

I waved, and he walked swiftly down the hall and out

the door. "I really know how to kill the romance in a room," I joked.

Allison pushed me into a chair. The kitchen was also bright white and festooned with various hanging baskets. A large vase of flowers sat in the center of the table and provided a beautiful tribute to spring. "What's going on? You seem blue," she said, sitting across from me.

"I'm not, really. My dad and Tabitha just arrived—"

"That's great!"

"But they kicked me out so they could plan my birthday. So I went to Sam's, and Victoria was there, kind of throwing herself into his arms."

Allison's lip curled with displeasure. "I know she's been through a lot, blah blah et cetera, but that lady is up to something."

"I don't know. She was very polite and gracious—"

"While hugging *your* boyfriend. He's yours, Lena. She needs to back off."

"I don't think it was like that. She was crying, and they were real tears. She misses her baby, of course. I would feel terrible in her place."

Allison still looked suspicious, and she was generally the least suspicious person in the world.

"Anyway. Enough about me. How are you doing in your resort house here?"

She spun around, waving at the airy kitchen. "It's a lovely house, and John and I are really enjoying being right in the center of town. We're treating it like a little spring break."

"When can you go back?"

Her face grew a shade paler. "Doug actually said we can go back now. They've cleaned everything up and taken down the crime tape. But I'm just not ready yet. Aside from the disturbing memories, and the fear that they will make me feel different about my own house, well—I'm afraid to face my neighbors."

"Why? You didn't do anything."

"No. But you saw how they were looking at us on the day you were there. And it's not just Eddie's death. I swear they just don't like us. Way back at Christmas, John and I noticed that everyone's decorations seemed to be thematically linked, as though they had gotten together to talk about it. But somehow we were left out of that conversation." Her face was suddenly vulnerable, childlike. "And then there were the renovations. One family started, with a new deck, and then they followed like dominoes: the screened porch, the new siding, the brick patio, the renovated basement. It was as if everyone was adhering to some sort of unspoken block-improvement plan. Except that John and I can't afford any renovations."

I stared at her for a minute. "Allison, your house doesn't need any renovations. These issues are in your mind. Haven't you ever had a nice conversation with one of these people?"

"Yeah, I suppose. But some of them seem judgmental. And I just can't face them right now."

"You did nothing wrong. You are the victim here! And all they should offer you is their compassion."

My phone buzzed in my pocket, and I checked the message, which was from my father: *We didn't mean to scare you off! Come home and give us the grand tour!*

I smiled. "My dad is asking for a tour of Blue Lake. Would you like to help?"

The old Allison bounced predictably back into place. "I would love it! This is my second day off, did I tell you?

They felt sorry for me at work, I guess. So I'm just rambling around in this big house. Let me grab my sweater, in case it gets cold later. You know this town and its weird weather. Text your dad that I'll join you."

"I can't. My battery just died. We'll have to tell him in person." I frowned at my phone for a moment.

She ran out of the room and I contemplated her last words. I had arrived in Blue Lake during a monumental thunderstorm, after which I had experienced the chill of fall, then the dreadful cold and plentiful snow of winter. This was my first spring, and I was happily anticipating summer in my sleepy little town; but Allison was right—the weather was always changing. It was best to give my father the tour while it still looked good outside.

Allison returned, her expression bright, and her good mood transferred itself to me. We walked back to Graham House and picked up my father and Tabitha, after which we explored Blue Lake: we brought them to the Bluebell Bakery to munch on their samples (Tabitha bought a coffee cake for Camilla). We let them peek into Blue Lake Coffee and enjoy its aroma. We showed them the eccentric wonderland that was Bick's Hardware, although we did not go in (I would wait to introduce Marge Bick, who was an acquired taste). We pointed out the various restaurants on Wentworth Street, in case my father and Tabitha ever wanted to wander alone; we showed them the second-run theater, where one could get popcorn *and* a drink for three dollars; we showed them the Laundromat and the florist (my romantic father bought each of us a rose), and then, roses in hand, we found the path that led to the pier, and then to the sandy beach of Blue Lake.

"Oh, it's lovely!" Tabitha cried. "And Camilla's house is just up there? Why, you're right on the lake! What a view you have!"

"It's amazing. I am incredibly spoiled," I admitted.

"She really is," Allison said. "John and I love our house, but we're farther out in the suburbs. We could never have afforded lakefront property, and Lena got to town and moved into a house at the top of the bluff, with this view."

"We can see the lake from the room Camilla gave us. Just wonderful. Your dad and I live by the ocean, but we have to drive a few minutes to see it. This is just serene," Tabitha said.

My father nodded. "It's just the way you described it, Lee."

"She is a writer, after all," Allison piped, sniffing her yellow rose.

Tabitha was finding colorful stones on the sand and slipping them into her pocket. I had done the same thing on one of my first days in town. "These will make a lovely centerpiece," she said. "Or I can put them at the bottom of a vase, and they'll stay bright inside the water."

"Tabitha's very crafty," my father said. "She's got home-made wreaths and wall hangings and things all over our house, and they're all beautiful." My father said this ear-nestly, and I realized why Tabitha loved him, and why I did. He was sweet and loyal.

"Ahhh. I could stay here all day," Allison said, gazing at the lake. "I always like to find the spot where the lake meets the sky, but I can't quite do it."

"It's a little hazy today," I said.

We had reached the foot of the steep red staircase that went up the bluff all the way to Camilla's backyard. I had finally grown used to it, but I feared it might be strenuous for my father and his wife. "These stairs are kind of tough. There's a bench halfway up; how about if you and Tabitha just take it at your own pace, then enjoy the view from the bench? I want to run up and make a quick phone call, see if Sam can join us."

"I thought he was going to stop by this morning," my father said, looking at his feet.

"He wanted to. He had an unexpected visitor."

"You go call; we'll savor the scenery," he said.

"Yes, you go up, sweetheart! Your dad and I have a different pace," Tabitha joked.

Her words chilled me, and for a moment I froze in place, hearing the word like a taunt in my head. *Hello, Sweetheart.* Such was the extent of my paranoia that for a wild instant I wondered if Tabitha could have been behind the note. Then I looked at her kind face, flushed with the exertion of our long walk, and shook off my ludicrous imaginings.

Allison and I moved up the stairs at a rapid pace; even now, after all this time in Blue Lake, my heart was racing at the top.

"That is a workout!" Allison said, laughing. "Ah. I'm glad my rose survived. It was a little windy down there."

"Do you want to stay for dinner? Or a late lunch? What time is it, anyway?"

She looked at her watch. "It's four o'clock!" We entered Camilla's kitchen and Allison set down her rose to adjust her windblown hair.

"Wow. Time flies. Let me find a vase. Do you want me to wrap yours in a damp cloth?"

"Yes, thank you. And then I'm going to go. As you saw, John is feeling romantic, so I want to dream up a nice little dinner for him."

"You do that. Have fun. And Allison—when it's time

to go back home, you'll be ready. You don't have to think about your neighbors or the mailman or anything. Just go live in your home and remember the good times."

She handed me her rose and I took it to the sink. "Okay, that's good advice. Now I have some for you. Don't be mad at Sam, but do tell him that he doesn't have to give in to everything that woman wants. She's not his responsibility. She's got family, and she's got bodyguards and stuff."

"I know—I saw one when I left Sam's. Hey—does one of her bodyguards have a beard? A guy about forty-five or fifty, with brown facial hair?"

"Why?"

"I—happened to see someone like that in town."

She shrugged. "I don't know. I just know she has body-guards, or at least one bodyguard. John saw him once, skulking around behind her while she waited for coffee."

"Oh well." I wrapped her rose at its base in a damp paper towel, then wrapped it again in tinfoil. "This will keep it moist until you get home."

"Great! It will be the centerpiece for my spaghetti dinner."

"Like in *Lady and the Tramp.*"

We laughed, and Allison gave me a hug. Then she waved and exited out the front door.

I put my own rose, a lovely peach color, into a bud vase that usually sat on Camilla's windowsill, and set it on the dining room table. My father and Tabitha appeared at the door, looking winded. "That's quite a climb," my dad said. "You weren't kidding."

"You two sit down and I'll make you some tea. I have to work for a little while with Camilla, but then I'm going to whisk you away for dinner. Does that sound good?"

"It does," my father said. "But I think Tabby and I are going to take a quick nap. Travel, and all that lake air, have got us feeling pretty sleepy."

"And then I'll want to change," Tabitha said. "I want to look nice for dinner."

"Okay—I'll check in with you in a couple of hours. Tabitha, if you want, I'll put your rose in this vase with mine."

"Oh yes!" She handed me her rose, a deep red shade—Eric London, you romantic devil—and they moved into the hallway and up the stairs. I tucked Tabitha's rose in the water with mine and retrieved my dead phone from my pocket, seeking out a charger from a kitchen drawer and plugging it into the outlet near the sink. Once the battery light went on, I picked it up and checked the messages, which I had not been able to do earlier. There were ten: one from Doug, one from Belinda, and eight from Sam.

I read Doug's first, which was a response to my Belinda update: *Thanks a million. I'm on it.* I smiled, then read Belinda's: *Don't forget I have some new things in the London File. And I'll put some Sam items in there, too.*

Finally I read Sam's messages. The first said, *Don't be mad at me. Can I come over and meet your dad?*

When I didn't respond, his tone grew more urgent. Now he probably feared I was one of those girlfriends who pouted and gave the silent treatment—which I was not. I dialed his number and he picked up on the second ring. "Lena?"

"I'm sorry. My phone died while Allison and I gave the grand tour to Dad and Tabitha. I'm not mad at you."

"Thank God. I really didn't know Vic was coming."

"Can you come to dinner?"

"I'd like to take you out, the whole London clan. Is that acceptable? We can drive over to Stafford and eat at Bonaventura."

"Oooh. That sounds lovely. I've only been there once, on a date with you."

"They've already seen Blue Lake and I'm sure they'll eat their share of meals at Wheat Grass, so this would be a nice change of pace."

"Okay, you're on. Can I invite Camilla, too?"

"She told me she and Adam are going to the theater tonight. I happened to call her a few times, looking for you."

"Ah." I smiled out the window. "You were worried."

"A little."

"You should know better. I'm not the type to run from a challenge."

"As I've learned."

"I miss you."

"I'll come by at six?"

"Good. See you then."

"Wear something red," Sam said just before he rang off. This was interesting; he'd never commented on my wardrobe before, except to say that I looked nice. Did I even have anything red? I ran upstairs to check my limited selection.

AT SIX O'CLOCK I was dressed for dinner in a pair of beige slacks and a red knit sweater, along with a silver necklace and some small diamond earrings that had been a Christmas gift from Sam.

Tabitha and my father were ready, too, looking refreshed and attractive in their dinner clothes. We chatted in the living room, and I pretended I wasn't nervous about Sam's imminent arrival.

When I heard his feet on the steps I leaped up and said, "Let me get that," even though he hadn't yet rung the bell.

I opened the door and Sam smiled at me. He was wearing black pants and a white shirt with a crimson tie. His messy brown hair had been tamed, and he resembled a boy going to church. "You look nervous," he said.

"I don't know why. But I am. Come and meet my dad."

Sam entered the room, and my father and Tabitha rose to shake his hand. "Mr. London, Mrs. London. I am very glad to meet you," Sam said, solemn and formal as a prince.

My father laughed and pulled him into one of his hugs. "Mr. London? You and Lena aren't sixteen, so you can call me Eric."

His wife leaned forward. "And I'm Tabitha. Oh, you are even handsomer than your picture in the papers," she said.

Sam actually turned red.

My father had let Sam go, but he was still looking into his eyes. "Son, Lena told us all you've been through, and of course we've seen it unfold in the press. We can't tell you how sorry we are for all that you've suffered."

His genuine sympathy disarmed Sam.

"I appreciate that . . . Eric. And I'm glad that people know the truth now, because when the world believed the worst—that was pretty unbearable."

Tabitha shook her head. "Well, we know you won't want to rehash it all, but just know that we always believed in you, because Lena did."

"That is very gratifying," Sam said.

I cleared my throat. If they kept going one of us was likely to end up in tears. "Dad, Sam is going to take us to

Stafford. It's about twenty minutes from here—it's the town where John works—Allison's John? There's a lovely Italian place out there."

"Terrific! We love Italian food." My father winked at Tabitha. "So many people want to take us out—we should have visited a long time ago."

"And I should have invited you," I said. "Now let's go, because by the time we get there I'll be starving."

We went to the door, and I called to the dogs to be good. Lestrade was off hunting for mice somewhere in the house. We piled onto the porch, and I locked Camilla's door.

As we drove toward the foot of the bluff, we passed a man walking along the side of the road. It looked like the bearded man who had glared at me in Wheat Grass. "Hey," I said, turning in my seat to double-check.

"What?" asked Sam, his gaze fixed on the path in front of him.

"That man—"

"What man?"

I twisted in my seat, craning my neck to look behind me.

"Dad, Tabitha, did you see that guy on the side of the road?"

"I only have eyes for this lovely lady beside me," said my father in a jovial voice.

Tabitha leaned in to give him a kiss and blocked my view out the back window. When she moved back, the road was empty, and then we turned onto Wentworth and I gave up with a sigh.

Half an hour later I had forgotten all about him.

7

In the rare light of the setting sun, the temple ruins glittered like gold.

—From *Death at Delphi*

BONAVENTURA WAS NOT as subtle as Wheat Grass, but it was still charming. The walls were parchment gold and decorated with framed photographs of art by the Italian Renaissance masters. The ceiling was a mural of blue sky with delicate clouds, and a real olive tree sat in a pot in the middle of the restaurant. On a ledge above our table were perched two antique lutes, and two guitarists strolled the restaurant, playing muted music.

A waiter invited us to come to the Tuscany Room, and as Tabitha and my father followed him, Sam held me back and whispered in my ear. "You look beautiful," he said.

I stole a quick kiss from him and said, "So do you."

He grinned at me. I loved to see him smile because it made him look young, boyish, in the same way that his moments of brooding made him look older than his thirty-five years.

We settled into a booth, where Sam and I faced my father

and Tabitha across a marble-topped table, at the center of which sat a small loaf of oven-warmed bread. Sam said, "I'm sorry that I wasn't able to meet you this morning, or join in your tour. I'm sure you know about Victoria."

"Oh yes," Tabitha said. "We followed every story, every day. Your poor wife! We were so relieved when they found her." She seemed to hear how this sounded, and said, "Not as relieved as you were, I'm sure!"

Sam nodded with a wry smile. "It was a miracle, and Lena made it happen. But then this man—Nikon Lazos—decided that he wanted to steal back his daughter. And Vic is devastated, naturally. She has a temporary home here in Blue Lake—I think it's important to her, somehow, to stay near the place where her daughter disappeared. It's so tough on her, I understand that, but it also puts me in an odd position. She wants me to be there for her, to be her confidant and supporter. But for me, life changed forever when she was gone."

"Of course it did," my father said. "You had to face a year of uncertainty and the disapproval of an entire town."

"The entire world, it felt like." Sam frowned down at his plate. I put a slice of bread on it.

A waitress appeared and told us her name was Gina. She took our drink orders and departed after sending a flirtatious glance to Sam, which he seemed not to notice.

"So Victoria came to see you this morning?" Tabitha asked, curious but trying not to seem that way.

"Yes. And Lena came by, which I love for her to do, and found Victoria crying on my shoulder."

"Ah," said my father.

"It was a bit awkward, actually," I said.

Tabitha shook her head. "I feel bad for her. But she has a family—parents and a sibling or two, doesn't she?"

Sam nodded. "Yes. And they plan to visit Blue Lake regularly. But they live in New York, and Victoria stays with them when she goes there for her various press conferences."

I started to butter my bread. "She and Sam shared an apartment there, which Sam was keeping while they were investigating Victoria's disappearance. Now that she's back, he's going to put it up for sale."

"I already did," Sam said. "And my Realtor has been inundated with offers. Apparently many people are willing to pay extra for the place where Nikon Lazos tried to frame me for murder."

"My goodness. It's all so unbelievable, isn't it?" Tabitha said, her eyes wide.

"Yes," Sam said. "Anyway, Victoria was especially upset because Athena turned seven months old today."

"Oh my," I said, setting my knife down and looking at him.

My father nodded. "That is hard. God, if anyone had taken my Lena away from me when she was just an infant—" My father sent me an affectionate glance. "It's amazing how quickly that bond is formed, between parent and child. But he wouldn't hurt the baby, would he?"

Sam shook his head. "Even Victoria doesn't think that. She knows Nikon loves his little girl. But he is also vengeful, and her fear is that he'll never let her see the child again."

"Poor Victoria," I said.

Tabitha looked near tears.

"Anyway, enough about this," I said.

Sam understood and slid an arm around me. "Yes. We're here to talk about you, and your life in Florida, and Lena's birthday. You're turning twenty-seven, aren't you?"

"Yes, I am."

"She was just a kid when I first met her," Tabitha enthused. "But always so talented and pretty. She looks very much like her mother, doesn't she, Eric?"

"Very much," my father said, his expression fond. His eyes held a trace of sadness. "We've all experienced the loss of a loved one at this table—a sad fraternity. But Sam, I fear you had to pay the biggest price. I'm very sorry for your loss."

"Thank you," Sam said. "It's a very long time ago now. Sometimes my family feels like it was a figment of my imagination." I leaned into his side, and his arm tightened around my shoulder. "But I loved them, and I know they loved me, and I take comfort in that."

Tabitha, who was always empathetic, stared at him with round, tear-filled eyes. "You have a great attitude. And now you have Lena," she said.

Sam smiled at her. "I do."

My father pointed to his right. "People are dancing. There's a dance floor. And they're playing a Sinatra tune."

"Ohhh," Tabitha said.

"Want to cut the rug, Tabby?"

She did, clearly. They excused themselves and moved to the center of the room, where a cluster of couples slow-danced to the romantic music.

"That's sweet," I said.

"Do you want to dance?"

"No. I want to sit and talk with you. I've barely been alone with you since you got back, you know? And the whole time I was in England I consoled myself that I would have tons of Sam time when I returned."

"I'm sorry. I always seem to be saying 'someday' to you.

But things are better than they were. We can be together openly now, and we can steal time together here and there."

"Yeah. Anyway. I'm sorry the conversation took such a personal turn. I guess Dad and Tabitha wanted to—you know—"

"I understand."

"Hey—on a different note. Remember a few months ago when you told me about what your dad said before they went on their trip? Something about good news, and your mom getting a letter."

"Yes." He tore a corner off his bread.

"I wonder—is it okay if I ask Belinda to look into it? Just in a sort of general background way?"

He shrugged. "You know what? I've decided that I need to live for the future, not the past. But if you want to pursue it, go ahead. I doubt she can find out anything useful at this point. The people with the information are gone." His voice was matter-of-fact rather than morose.

"You never know. Belinda has worked miracles before. She helped us find Victoria."

He shook his head. "It still amazes me—you and Belinda, the unsung heroes of the whole event. Victoria mentions you a lot, you know. How amazed she is that you were able to find her simply by using your computer and your ingenuity."

"Really? I always get the impression she resents me."

"She's shy around you because she doesn't know how to thank you. It's a big thing—I know just how she feels. You saved my life, too."

I waved him away. "This conversation is too intense. Let's just talk about silly things."

"One more serious thing. I heard from Doug about our ninja."

"Oh?"

"His lab guys couldn't make out a face. Doug thinks the person knew about the camera, maybe even wanted to be filmed. I can't imagine why."

"And fingerprints?"

"They dusted. Everything was clean. Just my prints and yours."

Another song started, and the Florida lovebirds opted to stay out on the dance floor. "And I don't suppose they know who killed Eddie Stack?"

Sam sighed. "No, but they know it wasn't me. Thank God."

I leaned against him and closed my eyes for a moment. "What's happening, Sam?"

It was a question that we'd been asking since the moment Allison had found a body in her backyard. *What is happening in this town?*

WHEN WE ARRIVED back at Graham House, Adam's car was still gone, which meant Camilla and he had probably combined dinner and their play. Sam and my father, to my great pleasure, seemed comfortable with each other, and in fact they sat in the front seat together while Tabitha and I had opted to talk about "girl things," as Tabitha put it, in the backseat. While the men in the front talked about sports, Blue Lake, and fishing, Tabitha wanted to know about clothing and jewelry shops in Blue Lake, as well as any promising antique barns. "I hate to be a cliché," she told me in a confidential tone, "but I do love shopping, especially when I'm on vacation!"

We climbed the porch, Tabitha and I, while the men locked up the car. I touched the wooden door and saw that it was not closed. Heathcliff and Rochester nosed it open on the other side. Their hackles were raised, and they whined slightly while Tabitha and I patted their heads.

Sam appeared behind me and pointed at the wood of the door frame, which was rough and jagged on one side. He said, "Lena, step away. That door's been forced open!" He pulled out his phone and called the police.

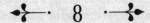

8

She first knew that she was being followed when she saw a shadow that wasn't her own. But when she spun around, ready to confront a stranger, she found nothing but the rutted path and the dense foliage around it.

— From *Death at Delphi*

CLIFF BLAKE SHOWED up to investigate; he said that Doug was in a dinner meeting with the mayor.

"What's all this stuff with Doug and the mayor lately?" I asked.

Cliff shrugged and put on that inscrutable expression that cops always wear. Then he climbed up onto the porch and frowned at the broken wood on Camilla's door. We had all remained outside on Sam's orders; in fact, Sam seemed the most upset, and he looked pale in the evening light.

Cliff looked at us, his brows furrowed. "This was done with a crowbar," he said. "You stay here and I'll make sure no one's still inside." He took his gun out of his holster and began to check Camilla's ground floor while we talked in low voices on the porch.

I kept my eye on Sam, occasionally peeking in at Cliff, who was now stealthily climbing Camilla's stairs. I had a moment of déjà vu—perhaps because, back in October, a police officer had also climbed Camilla's stairs, hunting for an intruder.

Finally Cliff came out, looking a bit less tense. "Nothing inside. Whoever visited has gone; but these two guys have done us a favor." He pointed at the dogs, then held up an evidence bag that seemed to contain a scrap of blue jean material. "This was on the floor, and there's blood on it. Whoever broke in probably didn't know Camilla had German shepherds. Looks like they attacked him."

Rochester and Heathcliff, seemingly aware that we were talking about them, sidled up to us to receive their praise. I knelt down and gave it to them, lavishly. "You are good boys!" Then I looked up at Cliff. "So it's not likely that he took anything, right? Not if the dogs were on him the moment he broke in."

"You can check out the house, but no, I'm thinking he came and went in a hurry." A little smile escaped him, and he looked suddenly approachable, even handsome.

Sam still looked upset. "The question is *why*. *Why* is someone breaking into Camilla's house with a crowbar? I don't like this at all."

My father said, "How about if Tabitha and I look around and see if anything is broken or disturbed?" Cliff opened the door, and my father led his wife inside, perhaps so that we could speak with Cliff in private.

I had a sudden memory. "Cliff! When we left to go to dinner, I saw a man with a beard walking up the hill. Remember I mentioned him, Sam?"

"Yes." Sam looked grim. "I wish I had seen him."

"I saw him, and I can describe him. Not only that, but I've seen him more than once! Belinda saw him, too. We were eating at Wheat Grass, and he was glaring at us. Do you think Adam can find out his name, maybe from customer receipts?"

Cliff looked interested. "Well, that is a great place to start. Thanks for the lead, Lena. Did Belinda happen to recognize this guy?"

I shook my head. "No—she barely noticed him. But he stands out: he has a bushy brown beard and scraggly eyebrows. It's hard to guess his age—he could be anywhere from thirty to forty-five, I would think."

"Had you ever seen him before?" Sam asked.

"No. That's why it felt strange to me that he was staring at me—I didn't know him at all. But then I wondered—"

"What?" Cliff asked. He had a little notebook out, which was cute. Doug did everything on his iPhone.

"Doug said something about there being reporters in town, trying to keep a low profile. When I saw him scowling, I thought maybe he was with the press, and maybe he was angry that he couldn't get an interview with Sam or me or Victoria. I don't know—that doesn't quite make sense as a theory, but that's what I was thinking at the time."

Cliff nodded and scrawled a few things in his notebook.

Adam's silver car turned in at the driveway and pulled in next to Camilla's where it sat at the foot of the porch. The two of them emerged, looking elegant in their evening clothes, and walked toward us. "Something's happened, I see," Camilla said.

I pointed at the door, rueful. "Someone broke in, Camilla, while we were at dinner. I locked the door, but they used a crowbar, Cliff says. Your guard dogs sent them off in a hurry."

She looked less distressed than she did curious. "Do we have any theories?"

I shook my head. Cliff said, "Lena saw an unsavory bearded character walking up the bluff. Seems a likely place to start. In fact, Mr. Rayburn, she says she also saw him at your place yesterday."

Adam raised his brows. "My restaurant? What time was this, Lena?"

"I was having lunch with Belinda—I think it was about twelve thirty."

He thought for a moment, then nodded. "Sarah did mention that she had a strange customer in the booth by the door."

"Yes, that's where he was sitting!" I said.

"He only ordered coffee and pie, and he seemed restless. Kept watching the cars in the lot. She said he paid in cash."

Cliff said, "Ask her if she remembers anything else, or if she had any conversations with the man. Can you let me know?"

Adam nodded. "Of course. I'll ask her first thing tomorrow."

Cliff put his notebook in his back pocket. "Meanwhile I'll ask around in town, see if anyone else has seen this guy. Let me get my fingerprint kit from the car and do a quick dusting of the door."

"Cliff, if we don't touch the broken area, can we go in the house?" Camilla asked.

"Let me open it up for you," he said. He did so, gingerly, touching the middle of the door, as he had done for my father. We went in and sprawled on couches in Camilla's living room.

We talked for a while about the break-in. Camilla said that as far as she knew she had never had one, although there had been intruders on her property in recent months.

Adam shook his head. "Something fishy is going on. First with this murder Camilla told me about, and now with a break-in? This isn't the Blue Lake I'm used to."

Camilla and I had exchanged a secret glance that suggested we felt there was a link between this and the note I received. But I had not told my father about the note, so we kept silent on that matter.

"You must think we live in a den of crime," I said to my father and Tabitha.

"No, of course not," my father said. "Florida has far more crime than this sweet little town. You're just not used to it here. Tabby and I have triple locks on our door and an expensive security system. There are those who prey upon retirees, you know."

"Ugh. I'm getting very disillusioned," I said.

Cliff had been delicately powdering all around the door, and now he was taking some photos. Sam stood up and said, "Cliff, we really appreciate this."

Cliff turned, surprised, and said, "Hey, just doing my job." He looked gratified, though. "I'll get out of your hair now. You'll need to get this repaired. I think Doug said Al Dempsey does emergency repair. He's on Pine Street, if you're looking him up."

"I know Albert," Camilla said. Camilla knew everyone. "I shall give him a call right now. Thank you for the idea, Cliff." She stood and went into her office. Over her white blouse and black evening slacks she wore a delicate silver vest shot with shiny silver thread, and she glimmered as she left the room. Adam's gaze followed her. He did indeed look love-struck. I wondered, briefly, about Camilla's husband, and how in love he must have been at the start with a twenty-four-year-old Camilla.

Cliff was packing up, and Sam seemed to want to talk

to him. I wondered why this particular break-in, despite the far more horrifying things Sam had suffered, seemed to bother him so much. "I'll walk you out," Sam told Cliff. Cliff said good-bye to us, and the men descended the steps together.

My father stood up. "You know, tomorrow Tabby and I want to go check out that resort town you mentioned to us."

"Meridien? Yes—it's lovely. Like Blue Lake, only fancier."

"So I think we'll go up, watch a show on that nice TV in our room, and then turn in for the night. We're early risers, as you know."

I stood up and kissed him. "Good night, Dad. It's so great to have you here."

He gave me a hug, I kissed Tabitha on the cheek, and they made their way upstairs.

Adam and I exchanged an uncertain glance. "I'll wait until the repairman gets here," Adam said, "and then I'll go, too."

"Don't rush on my account; I'm going to bed soon. I gave my dad the grand tour today, and I am wiped out."

"The Blue Lake air, perhaps," Adam said lightly.

"And I still need to write a bit tonight. Camilla and I are comparing notes tomorrow on a new project."

"I heard." He looked at me with his perceptive brown eyes. "She loves working with you, Lena. She feels years younger with you in the house."

"I feel the same. Not younger, but very happy."

He lunged forward and hugged me—something Adam had never done. "Thank you for making her happy," he said.

Before I could respond Camilla was back. "Albert will

be here within half an hour. He was most accommodating. Adam, Lena, would you like some coffee?"

I shook my head. "I'll say good night to Sam and head upstairs. It was a long day, and I want to do some writing before I conk out."

She nodded. "All right, dear."

I went outside and saw Sam still talking with Cliff by the police car. Cliff was nodding as Sam talked earnestly to him. Cliff saw me and clapped a hand on Sam's shoulder, saying some final words, and then he climbed into the car.

Sam watched him drive away, then turned to see me standing at the foot of the porch. "Hey," he said.

"Hey. What's with the secret conference?"

He moved toward me, his face unreadable in the growing dusk. "Not secret, just emphatic. It bothers me, Lena, that someone broke into your house. I don't care that they went into mine, or that they stole something, or even that they tried to frame me for murder—there's a part of me that's just been hardened against outside intrusions. But you—you're my Achilles' heel. I can't bear the thought of someone dangerous lurking around you, or Camilla. That note was personal. It had your name on it. And now this. Cliff said this looks like escalation."

"What does that mean?"

"It's a cop thing, but basically it's the idea that someone is getting more extreme. More angry, or more something. But why you? I wonder if Camilla should stay with Adam for a while, and you should come to stay with me."

I hugged him. "You're so sweet. But my dad is here, and I want to be around him. And we have the dogs. They bit whoever it was, remember? They'll protect us." A pickup truck turned into Camilla's driveway. "Oh, and look, this is Albert Dempsey, coming to repair the door."

Sam pulled me tighter, resting his chin on the top of my head. "This will sound selfish, I suppose, but I am also worried for me. I can't bear the thought of something happening to you."

"Sam, I'll be fine. Did Cliff reassure you?"

He sighed. "Sort of. He said all those things that cops always say. How they'll make it their top priority and be on the lookout for this bearded guy. How did I not see him when we left today?"

"You were concentrating on the road and your thoughts, probably. Sam, it's okay. Do you want to stay with us tonight? Camilla has another spare room, and I know she'd be happy to have you."

He nodded. "You know what? I do. But I have some things to do at home. Tell Camilla I'll be back at around ten, just for tonight."

Albert Dempsey emerged from his car with a toolbox in one hand, and Sam and I ascended the steps with him to point out the damage.

He whistled. "Someone really went after this, and they didn't bother to disguise it. This was a well-made door, and he had to work hard to get in there."

Sam and I exchanged a glance, and then he squeezed my arm. "I'll be back," he said, and he walked down the steps and to the road on swift legs.

ASIDE FROM A brief visit to Sam's guest room to kiss him good night, I spent a chaste evening writing a sample chapter for *Death at Delphi*, and then, in a moment of curiosity, I did what I always did when there was trouble in Blue Lake: I went to Google. I hunted for my same-old search terms, starting with Nikon Lazos. I got an immediate list of stories about Nikon's evasion of the police, about his apparent genius for hiding. There were some pictures of Baby Athena that I had not seen before and some follow-up stories on Victoria and what she was doing now. One of them was titled "Victoria West: Portrait of a Survivor." It was accompanied by a melancholy portrait of Victoria in New York, gazing out onto some body of water. I read for almost an hour, but the only thing that was slightly interesting was an article called "The Criminal Past of Nikon Lazos." This was written for the *London Times* by a reporter called Colin Wilde. According to Wilde, Lazos had been suspected, in his youth, of a number of robberies of wealthy families known to his clan. Greek police had suspected young Lazos when he was on the guest list at every home that had suffered a theft, from precious jewels to family heirlooms. However, Lazos had valid alibis for almost all of the crimes. One retired police officer clung to his theory that Lazos had been involved, but he was convinced that the young man must have had a talented accomplice.

This gave me pause. We had just suffered two break-ins: one at Sam's, one at Camilla's. We had also been questioning whether Nikon could be involved. Might this story be the key to something? I printed out a copy to show to Doug, Sam, and Camilla, and then I brushed my teeth and turned in, noting with a yawn that it was almost midnight. I fell asleep almost instantly.

At about two in the morning something woke me and I sat up in bed. With cobwebbed vision I peered at the blackness, sensing, rather than seeing, that someone was in the room.

I felt a scream rising in my throat but I managed a garbled "Who's there?"

Sam's voice, calm and reassuring, spoke. "Lena, it's me." He sat on the side of my bed and suddenly I could see him: his familiar form and comforting features. I dove into his arms.

"You scared me!"

"I'm so sorry. I didn't want to wake anyone, even you. I just wanted—to see you."

"Why?" I pulled far enough away to study his face.

"I had a bad dream," he said with a little smile, but his eyes were troubled. "Bad enough that I had to make sure you were all right."

"Oh, Sam. I love you," I said.

Then his mouth was on mine, and I pulled him back with me on the bed, enjoying his roaming hands and the cool scented breeze that floated in my window. "I missed you," he said.

"You've been home for more than a day."

"I missed *naked* you. In bed with me," he said, his lips on my shoulder.

"Mmm. Me, too. And this clandestine meeting is very exciting—you sneaking in here at two in the morning."

"I didn't have to sneak. Camilla assured me last night she wouldn't mind if I stayed in your room. I told her you would be uncomfortable."

"Well—it is sort of awkward."

"Feels very comfortable to me," Sam said.

"Stop," I said, laughing. "No, don't stop *that*."

"Okay," he said, and I giggled, and then there was no need to talk.

SAM WAS GONE when I woke, but Lestrade, who had been on his nightly rounds, was lying on the bed, snoring slightly.

I glanced at the clock; it was eight. I jumped up and hastened to get ready.

Sam, Camilla, Tabitha, and my father were at the breakfast table sharing coffee and rolls. Sam's eyes studied me as I walked in, and then he smiled down into his mug. My father stood up to give me a kiss, then looked at his watch. "Tabby and I are going to run out for some morning sightseeing. I know you and your boss have to work, so we'll get out of your hair."

"You'll have fun," I said. "And it looks like it's a lovely day." I gazed out Camilla's kitchen window at her expanse of yard and the distant lake, which glittered like silver under an azure sky.

"It does indeed," my father said. "Tabby, are you ready?"

She was. If I knew the signs of a woman who was ready to shop (and I did), I saw those in Tabitha London this morning. She was carrying a big purse and wearing comfortable shoes. She kept glancing at the door, and I suppressed a laugh. We waved and they vacated the kitchen; Camilla had kindly offered to let them use her car for the day.

I sat down and took a sweet roll, then gave Sam and Camilla copies of the article I had printed. "Let me know if this seems pertinent."

They read, dutifully, and Sam's eyebrows rose. Camilla said, "Interesting," then read some more, then said "Interesting" again.

"Something to share with Doug, right?"

Sam nodded. "This goes back what—thirty years? And yet it seems relevant to some of the discussions we've been having, and the idea that Nikon might have someone working for him in Blue Lake. I think I'll drop this off with Doug myself, if that's okay."

"Great," I said. Then, "Aside from this, are we all feeling better this morning?"

Camilla sipped her coffee. "I am delighted. How lovely to have you at our breakfast table, Sam."

Sam grinned. "It is nice. And you two are a beautiful sight for tired eyes. But I should run and drop this at the station, then go home and do some work. I'm relieved that last night was uneventful, but I don't think for a minute that the drama has ended. It rarely does in our part of town, does it?"

Camilla's laugh was tinged with regret. "There is some sort of strange cloud hovering over your house and mine, and I think it's been there for quite some time. Perhaps we should relocate."

"No way," I said. "I love this house and Sam's place, and I say we get to the bottom of this mystery once and for all."

"Let's do that, Madame Sherlock. You can get Lestrade to help you," Sam joked.

I was ridiculously pleased that he had worked my cat into the conversation; I got up and gave him a generous kiss. "Young love," Camilla said placidly, pouring some more coffee into her cup.

Sam kissed me back, holding my face in his hands, then stood up.

"Geez, I come downstairs and everyone leaves," I said.

"I'll see you later. Maybe tonight," Sam said. He touched Camilla's shoulder and said, "Thanks for letting me stay, Camilla. I hope your house has seen the last of its unwelcome visitors. I'll be stopping in now and then, and Doug has assured me he and Cliff will do the same."

"You're welcome anytime, day or night. No, just leave the dishes there. Have a fine day, Sam."

He waved and moved out of the room. I finished up my roll and stared into my coffee.

"He's a good man," Camilla said.

I nodded. "I would like everything to be over—all the uncertainty and strangeness—so that I could spend more time with him."

"Soon," she said. Then she clapped her hands once. "So—we are alone at last. Shall we work on our new book?"

This perked me up. "I have a chapter to show you. Did you write something?"

"Just some ideas in a little outline. Let's put them together and see what we have."

"Hang on—let me grab my laptop." I jogged upstairs and into my room, where Lestrade still lay like a tiny carpet on my bed, and ran across the floor to my gorgeous desk, where my laptop sat waiting for me. I grabbed it and flew back down the stairs.

Camilla had relocated to her office, and I pulled up my purple chair for our collaboration. I opened my Word document and set it in front of her. "Here's the chapter—just an idea of how it might start."

She handed me a few typed pages. "And here's an outline. Mark the things that you think would work in this story. These are just some ideas about Greece—how the setting can relate to the plot, some mythological references that might end up being good clues—that sort of thing."

We sat reading each other's ideas and making notes. Once in a while one of us would say, "Ah!" or make a pleased sound.

When I finished, I waited for her. She was still reading, her silver head bent toward the computer, her face intent, yet dreamy. Camilla was never happier than when she was immersed in a book. Finally she finished. She smiled and pushed the laptop away slightly.

"What do you think?" I asked, trying not to sound nervous.

"I think it's very promising. What a wonderful way to start—and what a romantic way for the two of them to meet. It actually would work well with some of the notes I made there."

"I know! I love the idea of incorporating a psychic character—an echo of the oracle of ancient times."

"Yes—it could work quite well. And I like the fact that, when a local guide and translator is unavailable, the British man offers to travel with her and be her guide. So perfect that he is a professor of classical literature."

"He can answer all of her questions, and he can inspire her ideas, because she wants to write a book set in Greece."

Camilla tapped her fingers on the desk. "But of course she's a woman alone. She can't just commit to climbing into a car with a strange man."

"But the local translator would have been a stranger! And she's looking for adventure—perhaps she is feeling like taking risks."

"Hmm. What if they have some tenuous connection? Perhaps a family member of hers has actually been in one of his classes, or—what if his father is also a professor? She can say she recognizes the name, but that surely he is not the right age, and he can smile charmingly and say, 'Professor Barclay Anselm is my father. I'm Curtis Anselm. You can call me Curt.'"

"Nice. The love for classics—and the knowledge of Greece—runs in the family. At some point they can call his father to clarify some arcane detail. They'll need him to help them solve the mystery."

She leaned forward, her eyes gleaming. "Because by that point they will have stumbled on something ancient— something that a murderer has already killed to protect."

"Or maybe to keep from the public eye. The murderer has his reasons why some antiquities should remain buried."

Camilla looked back at my chapter and nodded at the screen. "When they take the taxi together from Athens, she should confide something in him. Something that's been bothering her, perhaps, or something that brought her to Greece in the first place."

"Her own father died before he could take her here. He had asked her to go for years, and then he passed away unexpectedly. She feels remorse; she cannot take this journey with her father, and now she must make it alone, as a pilgrimage."

She sent me a shrewd look. "That will work. For her, a theme of loss. For him, a professional compulsion. For them both, a mystery that will bind them together."

"Oh my gosh! That sounds like the back cover copy!"

"This is good, Lena. I like it."

"Me, too. And I like you, writing partner."

She smiled, then yawned suddenly. "I might need some more coffee. I'm afraid I didn't sleep well last night, even with brave Sam in the house."

"Were you worried?"

She shrugged. "Not really. But my mind will try to work out puzzles, and my brain kept insisting to me that the dead mailman and my broken door are somehow connected. For the life of me I can't imagine how. If this is a puzzle, we have the pieces from opposite corners, but no other pieces to work with."

I leaned back. "How can we get those pieces?"

"I truly don't know. I feel a bit at a loss. In the past, we always had something to work with."

"Well, we have some things—we have the recording of the intruder in Sam's place. We have a phone call from Eddie Stack. We have the knife that was stolen. We have the weird note that was sent to me. We have the bearded man; I have to assume Doug and Cliff will find him soon."

"And we have a little piece of a blue jean material, with blood on it, compliments of my dogs."

"Surely they can do something with that? Some sort of DNA test?"

She shrugged. "I trust Doug and Cliff to do their professional best." She stretched. "I do apologize for all my rude yawning. Let me get that coffee. Would you like some?"

"No, thank you. For whatever reason, I slept well." I blushed slightly as I said it, but either Camilla didn't notice or she was too polite to comment. "Camilla, there is something I've been pondering."

"What is that?"

"Well, Sam asked yesterday—why you? Meaning me. And that is a good question. If someone out there is randomly targeting Sam and wants to get revenge on him through me, because I'm his girlfriend, I guess I get that. There have been pictures of the two of us in the paper."

"Yes."

"But if this is Nikon, and his motive is that he somehow blames Sam for the loss of Victoria, then why would I be involved? Unless he knew that I was the one who found her?"

"But he couldn't know. The articles in the paper only

said that Victoria was found because of the Blue Lake police and the invaluable aid of some Blue Lake citizens. Or it might have said 'women.' I don't recall."

"Yes, that's what I thought. I purposely asked Doug to leave me anonymous. So why would anyone link me to the rescue of Victoria?"

Camilla tapped her fingers on her desk blotter, thinking about this. Then she said, "Doug left you anonymous—but Sam didn't! Remember, in the interview with Jake Elliott? He said you were a primary reason why Victoria was found. He said he was grateful to you and that you had found a link that no one else had, something like that."

"And now that I think of it, Ted Strayer named me, too." I had tried not to think much about Ted Strayer, the evil tabloid reporter. "And back in winter, when the press first swarmed around us, Sam said something about me being the one who 'saved' him. I guess I just lost track of who said what because I tried not to focus on the press coverage."

"Yes, there was so much going on, especially once you and Sam became a public reality."

"We were suspicious that Nikon had something to do with Eddie, and the Arthurian sword, but—I guess I was trying to believe these notes were something else. Something less sinister. I suppose that was naïve."

"Don't worry over this, Lena. It could drive you crazy. Wait until Doug and Cliff unearth enough for us to really sink our teeth into, and then we will find this person and send them to jail. Meanwhile, we have a beautiful book in the works. Now, coffee."

She left the room, and I realized I felt better. Camilla had a gift for doing this—taking my worries and dissecting them until she lifted some of the burden from my spirit.

Now I looked over our notes with a feeling of euphoria and a sense of irony: while I hated the thought of unsolved mysteries floating around us in real life, I loved the ones that we were creating for our fiction.

This book, I knew, was going to be good, and this time I would have a large part in its creation.

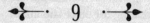

9

*"We'll need to call my father," he told her as they
bent over the old coin. "He's the only one I know of
who would understand the significance of something
like this."*

*"If he's an expert in this area," she said, "I wonder
that someone else hasn't consulted him with a similar question."*

*His eyes widened, and for the first time he looked
truly worried.*

—From Death at Delphi

BY NOON WE were ready to take a break, and Camilla said
that she wanted to go on a walk to sort her thoughts. "You
take some free time, dear. Go see one of your friends."

This sounded like a good idea, but I knew that Allison's
two-day break was over and she was back at the hospital,
so I called Belinda from Camilla's office. Lestrade, with
his feline audacity, had jumped on Camilla's desk and
started licking his paw. I scratched his head with one hand
while I held the phone with the other. "How's the library?"
I asked.

Her voice was wry. "It's fine. Are you calling for London
File details?"

"And also to talk to my friend Belinda."

She laughed. "I can meet for lunch again, if you want

to drive me. Darla told me that Willoughby's has opened their summer garden."

"Oooohhhh," I said. Willoughby's was a small diner in town, but a little-known secret was that the owner was a devoted gardener, and his outdoor eating area was a hidden paradise, filled with whimsical flower arrangements and tended with a loving hand. "I'm there. I'll pick you up in ten minutes."

"Great. I'll bring my notes."

I hung up, and Lestrade gave me a surprisingly judgmental glare.

"You're thinking that all I do is have meals at restaurants, aren't you?" I said. "I swear I do more than eat. Just not lately, I guess."

His fuzzy face remained skeptical. I kissed the top of his little head and said, "Keep an eye on the house."

AT THE LIBRARY I waved to Belinda, who was at the back of the room near her office, packing some things into a bag. At the front desk sat Darla, her dark hair pulled back in a thick braid. She was scanning in some books, and the regular beep, beep was one of the only sounds in the quiet space. I approached her with some reluctance, but she seemed not to notice. "Hello, Lena! Nice to see you," she said. Her eyes went to the door for a moment because some people had entered the library; she waved to them and then returned her attention to me. "How's everything?"

I summoned up a smile. "Just a regular workday. I'm taking a lunch break."

She nodded. "It must be amazing to work with such a famous author."

"I love it," I said. "Camilla is my hero."

"So cool." She finished scanning and pushed her pile of books aside. "How's Sam?" Her eyes were on the counter when she said it, and she was clearly working to make it sound casual. It wasn't casual, though; there was an intensity in her face, and a stillness in her form, that suggested my answer was important. I didn't know what she was up to; there was of course the chance that she was hoping to make money off any sort of story about Sam that she could sell—people had done it before. She had told me, though, that she had studied him for a class. I wondered vaguely if she could have fallen in love with his image—that, too, was a possibility. Sam did have an arresting image, to say the least.

"He's fine. His life is complicated, as always."

She didn't bother to hide her intensity now. "Is it? What makes it so complicated? I mean, they found his wife, right?"

"But her abductor is still at large. And Victoria's baby is missing. It's all—it adds stress to Sam's life."

Now her face bore what looked like genuine sympathy. "That poor guy. He's been through so much in his life. I'm amazed that he is so strong."

"Yes. Well, anyway—here's Belinda. Nice to see you, Darla."

"You, too." She wore a yearning expression that made me feel a bit guilty. For whatever reason, she was fascinated by Sam, and I was stingy with details. It wasn't like me, though, to discuss Sam's life with some stranger.

Belinda was wearing a mint green pantsuit today that made me think of ice cream. It was a delicate color which suited her slightly dreamy eyes. I said, "You have the nicest work wardrobe. I tend to always wear jeans and stuff."

She shrugged. "Some of it is years old. But you look

nice all the time, Lena. You always look like you're about to go off on some adventure. I can't explain it."

Darla leaned forward. "It's her enthusiasm. She looks full of life."

This made me laugh. "Yeah, right. Okay, Darla, I'll have her back by one."

Darla nodded and waved; a familiar-looking woman approached the desk with some books, and I paused for a moment, wondering where I knew her from. Belinda tapped my shoulder and pointed at her watch. She was on a timed lunch; Camilla had spoiled me in letting me have a flexible schedule. "Sorry," I said. "Our carriage awaits."

Belinda and I left the library and climbed into my car; I drove left out of the parking lot, back toward Wentworth Street, where Willoughby's sat unobtrusively in the middle of other storefronts. Minutes later I found a spot right in front of the little restaurant and felt a familiar glow as I looked at the sign. It was at Willoughby's that I had first realized my attraction to Sam, back in the fall when the whole world still believed he was a murderer.

"For some reason I'm starving," Belinda said, looking for something in her capacious purse. "I'm not having a salad today."

"Me, either," I said. "Must be the spring air making us hungry."

I paid the meter and we hurried inside, where Belinda asked if we could have garden seating. The waitress nodded. "It's getting a little crowded, but I have a table by the fountain that just opened up."

"Ah," I said appreciatively. The fountain was an antique shop find that the owner, Frank Attenborough, had placed in one corner of his brick-lined patio and refurbished to its original splendor. It was a circular stone fountain with a playful cherub frolicking in its center. Frank, who had a green thumb, had trailed ivy over the stone and tucked pots of bright geraniums and hydrangeas around the base. The sound of the sprinkling water was a restful accompaniment to the muted chatter of the people dining outdoors.

Belinda and I made our way outside, where the garden paradise was indeed filled with people, although we barely noticed our human companions on the patio. Frank and his wife, Deana, had outdone themselves this year, and for a moment we just stood in the doorway, breathing and letting the beauty invade us. Deana had done her usual job of scouring antique malls for gorgeous or unusual planters, and this year she had gone for earthenware pots in distinctive colors like red and deep gray and forest green. Into these Frank had planted a bright, sunny mixture of yellow blooms—yellow capsicums, orange marigolds, calendula, nasturtiums, orange chard, and cosmos. Mixed with these were purple-toned plants and bright green herbs with their variegated leaves. The color came from sages, purple basil, thyme, eggplant, beetroot, lavender, violet, geranium, viola, and petunia. As always, Frank had dedicated himself to the arrangement, probably for days, before he opened the patio. Rumor had it that he hired a high schooler each summer just to weed and keep the garden perfect.

"Oh, I needed this," Belinda breathed. "Look at our table—it's right next to the fountain! It's like a vacation back here."

It was. I indulged a brief daydream in which I bought my own house in Blue Lake and hired Frank to design my gardens, which would of course be vast . . .

We reached the table and tucked ourselves into chairs. "How are things going—in general?" I asked Belinda.

She pursed her lips at me, but her eyes were smiling. "You mean with Doug."

"Yeah, I guess."

"We talked. It was nice. And since then he's been—leaving me signs of his devotion."

I trailed a hand in the cool water of the fountain. "What does that mean?"

"Oh, this and that." A little smile escaped her. "A pot of roses on my porch. A present tucked under the windshield wiper of my car. Little notes left for me at the library."

"That's romantic, but why doesn't he just come in and talk to you?"

She shrugged. "I told him I needed a little time. I want to be sure—you know. I mean, there was an attraction between you two, right?"

"Months ago. When I first got to town. I would say yes, for me, but only until I met Sam. I fell for him pretty quickly, and Doug knew that. So it was nothing, Belinda. Nothing ever happened. He spent a few weeks hoping something would, maybe. And that was it. We were never together. Not like he wants to be with you. And he's a good guy—you know that."

Her eyes were bright as they studied mine. "Yes, I do. But I'm a good guy, too, and I deserve a man who will be devoted to me."

"You mean the kind who will leave you secret presents all over town?"

She grinned. "Yes."

"Don't make him wait too long, Belinda. Some other girl will snatch him up. He's handsome and young and single and super talented at his job. Remember how you had a crush on him before you even met him? Well, don't you think there are other women like that in town?"

This startled her, and she studied her menu without seeming to see it.

"Anyway, enough of my nosiness about your love life. Tell me what you've been finding out for the London File."

Her eyes lit up; they actually seemed to grow greener with her interest. "Okay." She put her menu aside and a waitress approached. It was Carly, the one who had waited on Sam and me the day we met. She was pregnant, and she wore an apron that said, "Bun in the Oven."

"What can I get you all?" she asked.

Belinda held up a finger. "I'll have a cup of the chicken rice soup and a club sandwich with chips."

I nodded. "The soup sounds good, and the chicken salad croissant for me. With chips."

Carly noted this on her pad and said, "And what to drink, ladies?"

"Iced tea," Belinda said. "It's so lovely and warm today, it's the perfect drink."

Carly nodded her agreement and I said, "Yes, I'll have that, too."

She went away to put in our orders, and Belinda pulled her large purse into her lap. "Okay. Who do we start with? Nikon Lazos or Sam?"

"You already have something about Sam?" I asked her, shocked.

"Yeah, a couple things. Nothing amazing, but still—he might not know this stuff."

"Start with Sam," I said.

She opened the file folder that she had started for me months before and removed a couple of clippings. "Well, here's the thing: Sam's mom was married before."

"What? Before Sam's dad?"

"Yeah. I traced her marriage certificate just as a matter of course and found that she had two of them. One in 1981 and one in 1979."

"Sam was born in 1982."

"Yes. She married his father in 1981. The father was significantly older, did you know that? By almost ten years."

"I didn't. I know he was a police officer."

"Yes—a decorated one. I'm still looking into details about him."

I stared at the fountain, where the stone Cupid seemed free of all care. "Tell me about the first husband."

"His name was Steven Randisi. I checked his school record and saw that he and Mrs. West attended the same high school. Maybe a first romance?"

I shook my head. "There's no way Sam wouldn't have known this, right? I mean, wouldn't you mention to your kids that you'd been married before? Why would it have to be a secret?"

Belinda was digging in the file again. "That's all I have so far, but I do have a death notice for Steven Randisi. He died in 1995 in an auto accident. He was survived by a wife and two daughters."

She handed me the obituary, which included a picture of the tall, thin Steven Randisi. He had not even reached forty years old. The thought made me sad.

"I don't know whether I should mention this to Sam, or not," I said. "He's got a lot on his mind."

"I'll give you this file. I made copies."

"Thanks. This is amazing work for only a day on the job."

She shook her head, dismissing this. "Okay. *Now.* I have

something to show you about our friend Nikon. Check out this picture I found—this is like pure gold, because you just don't find much personal stuff on him. I think this was taken at a relative's wedding."

She handed me the photo and I saw that it was the entire Lazos clan, grouped around Nikon's mother, Ariana, and his father, Aristotle. The two sat, proud and straight, while their eight children stood at attention around them; they all wore white.

Nikon was obvious and the most arresting. As the oldest child he stood directly behind his parents, leaning forward slightly with the arrogant, amused expression of a man who would never want for anything. Next were two women, seemingly the next oldest, then two more boys, then another three girls. All of the children had dark hair and dark eyes.

"They're like weird clones of one another," I said.

"Strong family resemblance," Belinda agreed. "Of course this is an old photo—about twenty years. Both parents are now dead. Lazos is fifty-three, but he was thirty when this picture was taken."

"Poor Victoria. I can't imagine any woman who could resist that man if he applied all of his charm. And I say this as one who despises Nikon Lazos."

"Yeah, he's handsome, all right. And look at the younger brothers—the Nikons junior. It's like the parents kept using the same recipe for making children."

I studied the picture carefully. "What do all these other Lazos people do? Wouldn't you think the Feds would be all over them?"

"I think they are. All the brothers and sisters lead pretty low-key lives. They're all rich, of course. But they're a tight family. I read an article about them in the *New York Times* that said no gossip about the Lazos clan has ever made it out of Greece. They probably own the whole country."

I pointed at the photo. "Look at this sister—she's holding a baby. They're probably all married, right? With families of their own. Interesting that Nikon didn't have children until Victoria."

"Yeah, I wondered about that. I mean, he seems like a giant playboy. But Doug said the woman he spoke to—his first wife—said that they had tried and couldn't. I guess you all spoke to her, right? That's how you knew you were on the right track about Victoria."

I sighed. "Yes, we spoke to Grace months ago. I wonder how she's doing now. She seemed happy and serene with her new husband. But she did warn us about Nikon's charisma and how he could get people to do things for him." I looked back at the photo. "Anyway, this baby looks a lot like Athena. It could *be* Athena. Victoria's baby really favors her father's side in the looks department. That seems unfair to Victoria. It's like he got absolutely everything, even the resemblance."

Our soup came, and we leaned back to let Carly set it down. When she left, Belinda said, "How is that going, anyway? Do they have any leads?"

"I don't know what Doug is doing, but I know that the other agencies don't communicate with him. He's just a small-town cop to them, and yet he broke literally every aspect of this case."

"Thanks to us," Belinda said.

"Yeah. Maybe the two of us should find Athena. Poor little kid must miss her mom."

Belinda smiled. "I've been working on it."

I leaned in. "Do tell."

"Everyone's focused on Nikon and Victoria and the

baby. But what about the driver? The man who stole the child? Who was he? How did Victoria happen to hire him? And how did he end up on Nikon's payroll? So I've been looking into him."

"Wait—I remember his name from Jake Elliott's article—Leonard Warren?"

"Leonard Wilson. Known locally as Len. He's from Indianapolis, and I guess he had started his own car company back in 2005. Nikon got to him, paid him off through one of his minions, and had someone follow Victoria West's travel plans. When he learned she was flying to Indy, he figured she would be hiring a car to take her to Blue Lake. He planted Leonard Wilson at the airport and gave him money to pay off whatever other driver showed up for her. Lots of money, I'm guessing."

"How do you know this?"

"Some of it was written up in the paper; some I hunted down through his contacts."

"Wow, Belinda! You should be a cop."

"That's what Doug tells me."

I sipped some soup out of my spoon. "So poor Victoria walked into another trap. She's not a foolish woman, and yet people tricked her twice in her life, and both times she lost something valuable. First her freedom, then her child."

"I'm going to keep looking into Leonard Wilson. There might be something there, some connection, that can help us find out where they took Athena."

"It's a good idea. You never know what the authorities are pursuing. Maybe they think some of these things are unimportant."

For a time we were quiet. I stared at the hypnotic fountain, and Belinda absently studied a pot of marigolds. We finished our soup, and Carly brought our sandwiches. I took a few bites of my sandwich and then said, "So what was the present?"

Belinda had been about to take another bite of her sandwich, but she paused. "What present?"

"That Doug left under your windshield wiper. What was in it?"

She laughed, then batted her lashes at me. "It was a notebook that said 'Investigator's Journal.' I've been using it, too."

"How perfect," I said, and we laughed while Cupid smiled at us with a whimsical, carefree expression.

WHEN I DROPPED Belinda back at the library, Darla was in front, helping a patron with a cane walk down the ramp. She waved at Belinda, then saw me in my car and waved eagerly. I waved back, summoning up a smile. I wasn't sure why I couldn't be friendlier to Darla; something about her just made me feel defensive, and yet I felt sorry for her, as well.

As I was about to pull out, I got a phone call. I slid the screen over and said, "Hello?"

"Hey, honey," said my father. "Tabby and I think Meridien Springs is terrific! But we'll be home by dinner and we want to take you to Adam's restaurant to pay you back for last night. You and Sam treated us to a really nice evening."

"Dinner at Wheat Grass? That sounds nice. I was just telling—I was just saying that all I seem to do is go to restaurants." No need to tell my father I had dialogues with my cat.

"Nonsense. You can ask Camilla to join us, if you want. Wear something really nice—we're going to make it a fancy evening."

This made me laugh. My mother and father and I had invented "fancy evenings" back when I was a little girl and saw a Grace Kelly movie. I had decided that I wanted to wear a dress like one of the many she wore in the film, so my parents decided we would be fancy once a month. The idea had died out long ago, but apparently my father was going to resurrect it as a form of nostalgia.

"Okay, you're on," I said. After I hung up, though, I remembered I really had nothing that would allow for this sort of dress-up game. As I had realized with some chagrin the previous evening, I was a casual-wardrobe person, and as someone who had only recently started getting a regular salary, I still had a limited number of items in my closet.

But I did have some money now, and suddenly I was yearning for a Grace Kelly dress the way I had when I was a kid. My car started turning onto Violet Street before I had even made the conscious decision to visit a realm I had never previously entered.

I was going to venture into Sasha's.

Sasha's, Allison assured me, was the place to get elegant clothing in Blue Lake. She said it was mainly for the country club set (and Blue Lake did have a country club), and that she had only gone there to look for bridesmaids' dresses.

"It's great, but kind of scary, and Sasha looks and acts like royalty, so you feel like you should be bowing to her all the time. I don't even know what country she's from. She sounds like a fortune-teller from the movies," Allison had enthused in one of our Saturday talk sessions.

Now I looked at the front of Sasha's, a brick building with a blue door, and summoned my courage. "I can be a country club person. I can talk to royalty," I said.

I got out and climbed the steps to find my Grace Kelly dress.

10

They went to the museum gala in Athens, convinced they would find their nemesis and the answers to their questions. As they moved among the glittering gowns and costly champagne, they felt a growing sense of menace.

—From *Death at Delphi*

THE INTERIOR OF Sasha's smelled like new clothes and expensive perfume. I moved tentatively across the polished wood floor and tried to look as though I belonged with the two glamorous-looking women who expertly flipped through the hanging dresses.

I touched a black gown with silver piping, and a woman appeared next to me like a genie. She was tall, blonde, and perfect, with hair that curved around her head in a smooth helmet. "You are looking for what?" she asked, smiling at me while her eyes assessed me.

"Oh—uh. Something fancy. I don't normally wear dresses, but I'm going to something elegant tonight, and I wanted to—branch out."

"Mm-hmm." She nodded with a wise expression, as though she and I both knew a secret. "Don't even touch that. Black is not your color. It would wash you out, terrible." She had an accent, but I couldn't determine what kind.

"I never really thought about—" I started, but she had clamped a hand on my arm and started leading me across the floor, trailing the scent of her lovely perfume.

"Here we go. I have your size—six, yes? Maybe eight. And your colors. You are gold tones. Gold, bronze, brown, tangerine, taupe, yes? Even cream and caramel. Oh yes!" She was gathering dresses and putting them over one arm. "I have you all figured out. Your name is?"

"Lena."

"Lena, lovely. Your brown silky hair, and this pale skin. We can draw out the color with these looks." She led me to a fitting room and hung the dresses on a hook. "You try on, then come out to me, then we decide."

I went in, half hypnotized by her strong scent and even stronger personality, and she closed the curtain with a swoosh. The first dress was a soft knit in a cream color, and it clung to my curves in a flattering way. I liked it, but it didn't seem the type of dress I'd wear for dinner with my father. The second dress was a one-piece knee-length gown with a chocolate brown slip and a gold scalloped sheath overlay. It was elegant, beautiful, and somehow perfect. I wanted a second opinion, so I opened the curtain and walked out, only to be swooped upon by Sasha. "Oh yes! You see? Look in this mirror here. Much bigger glass. Look at your face. See how this color brings out the rich skin tone? See how the silk hugs your form? And the scalloped gold neckline—you don't need jewelry! This is like Cleopatra. Just wear gold earrings. You have shoes?"

"Yes. Well, no."

"What size?"

"Six."

"You are so tiny." She walked away into an anteroom I couldn't see. The women in the store had stopped shopping and were simply watching. I would have done it, too. Sasha was fascinating.

"It does look great," one of the women said. "You should buy it."

"I'm going to," I said.

Sasha returned with a few pairs of shoes, and I tried them on. We settled on a pair of bronze sandals that suited the style of the dress and made my legs look somehow longer. "Ah," I said.

Sasha smiled at me smugly. "You take dress and shoes. You want more dresses?"

I thought about this. I had never had a professional stylist at my disposal. "I think I would like to try on the rest. And"—I looked at the women, who quickly turned away and feigned disinterest—"do you have any lingerie?"

I LEFT SASHA'S feeling both euphoria and guilt. I had spent more on clothing than I had ever done in my life, but I also had a nice new wardrobe and a better sense of what looked good on me.

The Blue Lake sidewalks were bright and sunny today, and I admired the storefronts and flowerpots on this block that I rarely visited. I was passing a little bookstore called The Hidden Cellar, which had an outside rack displaying newspapers, magazines, and paperbacks. A headline jumped out at me from the front row, and I gasped. It said, "West and London Forge Their Future." I moved closer; it was a tabloid paper, but one with a wide readership. The byline of the story belonged to someone named Joseph Williams. Not only had I never heard of this person, it sounded distinctly like a pseudonym to me. Doug was right: there were reporters hiding in this town, trying to cash in on the whole Sam West story. There was a picture of Sam and me with the headline—we were standing on Sam's front lawn and looking into each other's eyes. I recognized it as a moment that had occurred two days earlier, on his private property. Fuming, I went to my car.

I unlocked the driver's door with my remote control, but before I even got to the car I saw the envelope under the windshield wiper. My first thought was that Doug had decided to leave some sort of gift for me, as he had done for Belinda, and I was alarmed. Belinda would get the wrong idea! I moved closer and then the truth hit me: it was the same kind of envelope, the same inky black scrawl on the front, with the word "Lena" dominating the envelope.

I took out my phone and dialed Doug. I got his voice mail. I swore under my breath and looked in my contacts for Cliff's number; Sam had made me put it in after his conference with Cliff in Camilla's driveway. I dialed. "Detective Blake," he said.

"Cliff. It's Lena London. I wonder if you—I got another note."

His voice was alert, wary. "Where are you, Lena?"

"On Violet Street, outside Sasha's clothing store."

"I know where that is. Give me five minutes."

He hung up, and I stared at the thing under my windshield wiper. Cliff would show up with an evidence bag and tweezers and take it away, but suddenly I wanted to know what was inside; I couldn't wait a moment longer. I leaned in and grabbed one corner of the envelope between two fingernails. I got into my car and set the letter in my lap, slipping my longest nail under the flap to work it away from the envelope. I slid out the paper and opened it, still managing not to touch anything but the edges.

The message inside, once again on Sam West's stationery, made my stomach lurch:

Hey, Sweetheart!
Did you ever have a dream?
Did anyone ever destroy it?

I took the paper by the edges and put it on the passenger seat. What was this about? What dream were they speaking of? Were they suggesting I had destroyed something? Was this about Nikon and his idyll with Victoria?

A few minutes later a noise on my window made me jump and scream. I looked up to see Cliff standing there. I lowered my window. "I opened it. I didn't touch it with my fingers."

He nodded. "Where is it?"

"Here." I pointed to the seat. "It was under my wiper."

Cliff came around the car and opened my passenger door. As I predicted, he took out tweezers and put the note inside a bag. He disappeared, probably to stow it into his car, but he left my door open. A moment later he was back. He climbed into my car and sat in the passenger seat, turning to look at me.

"Are you okay, Lena?"

"Not really," I said. "It's weird. The wording, and the Sam West stationery. It's like they're reminding me, not just that they broke into his house, but that they're following me around. That they always seem to know where I am. I'm scared."

His face was calm. "I get it. It's a weird situation. But they're not going to do a darn thing to you, because Doug and I have stepped up patrols overall, and especially around Graham House, and around you. Have you noticed more cop cars?"

I thought about it; now that he mentioned it, I had seen those familiar white and blue vehicles quite a bit lately. I looked up, and one of them passed us where we sat, making me feel the truth of his words. "I guess so," I said.

"That's Officer Connolly," he said. "He's particularly good at spotting things that don't look right. He caught that purse snatcher that was running around last summer, I heard."

"I wasn't here then," I said.

Cliff patted my arm. "You drive home now; I'll be right behind you in my car. Nothing can harm you when I'm right there."

"Okay." I did want to be home, with Camilla, so that I could tell her about this and get her ever-wise interpretation of events. "Thanks, Cliff."

He left with the letter, sealed in the evidence bag, and I started my car. I waited for Cliff's car to appear behind me, and then I drove back to Graham House. Cliff came all the way to the driveway with me, then waited while I went to the door. I waved, and he waved back, and then he drove away.

I went into the house with my bags from Sasha's. I had felt so euphoric about the new clothing, but now it was the last thing on my mind as I locked the door behind me. I moved swiftly to Camilla, ready to lay my burdens upon her. She would know what to do about the note, the article in the newspaper, the general feeling of chaos that was descending upon me—but when I walked into her office I saw that she was in some distress. She sat with her hands pressed against her temples, her face creased in pain.

"Camilla! Are you all right?"

"Oh, Lena. I wonder if I could trouble you for a glass of water?"

"Of course." I went to the kitchen and ran some Blue Lake water—"most delicious in the U.S.," Doug always said—into a glass and moved swiftly back to her. "Is it a headache? Or do you think you have the flu?" I asked, putting the back of my hand against her cheek, which was cool.

"I'm not quite sure. If it's all right with you, though, I think I'll retire to my bedroom for a rest. I know we were going to do some work, but—"

"Don't be silly. Go rest until you feel better. Can I get you anything else?"

"No, no. I'll be fine. You're sweet. I'll just lie down for a time."

"Okay. Just so you know, my dad invited you to dinner tonight, if you'd like. He's taking me to Wheat Grass."

She took off her glasses and rubbed her eyes. "I must bow out this evening, I think. What time were you and your father meeting there?"

"Around six, I think." I consulted my watch. "It's three now."

"You enjoy dinner with him and with Tabitha. It will be an early night for me. Perhaps Adam is right and I haven't gotten over my jet lag after all."

This concerned me. I had thought Camilla was looking strong and even young, and yet Adam had been worrying about her health. Was I missing something? Was she hiding something from me?

Camilla saw my expression and waved it away. "Don't make this more than it is, Lena. It's just a headache. I'll sleep it off, I'm sure. You go put your packages away and enjoy the afternoon. I'll tell Rhonda she needn't make dinner at all."

"All right. If you're sure," I said. I went upstairs. Camilla's headache, distressing as it was, had been just the distraction I needed from my own worries, and now I felt better, stronger—ready to face whatever malicious person in Blue Lake was trying to terrorize me. I walked confidently into my room, where Lestrade, King of My Bed, examined the plastic dress covers that I laid upon it. "They're beautiful, aren't they?" I asked him. "I'm going to get all pretty for this evening."

I took great care, putting the clothes away with loving hands. I thought about calling Sam, asking if he'd like to come to dinner, but my father hadn't mentioned him, and we had all just dined together. Perhaps it was best if I spent time alone with my father and Tabitha.

I went to my desk and wrote for an hour, pursuing some of the ideas Camilla and I had just generated. I would show her tomorrow, when she was feeling better—because of course she *would* be feeling better? I never wanted to have to think of Camilla in decline; I had only just become a part of her life.

I closed my document and opened my e-mail, sending a few long-postponed notes to friends, filling them in on my Blue Lake existence. Some of them had sent questions about Sam West or the latest murder in town. I didn't elaborate on any of those, but spoke in general of Blue Lake's skies and soothing water.

While my hands were on the keyboard, I found that, as usual, I couldn't resist a little online sleuthing. First, I Googled "Joseph Williams, Indiana News X-Press." That had been the writer of the article about Sam and me. What popped up was just a paragraph on an "About Our Staff" page at the tabloid. While most staffers had photographs next to their biographies, Joseph Williams was merely a silhouette. Hmm.

I clicked on it and read, "Joseph Williams is an Indiana

writer who knows how to find the stories people care about. Contact him via the station at JWilliams@newsxpress.com."

This was very fishy indeed. I sent a skeptical look to Lestrade, then Googled "brothers and sisters of Nikon Lazos." This brought a few articles, most about Nikon with mere mentions of his siblings, but some were about individual brothers or sisters. One, Demetrius, had started his own bottled water company. Naturally, it had made him millions of dollars. I remembered a comment my mother had made when one of the wealthiest men in our town won the lottery: "Money goes to money, Lena," she had said wisely. "Somehow that's how it always goes."

Money. Joseph Williams, whoever he was, must surely be making money from spying on Sam and me. Might whoever was leaving me the notes be making money, too? What if Nikon had paid some local person to terrorize me? But of course, the question was *why.*

There were minimal articles about Nikon's other brother and his sisters. One sister had married a British industrialist and had relocated to the Isle of Man. Another had her own perfume line. The youngest had been kicked out of an expensive boarding school. How spoiled they all sounded, and it wouldn't be a surprise if they had an unrealistic idea of life and reality. Nikon certainly did; what if all of his siblings had as twisted a worldview as he had?

I closed my laptop, stretched, stood up, and looked at my watch. It was time to wear my pretty dress. Inspired by Sasha, I put on some perfume, then donned the brown and gold dress with some sheer hose and my new sandals. My thoughts darted back to Lazos's sister and her perfume, which was called Agapi. I shook my head; I didn't want thoughts of the Lazos family in there.

I combed my hair into a glossy sheet, then grabbed my purse and walked into the hall.

Camilla's door was closed, and the dogs were nowhere to be seen, which meant they were guarding her while she rested. I wondered if I should tell her that I was leaving, but I feared that if I knocked I might wake her. Instead I went down to the kitchen and wrote a brief note, saying that I was at dinner with my father, and we would all return sometime later that evening.

Lestrade strolled through the kitchen and jumped onto Camilla's windowsill to enjoy the evening sun. I scratched his head and told him I'd be back soon. "I know, I know— I'm going to another restaurant," I said. "But really I'm networking."

Lestrade was unimpressed. He twitched a whisker at me and then turned away, probably to scan for birds or bats.

I shrugged and left the house, turning the key in the new lock and trying the door afterward for good measure. It was solid and firm. Camilla had the dogs, and a phone next to her, and Adam just a call away, if anything were to happen. Meanwhile I scanned the area with vigilance, my fingers twined inside my keys in case I needed to use them as a weapon. I had the police number already dialed into my phone, should I see anything suspicious.

I realized, with some comfort, that whoever was writing to me had confined his activities to notes. This was a coward, I reasoned to myself, who wanted to intimidate me without any risk to himself. I tossed my head as I unlocked my car. Let him leave all the notes he wanted. Each clue would bring the police a step closer to catching him.

As I buckled in, though, I remembered the chilling words. "Hello, Sweetheart!" I would never like that word again. How could an affectionate term hold so much menace? Was this really about Nikon, or was it something entirely different? What "dream" had the writer seen destroyed? What did that have to do with me?

Driving the familiar route out to Green Glass Highway, I found my thoughts drifting to Athena, the lost baby. Did she know that she was lost? Was it certain that she was with her father? If so, was her father being good to her? Was he attentive and loving? Victoria had told various reporters how Nikon, her estranged lover, had focused all of his attention on her, lured her into a romance, and then essentially consumed her with his obsessive love.

What would it be like for a child, an only child, to grow up with a father like that?

Still pondering, I pulled into an open space against one wall of Wheat Grass. Although I knew I was about to have access to unlimited love and sympathy, I had decided not to tell my father about the notes. Why would I worry him when he was only in town for a matter of days? I paused to text him: *I'm here! Are you in the restaurant?*

A moment later, I got a response: *Yes—we have a table ready.*

In a Pavlovian response, my stomach started growling. I jumped out of my car and walked through the mild, flower-scented air to the front door. I pulled it open, ready to speak to whatever member of the waitstaff greeted me.

Instead, I saw a shocking sea of faces, with Sam and Camilla at their center, and they were all shouting "Surprise!"

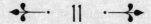

She felt the menace without seeing it; in the shade of the monuments she sensed its presence, palpable and intense. When she spun around, she found nothing but silence and a single purple heron floating weightless in the darkening sky.

—From *Death at Delphi*

I NEARLY FELL down. My party! I had expected it to happen later, closer to my birthday.

My father approached me now and gave me a hug and kiss. "I guess we succeeded! You're white as a ghost. Are you okay?"

"Yes—this is just a little overwhelming. Thank you, everyone!" I said, laughing a little. The crowd cheered and clapped and began to mill around. I tried to suppress the voice in the back of my head, taunting me even in this moment. *Hello, Sweetheart!*

Camilla approached, looking sheepish and quite pretty in a lavender dress. "Do you forgive me for lying to you?"

I stared. "How did you even—?"

"I waited until you went up to your room, and then I had Adam meet me at the front door. I felt like quite a conspirator, I must say."

"Where are the dogs?"

"I asked Rhonda's son to take them for the evening. She and her husband are here. Look at her lovely gown!" She pointed at Rhonda, who glimmered in black and silver. "But I wanted you to think the dogs were with me."

"I did! You thought of everything. And I'm glad you're not really sick. I was worried about you."

She sniffed. "I'm hearty as a horse. Look at the decorating job your father and Adam did." She pointed, and I noticed that the walls were draped with Italian lights, and a giant poster hung near the bar—it was a blown-up picture of me at one year old, playing with my father's typewriter. A caption at the bottom said, "Lena London: a writer since birth." Added to this were an assortment of pale pink and silver balloons hung tastefully around the room, and a large cake that looked like Rhonda's handiwork, which said "Happy Birthday, Lena—We Love You!" I scanned the room to see that in fact the people I loved best were all there: Sam, Allison, John, Doug, Belinda (hadn't I just dropped her at the library?), Marge and Horace Bick, Lane and Clay Waldrop, even some old friends who had driven in from Chicago. I waved at them, my eyes misting with sudden emotion.

Tabitha touched my arm. "We have a table in the center of the action. Come on in. Would you like a drink?"

I shrugged. Normally alcohol just made me tired. "Maybe. Some wine or something. Surprise me, Tabby." I had never called her this before, and she looked pleased.

Allison galloped up, dragging a smiling John. "Kiss, kiss. Happy birthday, my best friend. John and I are in charge of music, so we have to go mess with the sound system. Save us a seat." John managed to pat my arm before Allison dragged him away.

Sam appeared in front of me with a shy smile. "Happy birthday," he said. "Were you surprised?"

"I absolutely was, although I should have seen all the signs. Some detective I am. I actually thought Dad and Tabby were in Meridien."

"Your dad had me hanging balloons all day. He's a real taskmaster."

I studied his face. "You had fun."

He grinned. "I did. We are good friends now."

I leaned closer to him. The music started—some muted, big-band stuff Allison knew I found romantic—and I had to speak a bit more loudly. "When we get a chance, I need to talk to you—"

His face hardened. "Something's happened?"

"I got another note."

"Are you all right?"

I nodded. "I called Cliff and he escorted me home. This isn't the time to talk about it, but—"

He looked concerned, and a bit helpless. "Cliff has the note now?"

"Yes."

"What did it say?"

I told him. His face grew grim. "I am going to find this guy and punch him in the face. It's going to feel good, Lena."

I giggled. His warm hands, holding mine, made me feel stronger, more confident, less vulnerable. "I'll punch him after you do."

He sighed. "This is weird timing. Everyone worked so hard to get this together. I guess we can pretend for a couple of hours that nothing happened, right?"

"Sure we can. Because I see a pile of presents over there," I joked.

"Mine is the blue one," he said, tucking some hair behind my ear.

"Will I love it?"

"I hope so."

Doug and Belinda approached. They weren't holding hands, but they seemed comfortable next to each other. "Hey, birthday girl," Doug said. He gave me a quick kiss on the cheek, and then Belinda gave me a hug. "Happy birthday," she said.

I thanked them, then narrowed my eyes at Belinda. "What, did they pay you to distract me at Willoughby's?"

She shrugged and laughed. "You called me, remember? But Camilla had said she would try to nudge you in that direction. That dress is a knockout, by the way."

"Yes, it is," said Sam. He hadn't really taken his eyes off me since I'd entered the room.

"Thank you. Sasha helped me select it."

Belinda held up her hands. "Well, say no more. That woman is some kind of gypsy psychic."

"Maybe I should consult her on some cases," Doug said, looking distracted.

I noted, suddenly, that he looked tired. "Things are going slowly, huh? And hey, why is the mayor monopolizing your time so much these days?"

He looked surprised. "You heard about that?"

"Yeah. Cliff came out the other night because you were having dinner with him. And the mayor called you on the morning that you introduced me to Cliff at the house."

"Ah. That seems like a long time ago," Doug said. He sighed. All three of us were looking at him with curious expressions, and he laughed. "Okay, fine. The fact is, Chief Baxter is retiring, and the mayor wants me to consider taking his job."

"Police chief? Doug, that's amazing! You'd be great for

that job," I shouted. Sam and Belinda were saying similar things as we clustered around him.

He shrugged. "I don't know that I want it. It's lots of responsibility and desk work. I'm more of an on-the-street kind of guy."

Sam looked solemn as he contemplated Doug. "I think you deserve the honor, but I have to agree, I don't see you enjoying that role."

"He said I can take a couple of weeks to think about it," Doug said. "I'll need to go over the pros and cons with people I trust." He looked at Belinda, who bowed her head in silent affirmation.

I saw Tabitha waving at me and pointing at the tables. "I think Tabitha wants us to sit down. Oh God, there aren't going to be speeches, are there?"

"There might," Doug said. "Some of us might have some interesting stories to tell."

"I know I do," Belinda said, smiling.

"Me, too," said Sam. He took my hand. "Come on. I think the four of us are at the table of honor."

We were; it felt oddly like a wedding, and I felt grateful to the people around me for putting up with the rather awkward setup. Soon enough it didn't matter, though, because Tabitha brought me some wine, and three of Adam's waiters appeared, bringing us soup and salad, and my father walked to a microphone in the corner. I feared he would make me cry, but all he did was tell a funny story about my fourteenth birthday party, to which I had invited my writing idol, Camilla Graham.

"Camilla lived in London at the time, but Lena somehow found her address and wrote to her, saying that she loved her books and she'd love for Camilla to attend her party."

I stole a glance at Camilla, whose face was a picture of

surprise. "Camilla?" my father said. "Do you remember that letter?"

She looked shocked. "I do," she called. "But I had no idea that was Lena! Oh my goodness!"

The crowd laughed and clapped, and my father held up a hand. "What Camilla might not recall is that she wrote back to Lena, and we saved the letter to give to her at her fourteenth birthday party. It was her favorite present. And the other day I was looking through a box of Lena's childhood things that somehow came to Florida with me, and there was the letter. I'd like to read it now."

The crowd clapped again. I had forgotten the letter, and now I put my hands on my warm cheeks. How strange life was, with its curving path . . .

"'Dear Lena,'" my father read. "'What a charming invitation I have received from Chicago today in my London flat. I must say it was the highlight of my day to receive your picture and your sweet compliments about my books. Were I in America, I would be happy to attend your party. As luck would have it I am in London, and I will be giving a lecture on the very night of your birthday. Why don't we make an agreement that we will think of each other at our respective events, and feel a warm glow knowing that someone in another country is wishing us well.'"

Everyone clapped again, and Adam kissed Camilla on the cheek. She waved at me from her table, which she shared with my father, Tabitha, Adam, and the Bicks. I waved back.

Then my father was handing the mic to Tabitha, who spoke of meeting me for the first time and knowing that I was special. She handed the mic to Doug, who told the story of finding me on the side of the road, where my cat was making me late for an appointment by tearing around the inside of my car. Doug had soothed him with catnip and I had managed to go to my interview with Camilla on time—and the rest was history. Belinda went after him, explaining that we had met in a library and had bonded over our shared belief that a person could pursue clues in order to find solutions to mysteries.

More applause and some laughter. Then Allison came up to tell everyone how long I had been her best friend, and that she had picked me out in high school as a likely candidate for friendship because I looked smart, pretty, and loyal. "And I was right about all three," she said. I applauded with everyone else and blew her a kiss.

When Sam went to the mic the room grew silent. Not only did everyone in the room know I loved Sam West, but they also knew that, for more than a year, he had avoided microphones and any attention at all. But he was doing this for me. "On the day I met Lena London," Sam said, "I was very rude to her. I thought she had climbed up the bluff to stare at me—people had done it before—and I was not in the mood to talk to her, even though I thought she was very pretty."

My cheeks grew warmer still. No one made a sound. Sam smiled. "But she wasn't intimidated by my bad attitude. She was walking those two giant beasts of Camilla's—I don't know how she kept them both under control—and she just sniffed at my rudeness and said she needed to be on her way."

Some gentle laughter. "The next time I saw her she was walking past my place in that jaunty way she has. She was like a siren moving down the bluff. I felt compelled to follow her, all the way to Willoughby's, where she intended to have breakfast with Allison."

He pointed to Allison, who waved. "Allison, I can't tell

you how grateful I am that you had to cancel that day. Because it meant I got to have breakfast with Lena, and after that we were friends. And the most amazing thing was that Lena believed in my innocence when no one else did—except you, Camilla—and she kept working and trying on my behalf, even when I was arrested for a murder that never happened."

Some rustling and gentle rumbling in the room. Someone reached out and patted Sam's arm. "Somewhere in there I realized that I loved her. And then she defied all odds and found proof that Victoria was alive. I was pulled out of a cell in New York and told that I was free to go. On the plane back to Indiana, I spoke to my lawyer, who said that someone in Blue Lake had found the evidence we needed. And I didn't even need to ask him who that person was. I knew it was Lena."

The room burst into applause and Sam lifted his glass to me. "Happy birthday, Lena. There is no gift I can give you to match the one you've given me."

AFTER THE TOASTS came a delicious dinner of almond chicken and fresh green beans with duchess potatoes. At my request, Allison sang a song she had sung in our high school production of *Guys and Dolls*; John accompanied her on the piano. She was a consummate performer, and her voice had only gotten better with time. The crowd loved her and made her do an encore, for which she had selected "Birthday," by the Beatles. It became a raucous experience with audience participation.

After dinner, while everyone was partaking of Rhonda's beautiful cake and Allison was starting to play some dance music in hopes that people would hit the floor, I sidled up to Sam, who was talking seriously with Doug. "I'm just going to get a sip of fresh air," I said. "I'll be right back."

Sam latched on to my arm and pulled me against him. "I told Doug," he said.

Doug nodded. "I'm going to leave soon and talk to Cliff, see if we have anything to go on. This seems to be escalating."

"Cliff said that, too, but escalating into what? I don't even understand the notes," I said in a low tone.

Sam stroked my hair. "Anyway, I don't want you going anywhere alone. Let me run to the washroom and I'll go out with you." He pointed at his beer with a helpless expression, and I laughed.

I was left with Doug, and we had identical reactions: we looked around to see where Belinda was. Neither of us wanted her getting the wrong idea. She was talking with John; she waved at us with a placid expression. I shrugged. "I certainly don't want to worry every time I talk to you. You're my friend, you big blond lug."

"I know. I always will be. Just let me lock this down with Belinda first, and hopefully things will go back to normal."

"She's not still worried that you and I—?"

"I don't think so. But maybe I'll go over there just the same. Don't worry about the note. I'll get the lay of the land tonight, and we'll figure things out tomorrow. Just enjoy your party."

He moved off toward Belinda, whose blonde hair glinted in the glittering lights.

Sam wasn't back yet, but I made my way to the door. The wine and the public focus had raised my temperature to an uncomfortable degree, and I needed some cool night air. Outside of Wheat Grass I got just what I wanted: a soft

May evening with a gentle breeze, still scented with the lilac trees that sat at intervals against the wall of the restaurant.

"Ah," I said to myself. Perhaps I was an introvert; I had loved my party, but I was also greatly enjoying the silence and semidarkness.

In the glow of the landscaping lights around Wheat Grass, I saw movement. A man was emerging from the shadows and heading toward the parking lot—a man I thought I recognized.

"Hey!" I yelled without thinking. He turned, and I realized I was right. It was the man with the beard.

He hovered there, seemingly uncertain. Fueled by the confidence that Sam would join me in a moment, I walked toward him. I couldn't let this man disappear. "What are you doing here? Who are you?" I asked.

"Nobody. Just goin' back to my car."

"From where? You weren't inside."

"Just takin' a walk. It's a nice night."

He wasn't making eye contact as he talked. For the first time I noticed that he had something in his hand—a camera. "What is that? Were you taking *pictures*? Oh my God. Are you Joseph Williams?"

He stared at me, his expression blank. "No. I'm not doing anything. I have to get goin'."

"No, you don't. Not until I get some answers. I looked you up—I know all about you!" I said, angry now at the memory of his intrusion into my life, Sam's life. "And why did you break in to Camilla's house? Just to get more dirt? More information? I suppose your bosses told you to do it?"

Now he looked afraid. "What do you know about them? They said you didn't know anything about them. Don't say a word—they'll get mad."

I stood my ground. "I think I can hold my own against those cowards. How dare you all try to make a living off people's pain? Their private lives?"

"What?" he asked.

"Give me that camera."

"No. I gotta go, lady."

"You're not going anywhere. You broke the law! You broke into someone's home! And there is a police officer right behind me in that building who wants to talk to you." I turned and made a show of yelling for Doug.

With an exasperated sound, the bearded man pocketed his camera and grabbed my arm in a surprisingly fierce grip. "Come on," he said.

"What? Let go of me!"

He was dragging me now, his hands on both my arms in such a way that I couldn't fight back. "You done this. Now I'm in trouble either way. If you're gonna call them anyway, I guess I'll take you there. You're not supposed to know." Then, muttering under his breath, he said, "No way I'm dealin' with that snake lady when she's mad." He had reached a nondescript car, a beige rectangle in the dim lot.

"Stop it! Let go!" I cried. Hurt and frightened, I tried in vain to turn around, to find the door that I prayed Sam or Doug would walk through. In desperation, I screamed, knowing I wouldn't be heard over the music inside.

A moment later a car screeched into the turnaround driveway. I was still struggling and screaming, and then suddenly I was free, and the man was grappling with someone else. It was Cliff.

For a moment it looked as though Cliff had control; he had subdued the man and was reaching for his cuffs, but then the bearded man punched him in the chin and Cliff staggered backward, then fell. The bearded man ran around the side of his car and got in. A second later he tore out of the parking lot.

Cliff was on his feet. "You all right?"

"Yes—go ahead."

He ran to his car and drove out at high speed, his Mars light flashing.

I stood there, suddenly shaking with delayed fear and horror. I made my way back to the door just as Sam was coming out, along with Doug and Belinda. They were talking and laughing, but they paused when they saw me.

Doug's cop face snapped into place. "What happened?"

I started to cry, infuriating myself. "Lena?" Sam asked, looking horrified.

"I was here," I managed, "and I saw someone. It was the—the—man with the beard."

Sam pulled me toward him and I winced. "What did he do?" he asked. His face looked deceptively calm.

"I confronted him—"

"Lena!" Doug said, his expression dismayed.

"I asked if he was Joseph Williams, that reporter. Now I—he didn't seem to respond to that. But he said he had bosses. He called them 'they.' He grabbed me hard. I think I have a bruise. He was trying to put me in his car."

Doug was looking around. "What happened? Where did he go?"

"Cliff came out of nowhere. Thank God. I was screaming, but I don't think you heard me."

Sam closed his eyes. I thought he was going to faint. Then he opened them and I was afraid of what I saw. "Did Cliff get him?" he asked.

"They were fighting. He punched Cliff, and Cliff fell,

and then the bearded guy got back into his car and drove off. Cliff ran to his car and followed him. That's all I know."

Doug's face was grim and intense. He patted my arm. "You go inside. They'll take care of you. Belinda—I'll text you."

He ran into the darkness, to wherever his car was, probably already radioing Cliff.

Belinda waved good-bye to him, then turned and held my hand—the one Sam wasn't holding. It was silly, but extremely comforting.

Sam leaned into my side and kissed my hair. "Why did I let you go out here alone?"

"Don't," I said. "I know I shouldn't have confronted him, but I couldn't just let him go. I was having a nice time, feeling the breeze, smelling the flowers. He just came out of nowhere, and we needed to know who he was. He had a camera!"

His arms tightened. "You've seen him three times. Do you think he's been following you to take pictures? Or is this a more . . . predatory sort of thing? Do we assume that this is Nikon, too?"

Belinda's hand tightened on my arm. "Oh my God! You saw that man at the restaurant! You even pointed him out to me. He gave you a bad feeling even then, and I just blew it off."

"You couldn't have known," I said.

My father peeked out the door. "Lena, they want to— Lena? What happened?"

Sam filled him in, tersely.

He looked upset and worried. "Oh, my poor baby. Why would someone, just out of the blue—?"

"Dad, it's a long story. It might go back to some of the stuff that happened to Sam. Doug's looking into it.

Meanwhile—I hate to ask this—but is there any way to cut the party short?"

My father nodded. "Of course. We were just going to have you open gifts, but we have little party favors. I'll have Tabby start giving those out and telling people that Adam needs to get ready for tomorrow's crowd."

"Dad? This was the best party of my life. And I'll always remember it that way."

He leaned in and kissed me. "You're my sweet girl. Give me one second; we'll take care of this."

People began to leave, good-naturedly, clutching beautiful gold gift bags that Tabitha had obviously made with great care. I managed to say heartfelt good-byes to all of them, and then at last I was inside with just my father and Tabitha, Camilla and Adam, Sam and Belinda, Allison and John: my inner circle.

To these few I confided what happened, and they expressed dismay. Sam explained that Cliff and Doug were both in pursuit of the perpetrator, but Doug had not returned, and we waited, somewhat tensely, for word from him. It was ten thirty, and I was suddenly very tired. Adam's waitstaff had cleaned up the tables and taken down the decorations with quick, deft movements.

"Don't let this ruin your birthday," Allison said, pouting slightly. She and the others had worked hard to make the evening perfect.

"It won't. Nothing could. All of you threw me such a lovely party—I'll never forget it. Thank you."

Camilla looked troubled. "But we need to get to the bottom of this immediately. Lena was assaulted. This man's behavior has escalated; first he lingers around her private party—then he decides he has to take her somewhere? Why?"

Sam spoke quietly. "I think I know."

We all looked at him. Everyone was curious, except for Camilla and me, who knew what he was about to say.

"This is about me," he said.

"What do you mean?" asked Tabitha.

Sam sighed. "A few days ago a man was killed just behind Allison's house. I'm sure you've all read about it in the paper. I won't go into detail, but whoever committed that crime tried to frame me for it. Luckily Doug saw through the attempt, and what we were left with was an act of aggression against me for unknown reasons."

"More than aggression," Camilla said. "An act of hate."

"Yes. And now someone in town has been targeting Lena. Leaving her notes on stationery stolen from my house."

"What?" my father said loudly. I patted his arm.

"I didn't want to involve you," I said.

Sam nodded grimly. "Anyone who reads the tabloids knows about my relationship with Lena, thanks to an unscrupulous reporter and a story he printed a few months back."

My father's mouth hung open. "You're saying someone tried to kidnap Lena because they wanted to get back at you?"

I shook my head. "He didn't exactly try to kidnap me. I mean, he did, but it was in reaction to our discussion. He acted like it was his only option, because of these bosses he spoke of."

"Who are they?"

I shrugged. "I don't know. But he said 'them.' And—oh yes! He called one of them a 'snake lady.' And he said I wasn't supposed to know about them."

"What?" Sam said, turning to me.

"He said he didn't want the snake lady mad at him, or something like that."

My father's face was a picture of confusion. "But how does this relate to Sam, or to you?"

I sighed. "If it's reporters, hiring a paparazzo that got out of control, then they just want more stories about Sam. But if it's more sinister than that—and all the details Sam just gave you might suggest that it is, then that's the part of this that is totally irrational. Sam did nothing, except exist. And when Victoria was freed, she didn't resume her relationship with Sam. But someone might interpret it differently. After all, Victoria has a house in Blue Lake, and she visits Sam often, looking for comfort. Someone with a twisted mind, who sees this as a battle, might perceive that Sam is temporarily 'winning,' and that he, the 'loser,' has been humiliated. Our theory is that somehow he has made that Sam's fault."

I turned to Camilla. "I think you were right all along. This is Nikon."

Allison shook her head. "I don't get it. What does that have to do with the dead man in the woods behind our house?"

John looked pale. Allison told me he still felt guilty about the fight he'd had with Eddie, which seemed ridiculous in retrospect. He said, "He wouldn't kill a man just to make a point, would he? He wouldn't just select a random stranger and murder him?"

We were silent, pondering this. Had the murderer known that Eddie Stack was offering information to Sam? Had Eddie died because of that? Or was his death unrelated to that phone call? In any case, Doug had sworn us to secrecy about Sam's message from Eddie.

The door opened and Doug walked in. "Let me guess what you're talking about," he said with a rueful smile.

"What have you found?" asked my father.

Doug sighed. "Cliff kept on him. Blue Lake is lucky to have him—he's a bloodhound. But about two miles down Green Glass Highway the guy he was chasing cut his lights, and Cliff lost track of him. He probably darted down one of the side roads, and Cliff did backtrack through a few of those subdivisions out there, but he never found the car again."

We absorbed this in silence while Doug found a seat next to Belinda and put his arm around her. "The good news is that we got his license plate and his photo, thanks to our traffic light cameras. He ran a couple reds, and we got a nice snapshot. We'll have him identified by tomorrow."

"Thank you, Doug," Sam said. "You guys are great."

"Why was Cliff there, anyway?" I asked.

"What?" Doug had been smiling at Belinda, but now he looked back at me.

"When the man grabbed me—I realized that none of you would hear me because of the music, and I was really scared, and then Cliff just appeared out of nowhere. Why was he there?"

Doug's brows rose, but then he shrugged. "He was driving, out on patrol. I guess he was just in the right place at the right time."

I stole a glance at Camilla, who clearly found this as unlikely as I did.

Now Doug was all business. "Okay, listen. Until this guy is caught, I want to suggest some new living arrangements. Camilla, I'd like you to stay with Adam for a while."

Adam's face brightened. "We can go pick up some of your things this evening."

Camilla nodded. "All right. Perhaps that's best."

Doug said, "And Lena—"

Sam's arms tightened around me. "She can stay with me—she and her family. I have security; I've repaired it since—the incident. And I certainly won't be leaving her side."

I shook my head. "What about the dogs? And Lestrade?"

"That won't be a problem," Doug said. "Because I'm going to stay at the house. If that's all right with you, Camilla?"

She smiled. "I feel much better about the arrangement knowing that you'll be there to guard the place. I don't relish the thought of another break-in." Suddenly she turned to me. "Lena! The dogs bit the person who broke in. Was the bearded man limping?"

I thought back; the shock of the experience had made everything seem surreal in retrospect. "I—don't know. He certainly seemed to move in lunges; but I was distracted . . ."

She nodded. "Of course you were; he scared you out of your wits. No matter. They'll know soon."

"We will," Doug said. Then he stood up, looking brisk. "Adam probably wants to close up here. Lena, I'll ask Sam and Adam to escort you two back to your place so that you can pack whatever you need. Then you can relocate for the evening." He turned to Belinda. "I'm sorry to say I'll have to take you home so I can go set up shop at Graham House."

Belinda's eyes were bright. "Well, it certainly will make an entertaining story. Darla has been living on this stuff, so you'll make her day tomorrow."

I stiffened. "Darla knows about this?"

"No, nothing secret. But she's read about the crimes in the paper, and of course you know about her fascination with Sam. Now if I tell her someone tried to kidnap you she'll probably lose it."

Doug listened to this with an attentive expression. "Who is this woman?"

"*Darla*," Belinda said. "She's worked at the library for the last month. You talk to her whenever you visit me."

"Right," Doug said, making some sort of note on his phone.

We were all standing now, and I said, "You know what upsets me? If this is Nikon, he just keeps jabbing at us, from wherever he is in the world, paying his minions to do his dirty work. Meanwhile we can't do anything to him."

"Not true," said Sam. "I've been thinking about this. Did you know Jake Elliott is in town?"

"Elliott? The reporter?" Doug asked.

"Yes. He ended up helping us a lot with his stories a few months ago. What did he call it, Lena—'shaping the narrative'? I think we should call him. He's here to talk to Victoria, of course, but I want to tell him about the murder. The frame-up. The attempted abduction. I want him to expose Nikon in the press. Let him shape our story in such a way that we look strong and Nikon looks like a petty fool."

"That sounds good," Allison said. Tabitha and my father nodded their agreement.

Doug pointed at Sam. "Talk to him tomorrow, then. Let me know if he wants a quote from the police."

We all cleared out then, and Adam locked up his restaurant for the night. I thanked everyone again, and we bundled into our cars and headed for our respective destinations. I had come alone, but Tabitha insisted on riding with me, which I appreciated. Her soothing voice told me all about my father's summer plans, and it helped to distract me from the dark shadows that loomed along the edges of the road.

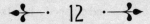

12

She turned to him, feeling helpless. "What now?"
"Now we wait," he said.

—From *Death at Delphi*

IF OUR VISITORS had appreciated the grandeur of Camilla's house, they were just as impressed with the stylish elegance of Sam's. A local woman who was Marge Bick's cousin cleaned Sam's house every other day, and that helped to keep it always gleaming.

"Oh my," Tabitha said as she drank decaffeinated coffee at Sam's kitchen island and gazed around his large, lovely space. "I am so glad to know that when the world was treating you badly, you had this haven, and you had Lena."

"I agree with you on both counts," Sam said with a smile. "When you finish your coffee, I'll show you the guest room. It will be neat to use it—I've never had the chance."

My father nodded. "Thanks for putting us up. We sure don't want to cramp your style. I get the impression you and Lena haven't gotten to be alone much lately."

As always, my father saw straight to the center of things.

"We're working on it," Sam said. He smiled at me and something inside of me twisted pleasantly.

"Oh my," Tabitha said, fanning herself with her hand.

My father stood up and clapped a hand on Sam's shoulder. "I'll be glad, when I head back to Florida, to know that Lena has not one, but two homes here, and that she's loved in both of them." He turned to Tabitha. "I'm about ready to turn in. How about you?"

Tabitha nodded, pushing away her coffee cup. "Yes. It's been a long, eventful day."

"Tabitha," I said. "Those gift bags you made were amazing. I don't know how you did it all. You must have been so busy, and all for me. Thank you so much," I said.

If Tabitha hadn't loved me before, she clearly did now. She glowed as I gave her a hug, and then she moved toward my father and took his hand. He smiled at us both. "Lena, if it's all right, Tabby and I really are going to see Meridien tomorrow. You have things to do here, I'm sure."

I hugged him, too. "Thank you so much for the party, Dad. Despite the—event—I will always remember how beautiful it was."

"And I'll remember how beautiful you were, my daughter. I've never seen you look like this. You're luminous."

"It's the dress," I joked.

Tabitha said she wanted to look at the stars, so my father accompanied her out onto Sam's deck. Sam touched my arm and said, "We packed up your presents to open tomorrow, but I want you to open mine now."

"Okay," I said, pleased.

He pulled a little blue box out of his pocket and handed it to me. The paper was lovely, but I tore it anyway, then lifted the lid to find a delicate silver charm bracelet under some silver tissue paper. "What is this?" I said, examining it. The first tiny charm was delicate and pretty, and clearly handmade. "Is this—a waffle?"

Sam grinned. "Every charm has something to do with the way we met. You ate waffles at the diner."

"Of course. And at your house, when you made them for me. Let's see, what's this one—a cigarette!"

"Because you helped me stop smoking."

"And a little German shepherd. Because I was walking them when we met."

He nodded, smiling. "And of course there's a little book there, because you are a famous author."

My eyes were spiked with tears. "This is the most thoughtful gift I have ever received. This is expensive silver, and you had someone handcraft it—"

"Did you see the last charm?"

I looked. It was a silver heart with a red stone in its center. "That one represents me falling in love with you." His face was earnest, handsome, irresistible.

"I love this. I'm going to wear it all the time. But I don't want to explain it to people. I just want it to be our special secret. To remind me of you, every day, forever."

Sam leaned in, about to kiss me, but my father and Tabitha came back in, loudly proclaiming that Blue Lake had the most stars they had ever seen. I tucked away my beautiful bracelet, and Sam led my father and Tabitha upstairs, where I could hear her saying "ooh" and "aah" over the spare room. I put the coffee dishes in Sam's sink, suddenly weary, and then headed upstairs with my little blue box.

Sam's room was warm and quiet. I went into his bathroom with the overnight bag I'd brought with me and changed out of my lovely dress into something else that I'd bought at Sasha's—something I'd been eager to wear for Sam. Despite the draining events of the evening, I still wanted to wear it for him, and this desire had intensified when Sam had smiled at me in the kitchen—his smile managed to convey such intimacy, such intense focus, that I couldn't think of anything, now, but being alone with him.

When I went out again Sam had turned the lights down and lit his fireplace. "You can just tuck yourself in and relax," he said, stoking the flames. Then he looked up at me. "What—is that?" he asked, almost stuttering.

"Something I bought to wear for you."

"I was thinking you should just rest," he said, swallowing.

"I'm not elderly, Sam," I said. "I think I could use a nice, physical distraction."

"You *are* a physical distraction. What color is that?"

"It's called 'peaches and cream,'" I said, moving toward him.

He pulled me into his arms and kissed me, his mouth warm and alluring. "It's lovely," he said. "*You* are lovely."

"You are sexy."

Suddenly he swooped me up into his arms and carried me toward the bed. I giggled, then covered my mouth. "I don't want the visitors to hear," I said.

His lips were warm on my ear, turning my bones to water. "Then we'll be very, very quiet," he said.

THE FLORIDA CONTINGENT left for Meridien the next morning—a lovely, blue-skied morning with the scent of the lake in the air. "Enjoy your shopping," I told Tabitha as I waved them out the door.

Sam was making coffee. I paused in the doorway to the

kitchen, admiring his trim waist and the deft movements of his hands. The buzzing of Sam's phone on the counter brought me out of my reverie, and he snapped it up with his right hand. "Sam West." He listened for a while, then turned to look at me. He gave me a slow smile that had me blushing like a teenager. "Yeah, that will be fine. We're just about to have breakfast." He hung up and said, "That was Doug. He's got some information."

"Okay. That's good, right?"

"Probably. Here—drink your coffee." I sat down in front of the mug he had poured me, and he pressed his lips to my neck, lingering slightly before he pulled away. "I don't have waffle ingredients today, so it's going to be egg and tomato sandwiches."

"Wonderful. Thank you."

"Did you sleep all right?" he asked, back at the stove.

"Very well. Eventually."

He grinned. "Me, too. Lena?"

"Hmm?"

"I wonder—"

Now it was my phone that rang. It was Belinda. "Just a sec," I said, and I answered it. "Hey! What's up?"

"Lena, you're at Sam's, right? Can I stop by?"

"Sure, why not? Doug's going to be here, but I don't know why—the more, the merrier. Have you learned something?"

"Yeah. About Sam, not about Nikon."

"Okay—we'll be here. See you in half an hour?"

"Great." She rang off. It was shaping up to be a busy Saturday. I looked at the man across the room and felt a pang of remorse. "Sam? There's something I was supposed to tell you the other day, but I wanted to wait for a quiet moment, and then so many things happened . . ."

He moved a spatula in his pan. "Okay." He turned to look at me. "About what?"

"Belinda was looking into some things about your family. Because I asked her to, remember? And she found out something about your mother. I'm sorry I didn't tell you this sooner."

He turned off the heat under his pan and walked back to the table. "My mom?"

"Yes. Belinda found that your mother had been married twice."

"What?" He sat down, brows raised. "That makes no sense."

"Belinda said it was a guy your mom went to high school with. She married him in '79. She never mentioned it? Your dad didn't, either?"

"No." He looked less upset than he did flabbergasted. "I—this is so bizarre. She would have been just a kid. She was only twenty-two when she married Dad."

"Belinda thought maybe it was a high school romance. Apparently they either had it annulled or divorced a couple of months later. A mistake made by two inexperienced kids."

Sam nodded. "Well, it's not like it's a deep, dark secret. But why wouldn't she have told me and Wendy? It's—shocking."

"I'm sorry to spring it on you like this, but Belinda is coming over—she said she found out something else."

He rubbed his face for a moment. Then he looked at me. His eyes were deep blue and slightly sad. "Whatever it is, Lena—it just doesn't matter. How could it possibly, after all these years?"

I nodded. "I guess. Are you okay?"

"Yeah. Are you ready for breakfast?"

"I am. I'll slice the tomatoes."

DOUG ARRIVED AS we were washing up. Sam poured him some coffee and we sat down at the table. "We know who he is," Doug said, handing us a photo printed from a traffic camera. "His name is Wally Kallis. He's a thug who's been in and out of jail in both Indiana and Illinois. He's been out since he finished serving a sentence last year for breaking and entering."

"Do you think he's the one who broke in at Camilla's?" Sam asked.

Doug nodded. "We're fairly certain. Cliff took fingerprints, which we'll check for a match today. The question is *why*."

"Or *who*," I said. "As in who hired him. Right? I mean, he was scary, but he didn't seem to have any—personal intent. This isn't necessarily related to Eddie Stack, or to Nikon. It could be some tabloid going beyond the bounds of the law. Hiring unstable people as paparazzi. I mean, he was holding a camera."

Sam and Doug exchanged a glance. "You're probably right," Doug said. "Once we get Kallis—which I hope we will do today—we'll know the answers to these questions. But I want you to study the photo carefully, and consider the name. Has either of you ever encountered this man before? Heard his name in the past? We have to rule out any possible connection."

I shook my head. "I know I've never seen him. Aside from our three encounters, I mean."

"Me, either," Sam said. "I spent a year trying to avoid

people in this town, so I can count on one hand the number of strangers I've met. He's new to me."

"Any chance he was the man who broke into Sam's?" I asked.

Doug shook his head. "We don't think so. Kallis is quite tall. Based on the video, we're estimating the height of the person in the video to be about five foot eight or nine."

He took a sip of his coffee, then held up a finger. "By the way, I can tell you that your little letter opener was not the murder weapon in the Stack murder."

"No?" asked Sam, looking relieved.

"He was shot. The knife was plunged in postmortem. A weird, vengeful touch, probably done in the middle of the night."

Sam and I exchanged looks of surprise.

A knock sounded on Sam's door, and he rose to look at his security screen—a little monitor next to his refrigerator. "It's Belinda," he said. "I'll go let her in."

Doug brightened, and I smiled. "How are things going?" I asked.

He shrugged. "She wants to be sure that I'm sure. I get that."

Sam came back with Belinda, who wore a pair of faded jeans and a navy blue peasant blouse embroidered with white flowers. A large purse was slung over her shoulder. "Hey, everyone," she said, her green eyes lingering on Doug.

He sprang up and gave her a quick kiss, then pulled out a chair for her. If he'd been wearing a jacket, he probably would have flung it on the ground for her to walk on. I almost laughed out loud.

"Thanks for letting me drop by," she said. "I had a few more things I wanted to share. You might consider them significant."

"About Nikon?" Doug asked.

"One of them is." She put her purse in her lap and pulled out some file folders. "I was digging deeper into the Lazos family. As you know, it's hard to find anything about them at all. How can you be so rich and keep such a low profile?"

"If you have the money, you can buy the low profile," Doug said.

She shrugged. "Well, I found an interesting story about Nikon and one of his brothers. The youngest brother, I think. His name is Demetrius."

"I read about him the other day. He has his own bottling company," I said.

Belinda didn't seem to hear me; her nose was in her file. "Back in 2010, Nikon and Demetrius had a huge falling-out—it wasn't clear why—and the rumors of a rift in the Lazos clan made it into the papers—first in Greece, then all over the world, when people picked up the story. The amazing thing is that the reporter actually got a quote from Nikon Lazos." She pushed the clipping over to us, and Sam picked it up.

"'There is no excuse for betraying your own family,'" Sam read in a wry voice. "'My brother has made the decision to break faith. He will have to live with the consequences.'" He set down the paper in disgust.

I looked at Doug and Belinda to see if they shared my reaction. Then I said, "Nikon is a piece of work! I really think he might be insane. I wonder what his poor brother did—maybe told him he was out of line? Commented on how badly Nikon had treated his first wife? Laughed about the fact that she escaped from him?"

Belinda shrugged. "But the article implies that after this, the siblings took sides. Some with Demetrius and some with Nikon."

"Can I keep that clipping?" Doug asked.

"Sure. It's just a computer printout," Belinda said, putting it back in the folder and handing the whole thing to him.

"You're amazing," Doug said.

Belinda blushed a little. "The feeling is mutual," she said.

He got up. "If that's all, I need to head out. Sam, Lena, keep me informed. Belinda—can I talk to you for a minute? Maybe you can walk me to my car."

She said, "Sure," and stood up, but turned to me and said, "I'll be right back."

I exchanged a surprised glance with Sam, and we waited for a few minutes. Sam reached across the table and played with the tips of my fingers. "He's trying to out-romance me," he joked.

"He would lose."

"Belinda won't think so. I'm glad to see them back together. Were they off for a while?"

"Yeah. But they seem to be back on."

Belinda came back in, her face pink, and said, "He just wanted to ask me something about my research."

Sam and I burst out laughing, and finally Belinda laughed, too. "Okay, stop making fun of me."

I pointed at the remaining file. "Fine. What do you have in there?"

She looked at Sam. "First, I will tell you that you don't need to hear this. I can take it away and you can remain in happy ignorance if you'd like. But I did find out something about your parents that you most likely did not know. And it—well, it potentially affects your life."

Sam studied her for a moment. "If it were you, and this information were out there—would you want to know it?"

"I would," she said without hesitation.

He folded his hands on the table. "My mother and father told me once, just before the plane crash, that they had news for me. We were going to talk about it, and then my family was killed. Is there any chance that this could relate—to that? I know that's a vague question."

"So I'll give a vague answer—it's possible."

We sat for a moment. It was not tense, but companionable. Belinda seemed content to wait, probably reliving her recent romantic encounter with Doug, and Sam seemed willing to contemplate his options without having to make a rushed decision.

I got up to retrieve the coffeepot and topped off everyone's cup.

Then I sat down. Sam said, "What do you think, Lena?"

I thought about it. "I think that, whatever it is, it won't change how much you loved your family. But who knows? It might offer you insights into your parents—back when they were young—that you never had before. It might make you love them more."

He shrugged. "Okay. Let's hear it."

Belinda opened the file. "I found an article that I think actually chronicles the way your parents met. This is an article about your dad, David West, when he was an officer in Upstate New York. A young woman had been accosted by a purse-snatcher, and he saved the day. Helped the woman to her feet, apprehended the perpetrator, arrested him, then returned to check on the woman. The woman was your mother."

Sam hadn't looked at the article yet. "Why would they put an article about a purse-snatching in the paper?"

"Human interest, of course. Your mother was young and pretty, and the officer was young and handsome. But it was mostly about where the attack occurred that captured the public interest. It was just outside an obstetrics office." She turned the article toward Sam so that he could see the picture. "And your mother was nine months pregnant."

Sam said, "What?" and pulled the article toward him. He stared intently, and Belinda turned to me.

"I seem to always be informing people about pregnant women," she said lightly, referring to the time, months earlier, when she had learned through her research that the missing Victoria had been pregnant.

I gave her a half smile, then turned my attention to Sam, who was clearly struggling with various emotions. "This was 1979," he said. "Right around the time she got divorced, or whatever. She had a baby."

Belinda's voice was encouraging. "Your dad was called a hero for coming to the aid of a pregnant woman. Apparently he continued to check in on her, and they started dating. I found a follow-up article."

She pulled it out; it was dated August of 1980. The headline read "Hero Cop Proposes to Woman He Saved." In this picture Sam's parents posed once again, but she was clearly not pregnant.

"Does the article mention what became of her baby?" I asked.

Belinda shook her head. "No. And I can't find any records about an adoption. If it was a closed adoption, then there might be no way to access those files."

Sam leaned back in his chair and looked at the ceiling. "You're telling me my mother had another child. That I was not her first child. And that she never told me I had a sibling other than Wendy somewhere in this world."

Calmly, Belinda pushed the second article toward Sam. "Many, many people didn't tell their children these things.

Often the women were made to feel ashamed about their pregnancies. We don't know what your mother's circumstances were, or what sort of input this divorced husband would have offered. I'm guessing none. Perhaps the marriage occurred because of the pregnancy, but that sort of thing doesn't often work, especially with people who are essentially kids."

Sam shook his head. "My mom *loved* babies. She was wild about them. She wouldn't have wanted to give hers up."

"Maybe it wasn't her choice," I said. "Parents can be very persuasive. They can assert pressure, as can social groups. Think about your mom's parents. Would they have wanted her to keep the child?"

"I don't know," Sam said.

"Are they still alive?" I asked suddenly. "We could just ask them!"

He shook his head. "My grandfather died five years ago. My grandmother is in an Alzheimer's facility. My dad's parents are dead, too."

We sat and thought about that. Then Sam sat up suddenly and touched the file in Belinda's hand. "Can you find out for me? Can you find this baby?"

"I can try," she said.

"What if the letter my mom received was from this long-lost child?" Sam asked. "My father said that it was good news, but something that the whole family had to discuss. He said that *my mother* had received a letter. And it was a big enough deal that they wanted to talk to me about it personally."

He turned to me, suddenly eager. "Lena, do you think she might have received a letter from this lost child? Do you think she was going to make contact with him or her?"

My favorite Camilla Graham novel came to my mind;

it was called *The Lost Child*. Indirectly, that book had brought me to Blue Lake, and to Sam. And now here was Sam, saying the words "lost child" and making me feel that my life had folded in on itself. "It could be, Sam. This is certainly something big, something you didn't know. It's a secret your mother had, and now you share it with her."

He looked sad. "I wonder if she answered the letter before she died. If she said anything to that child. Otherwise, I wasn't the only one who suffered when that plane went down."

This was a sobering idea, yet I also found it invigorating. If Sam were right, it meant that in the time of his worst grief, someone else, somewhere in the world, had been grieving with him.

It meant that Sam had family.

13

When they finally found Phanessa, the woman who locals said was psychic, she faced them with a grim expression. "The past is a dormant volcano," she said with quiet solemnity. "It will inevitably erupt and endanger everything built upon it."

—From *Death at Delphi*

BELINDA READIED FOR departure, promising to pursue her research. "You can come by the library on Monday," she said. "I'll probably have something by then."

We thanked her and I walked her to the door. "Sam will need some time to think about this," I said. "But he'll also want some answers. If need be he can probably get his private detective to work on it."

Belinda stiffened and I realized that she was actually quite competitive. "Give me a chance. I think I can do it," she said. "It will involve a lot of file searching."

"We'll check in Monday, then," I said. "Thanks, Belinda."

She waved and walked to her car. I went back in and found Sam staring out the window. "A lot to think about," I said.

"Yes." He didn't seem ready to talk.

"Sam? You need time to process this, and Camilla texted me and said we should both try writing in our new locations—she thinks maybe they'll inspire us to new ideas. But I thought I might cross the road and sit on that bench that overlooks the bluff. Would that be okay?"

He shook his head. "Not with that weirdo on the loose. I'll go with you."

I was about to protest, but he held up a hand. "I won't get in your way. I'll bring some work, too, and stay behind you. You can have the lake view and your solitude, but you won't have to worry about some criminal grabbing you."

This was wise. "Okay. Thank you. It just seems so beautiful and warm today, and there aren't many bugs yet."

"It's a good idea. I know you want to write." He touched my hair. "I'm in love with a writer. That sounds glamorous."

I pointed at the jean shorts and T-shirt that I was wearing. "Not so much. But I like the 'in love' part."

He bent to kiss me, his lips lingering and warm on mine, and then I collected my laptop and my sunglasses, and Sam picked up a file folder that he'd been going over that morning. "Okay. Let's go look at the lake," he said.

Camilla, it turned out, was right again. I had seen the little bench tucked into the trees, halfway between her house and Sam's, but I'd never sat on it or studied Blue Lake from that particular vantage point. Ideas were already bubbling to the surface of my thoughts, starting with some images of setting. I could imagine that I was looking at the Ionian Sea. The lake was calm today, with waves that appeared like froth on its deep blue surface, and the sky, pale and speckled with clouds, spoke of eternity with its vast and sunlit expanse. How strange that I tended to think of the sky in a limited sense: the Blue Lake sky, the Chicago sky. This same sky hung over Delphi, over the whole world.

I opened my computer and tried to capture some of these

philosophical thoughts and shape them into the narrative of our heroine, Lucy Banner. My hands flew over the keys, but my eyes stayed on the lake, the sky, the elusive, amorphous clouds . . .

A shadow fell across my screen. "Lena?"

I started and looked up, shading my eyes. Victoria West stood next to me, clad in a pale yellow spring sweater and a pair of faded jeans. She looked ridiculously elegant.

"Oh, uh—Victoria. Hello—uh," I stammered. She was the very last person I had expected to see. "You'll want Sam. He's back there in the trees, trying to be unobtrusive while he guards me. I had a—an incident yesterday."

"Yes, Sam just told me. Smart of him to keep an eye on you. He's chatting with Timothy right now—that's my bodyguard."

To my horror, she sat down on the bench next to me and stretched out her long legs. "It's actually you I want to speak with, Lena."

"Me? What—how can I help you?" I closed my computer and set it on the ground. I hoped that I didn't sound as uncomfortable as I felt.

"I just thought it would be good if we talked. We never really have. And I've heard such nice things about you." I ventured a look at her face and was treated to a disarming smile—a smile so genuine it made me feel a bit more at ease.

"No, we never really have. And I never got to say that— I'm sorry for all you went through, Victoria. Even before Athena—it sounds like it was difficult."

She sighed and looked at the lake. "Well, thank you for that. Truly it was nothing compared to what poor Sam had to endure. I've been looking back at the headlines, watching news videos on YouTube . . . that was quite a witch hunt. Poor Sam. And I'd treated him abominably before I even got on that damned yacht. I wasn't a good person, Lena. I was selfish and indulged, and I was experimenting with drugs and alcohol like a teenager."

I had nothing to say to that.

"I suppose I still live the privileged life. But I like to think I grew up—finally—during this experience. Only took me thirty years, right? And that's probably because it was difficult. I was forced into adulthood by the reality of my circumstances." She looked at the sky and brooded about this. "Toward the end," she continued, "when I realized who Nikon really was—then it was hard, very hard. Especially when Athena was born, and I wanted nothing more than to show her the world. I would spend long days with her, trying to plan escapes that I knew, deep down, could never happen. You saved my life, Lena. And Athena's life."

"Not really. I just—I tend to be very curious. And I find Google to be a very helpful tool."

She laughed and pushed some hair out of her face with a graceful hand. "Sam and I talked about what we went through, and we agreed that there must have been some sort of divine plan of suffering and redemption. Because as a result of my fateful meeting with Nikon Lazos, I got my beautiful child. And Sam got you."

She turned her green eyes on me. "You're young, but you have a wise face," she said. "You have healed Sam, or almost healed him. Without you he would not have come out of this as well."

"I hate to contemplate that."

"So do I."

We sat for a moment, looking at the lake and thinking our thoughts. I said, "I tried to imagine what your voice would sound like, back when we were looking for you.

Now that I've seen you and heard you—it's actually quite close to what I imagined."

"Is it?" She looked amused. "And how does my voice sound? Spoiled?"

"No. Cultured, elegant, but also fun-loving. It's a nice voice."

She turned toward me on the bench. "You're very generous, aren't you? You helped to find me, and now here I am, making demands on your boyfriend, monopolizing him sometimes, and you're telling me I have a nice voice."

I shrugged. "I understand why you need to talk to Sam. You two have a long history."

She laughed. "How very careful you are at choosing your words. You are far too polite, Lena." She sighed and tucked one of her legs under her on the bench. "I want you to know there's nothing to worry about. I have no designs on Sam. And even if I did, it's clear that he is far too in love with you to ever consider someone else."

"I would like to think so. I certainly do love him."

Victoria West touched my hand. "If I could pick a wife for my ex-husband—someone to make up for all of my own matrimonial failings—I could not find a better candidate than you."

"Thank you." I smiled at her.

Her eyes were back on the lake. "The truth is, Lena, I've only fallen in love once in my life. And until that moment, I didn't know what love was."

"Do you mean—with Nikon?"

Her lovely mouth curved into a frown. "Nikon! Ugh. A passionate lover who turned my head for quite some time, yes. When I think of how stupid I was, falling for him because he was foreign and mysterious, and older, more experienced. And so very, very rich. He made such a big deal of our boarding the yacht—our big adventure, our secret future together." She shook her head. "I'll confess it never once dawned on me to tell Sam or Taylor or my family where I was going. I would contact them later, once the excitement was over. But looking back, he was selfish even then, because his people knew all about it. His brother and sister were there to see us off—the only two of his clan I ever met—and he was always surrounded by his friends and advisors. Several of them crewed the yacht. But I—had no one." Her face turned hard for a moment. "No, I realized soon enough that I had never really loved Nikon."

Her gaze dropped to her lap. "I was talking about my baby."

"Oh!"

"Lena. I didn't even know if I would love her, do you know that? I didn't know much about children, and I had planned never to have a child, but Nikon swayed me with all his rhetoric about family and children and how they are the best parts of ourselves. He said things about planting roots, and the strength of the family vine. Well, anyway, I was pregnant before I knew it, and he made such a big deal out of it that I enjoyed my pregnancy, for the most part—never letting myself think of what life would be like after she was born. What it would be like to have a child, to raise a child."

She wiped at her eyes. "I wanted to give birth on the mainland, but of course Nikon insisted we had to have the utmost privacy. He set up his own little hospital on the yacht and brought in some doctor—well, you know the story. But you don't know how lonely it felt. I was in this white room, surrounded by medical staff who were strangers. I wanted my mother and father. I wanted my sister. I wanted Taylor. I even wanted Sam, because he had always been kind to me.

"And I knew that beyond the walls of that boat was an even lonelier view—a foreign country, people speaking a language I didn't know, and a sea that kept me away from the world I had once known. Nikon would wander in and out, and I fixated on this ring he always wore, a silver ring with an inlaid jade snake. I just kept thinking *snake, snake*."

Her voice was so sad that I took her hand and held it. She looked surprised, then gratified. She put her other hand over mine. "Then I had Athena, after nine hours of labor. She was tiny, with smooth pink skin and tons of black hair. Her eyes looked black, too, but I think they'll be green. Like mine."

"She's beautiful. I saw her—that day that you brought her to Sam's. She looked right at me, Victoria."

She nodded, happy to be talking about her daughter. "She is magical. They say it takes weeks and weeks for a baby to smile, but my Athena saw my sadness, and she smiled at me almost right away. Just looked into my eyes and smiled."

To my distress, Victoria burst into tears. She lifted her hands to cover her face and I, at a loss, slid closer on the bench and gave her a half hug.

She threw herself at me, wrapping her arms around me and crying on my shoulder. Her grief was so palpable it brought tears to my own eyes. "We'll find her, Victoria. I know we'll find her," I said, patting her back.

"My baby," she said. "I miss my baby girl!"

Sam approached; perhaps he had heard her crying. "Vic," he said. "Do you need anything?"

She pulled away from me, trying to compose herself, wiping at her wet face. "Oh God. I just cried all over Lena."

"It's all right," I said. "I know how hard it must be."

Sam handed Victoria a tissue and she blew her nose. "Oh, I'm a mess, aren't I?" She stood up. "Well, Lena, I'll leave you to your writing. I read your book, I meant to tell you. Sam lent it to me, but I'll have to buy my own and have you and Camilla sign it. It was terrific—a wonderful distraction. I may have to read them all."

"The rest are all Camilla's—you will love them."

She patted Sam's arm affectionately and included us both in her watery smile. "You've both done so much for me, but I'll ask one more favor. If you and your librarian friend could put your heads together and work your intelligent magic to figure out where he might have taken Athena so that I can get her back before she forgets me—"

Her voice broke on the last word, and Sam pulled her into a sideways hug. "We'll find her, Vic," he said. "I promise we will."

She cleared her throat. "Okay, enough of my pity party." She looked at Sam. "I just miss her little face so much."

She waved at us and started through the trees, where I now saw her bodyguard was waiting for her. He was big and burly, but seemed quite tender in the way that he dealt with Victoria.

I looked at Sam and wiped at my own eyes. "Well, she just broke my heart."

Sam sat down beside me and looked at the lake. "What did she want to talk to you about?"

I shrugged. "Her gratitude about the rescue. You. Baby Athena. Love."

"Ah."

"I'm glad she came to talk with me. Was that your idea or hers?"

His blue eyes were innocent. "Totally hers. I would not have thought putting the two of you together was the greatest idea, but it seems to have cleared the air."

"I'll bet she's changed a lot, huh? Since back before the whole Nikon thing."

"In many measurable ways." He nodded at the clouds before us. "But in many ways, she's the same."

I picked up my laptop. "I think I got some good impressions down for now. The wind is getting a little chilly."

Sam took my free hand and we walked back to his house, where he started preparing us some lunch. I called Allison, who said that she and John had moved back home. "It's not as bad as I thought," she said. "I'm not constantly picturing poor Eddie. Someday we'll be able to put this behind us."

"Good for you," I said. "And are your neighbors being nice?"

"Sort of," she said. It sounded as though she was doing dishes while she talked. "I mean, a few of them came over, asked what was going on. Some of them wanted to talk about Eddie. You know that old guy that you told me was being rude to Sam? Mr. Hendricks. He actually invited us over for dinner, but John thinks he has ulterior motives and just wants to grill us at length rather than grilling for us, which is what he said he would do."

"Huh. I didn't care much for him."

"Yeah, he's not the best. We managed to get out of the invitation for the time being. Oh, and the worst thing is that we saw Eddie's wife, Doris. She was at Bick's Hardware while John and I were getting some supplies. She was very polite, but it was awkward."

"She certainly can't hold you responsible for the fact that Eddie was found near your house!"

"No," she said, her voice trailing. "Unless she thinks we had something to do with it. I don't think she does, though. She told us Doug has been over to her place a lot, asking questions and giving her some insights. Doug told her he may have been killed by a stranger."

"Really?' I said. I had thought Doug was convinced, as we were, that Nikon was somehow responsible.

"Yeah, well. He's working on it. I don't even want to think about it, to be honest."

"So who is this Doris Stack? Have I seen her before?"

"Probably. She works at Dilley's on Green Glass Highway."

"The grocery store? Is she the dark-haired woman who works at the service counter?"

"Yeah, that's Doris."

"I know her! Oh, the poor lady."

"Yeah. They don't have children. I don't know if that's good or bad. But they couldn't have had more than one, anyway; they've only been married a year."

"Oh, right. You mentioned that." I sighed. "Sorry to bum you out. The good news is you're back in your house, and you can listen to your birds again."

"I did miss *them*," Allison said with a return of her spunky tone.

I MADE A call to Camilla, as well, and read her some of what I had written on the bluff.

"Oh, I like that, Lena! 'The sky that hangs over the whole world.' A nice way of capturing the limitations of human understanding, that we think it hangs only above the place where we live. Yes—as the book goes on, Lucy should grow more and more philosophical. This is what will ultimately bond her to the classics professor."

"Oh yes! Perfect. Maybe they can share a surprising love for Plato, or have a debate about his theory of Forms."

"Good." I could hear her tapping away at her keyboard, logging some of our ideas. "I also did some research about the Greek ethos. The people in this little Greek town where she's staying would be very closemouthed about information. When Lucy starts to ask, she will get nowhere. It's not just that the Greeks have a strong sense of family, it's that they consider this an obligation."

"Funny. I spoke with Victoria West this morning."

"Really?"

"Yes. I was writing on the bluff—don't worry, Sam was guarding me—and she appeared there. She said she wanted to talk to me, and she mostly just said that—well, that she was grateful, and that she doesn't have designs on Sam."

"I should hope not," Camilla said.

"Anyway, she talked a bit about Nikon, and said that he talked her into having a child because he was so big on family, and talked about the family vine, or something. Interesting that you researched the same idea."

"The Greeks, my research tells me, wanted to preserve tradition, and family was a way to do that. One valued not only the immediate family, but connections that went back many generations."

"So Lucy would be seen as an interloper."

"Yes. We'll have to give her a local contact—someone she befriends who is a native Greek."

I thought about this. How would an outsider find a way

in? "Lucy can know first aid," I said. "And she can help someone. Later, perhaps their gratitude will overcome their reserve."

"That has layered possibilities. You are a natural, Lena. Oh yes—first aid. We'll have to think: Will she save someone from choking? Help a woman deliver a baby? Make a tourniquet for someone who has been wounded? Treat a snake bite?"

"If she makes a tourniquet, perhaps someone has suffered a bullet wound. Perhaps, because she stumbles across this crime, it will make her a victim herself."

Camilla was tapping away. "Give me a moment," she said.

"Sure." I thought about what we had said, and how much I loved brainstorming. It gave me a full and satisfied feeling. "I wonder if that Greek feeling of family is what makes Nikon so certain that Victoria is in the wrong. That she betrayed him because she left and didn't resist the intrusion of authorities. From that perspective, Victoria abandoned her own."

Camilla was silent for a moment. "A good point. And if he couldn't get Victoria to acknowledge his family, at the very least he would feel obligated to reclaim his daughter."

 · 14 ·

There is the story people tell, and the story which is true.

—From *Death at Delphi*

MY FATHER CALLED that evening and said that he and Tabitha would be home rather late, and that Sam and I should have dinner without them. Sam said he would make something, but I suggested we just order food from Wheat Grass, which we did.

An hour later we sat at Sam's kitchen table and ate our meals in relative silence; we were clearly each distracted by our own thoughts. Finally I said, "Hey."

He smiled. "Hey. I'm not being polite, am I?" He poked at his salad.

"I wasn't making much effort, either. What are you thinking about? Belinda's bombshell? Are you doing okay with that?"

"Yeah. I was thinking about that, but I was also realizing something. The last few days, when I went to town or ran errands, I always saw a Blue Lake police car."

"That's not a surprise. Doug said they would be watching us."

"Look out the window. They're watching right now."

I got up and went to the front door, then peered out. As Sam had suggested, there was a white and blue squad car parked near a tall streetlight; I could just make out Cliff at the wheel.

I went back into the kitchen and looked at Sam. "Huh," I said.

"I'm not sure what to think."

"I see what you mean: why the double-duty? Doug is already at Graham House, right? So why does he need Cliff down the street? Who's guarding the rest of this town?"

"Right. And who's to say he's guarding us, Lena?"

"What do you mean?"

"How do I know they don't suspect me? Let's face it, I've long since ceased to believe that the police will leave me alone just because I'm innocent. And yes, Doug knows someone stole that knife—but for all he knows, it could have been me. Right? Creating an elaborate little sting operation that would allow me to commit murder."

"Oh, don't be ridiculous. He doesn't believe that for a second. And he just told us—Eddie was shot, not stabbed. So you stealing your own knife would be kind of ridiculous."

"Why Cliff, then? As you said, Doug is within hail. And shouldn't they both be off duty by now?"

"You're just being paranoid. And making me paranoid, too! The fact is they feel bad that weird man was stalking me all over town, probably leaving the notes, and now they want to make sure that nothing else happens on their watch. That's what it is. Eat your salad. It looks delicious."

"It is. But your pasta looks good, too."

"Here, let me put some on your plate." I shared some of my ravioli, and Sam West smiled at me. Our romance was rooted in the sharing of food.

"Thank you. I eat more when I'm around you," he said.

"Good. You were looking too thin there for a while." We both ate for a moment, and I sipped my wine. "Sam."

"Hmm?"

"Do you think they'll find Athena?"

He rubbed his jaw. "I really don't know. Nikon's a slippery guy. I want them to catch him. I would really love to see that man face-to-face. He has a lot to answer for, Lena. What he did to Victoria, what he did to me, what he just tried to do to you."

"If that was him," I amended. "He could be anywhere. But I would like to see him, too. Especially now that I heard things from Victoria's side. I said as much to myself when Nikon's thug stole that baby. I was standing in the road, in the snow, thinking: I'm going to meet him, and I'm going to get revenge. I sound like someone from Greek mythology, don't I?"

Sam shook his head. "Everyone feels that way about the man. We need to lure him out." Sam sat up straight. "That reminds me. I never called Jake Elliott. Do you mind if I do it now?"

"Go ahead."

Sam went to his kitchen counter and picked up his phone; he dialed a number and started talking in a low voice. I sipped my wine and looked out Sam's giant windows onto the shadowy back lawn. How strange that every house in Blue Lake seemed to border on woods: Sam's, Allison's, Camilla's. I thought of poor Eddie Stack, and the location of his body. Had he been trying to reach the woods when someone shot him? Is that why he had been just on the verge of the trees? Or had he simply been taking a shortcut from one block to another?

Suddenly Sam was standing in front of me. "Elliott says he could come over now. Would that be okay?"

"Sure. I'd like to see him again."

"You hear that, Jake?" Sam said.

I heard Jake Elliott's gruff voice, and Sam grinned at me. "He says that's what all the girls say."

JAKE ELLIOTT SHOWED up about half an hour later; Sam poured him some wine and pointed out a platter we had quickly assembled with crackers and hard cheeses.

Elliott limped into the living room; he was still recovering from a severely broken leg, but other than the limp he looked healthy and interested, as always. His bald head gleamed in the lamplight, and his dark eyes were intense as he studied us both.

"So. You have an agenda, and you have lured me here with promises of Nikon Lazos details." He plopped onto Sam's couch and smiled his charismatic smile.

"Yes, we do have an agenda, but you can pick and choose what you think is appropriate. You're the professional, but you said that stories shape the narrative, right? We want to expose Lazos and make him feel weak, even emasculated," Sam said.

"Really? And why the sudden desire for this? It can't be just that he stole his daughter, because that's old news."

So we told him: About Eddie Stack. About Sam's stolen knife. About the man with the beard. About my attempted abduction.

Elliott's eyebrows kept rising higher and higher as he took it all in, and then he pulled his phone from his pocket and said, "Do you mind if I take notes?" Then he fired off his predictable questions.

"Have you ever seen this bearded man before?"

No.

"Did you have any previous knowledge of Eddie Stack?"

We had not. "Although it turns out I'm familiar with his wife. She works at the service desk at the grocery store on GGH."

"What?"

"Oh, sorry. That's what some of the local people call Green Glass Highway."

Elliott frowned. "I despise acronyms," he said.

I sniffed. "Anyway, what do you think of writing something to expose him?"

Elliott nodded. "It's a good story—but are you sure it would have the effect you want—that it would anger him and draw him out? Or would he just feel persecuted?"

Sam shrugged. "It doesn't really matter. We would be attempting to smoke him out, and whatever strong emotion he felt might get him to make a move—to do something stupid."

"He hasn't made too many mistakes so far," Elliott warned. "The guy is like Teflon."

He took a piece of cheese and two crackers and made a tiny sandwich, then popped it into his mouth.

I studied him, then said, "Hey, who is Joseph Williams? Is that a reporter you know?"

He wiped his hands off and chewed his crackers. I waited until he swallowed, at which point he said, "I know who you mean. I saw the story. But that's not a national rag, and I don't know the name. It's pretty clearly an alias."

"That's what I thought! And it has to be someone from

this area, because they had a picture of Sam and me. Who could get that kind of access?"

"Anyone," Elliott said. "As long as they're willing to spy."

I frowned at this. The bearded man and his camera . . .

Elliott leaned back on the couch. "So tell me this: what's Nikon's motive? He got his daughter; he wins. So why lash out at all of you?"

Sam pointed at him. "That's what you have to make clear. That he's a control freak. That he can't bear to lose on any level. That he sees Victoria as a disloyal wife and me, somehow, as a romantic rival. Rationality doesn't seem to enter into it."

He typed some more into his phone. He was grinning while he did it, which I pointed out to him.

"Sorry," he said, still grinning. "But a good story is pure gold to me. And while Victoria West has been making my life worthwhile with a lot of interviews about her life with Lazos and a world without her daughter—well, this is better. It suggests future conflict."

"For whom?" I asked.

Jake Elliott looked at me with his clear brown eyes. "For whoever loses. One way or the other, there are people at risk here."

"There's a lot we don't know," Sam said. "Almost everything is a mystery, in fact. But our biggest question is about the mailman. Why Eddie Stack? What does he have to do with the rest of us, and with these puzzle pieces?"

Jake Elliott nodded. "And is any of this off-limits? Anything the cops don't want me to use?"

Sam's face closed off slightly. "You can ask Doug. He's up at Graham House right now. Guarding Camilla's kingdom. Oh yes—we didn't tell you about the break-in, did we?"

Elliott's eyes were almost twinkling. "You did not."

Sam began to tell him about it, and we heard his front door opening. My father and Tabitha entered, looking exhausted after their day in the fresh air. "Hello," my father said. "Did we interrupt a party?"

We stood up, and I introduced Jake, whom Tabitha immediately flattered by remembering his name from the AP articles. "We really admired your story about Sam," she said. "You changed the way people looked at him, and it was powerful journalism."

Elliott beamed at her. "Thank you very much. I was lucky that Sam trusted me enough to confide in me."

We chatted for a while, but soon my father and Tabitha wished us good night and went up to their room on the second floor.

Jake Elliott looked at his watch and nodded. "I have to go, too. Sam, thanks for the call. I'll see what I can find to corroborate your ideas."

Sam thanked him and shook his hand, and then I did the same.

Elliott left, and we stood in the silent room.

"Just another day in Blue Lake," Sam said with a crooked smile.

Before we retired for the night, I went back down Sam's entrance hall and peeked out the front door. The police car was still there, pale white under the streetlight.

My spirits plunged. Sam was right; it couldn't be a good sign that they were sitting outside his house, almost as though they expected something to happen.

What did Doug know that we didn't know?

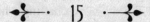

15

When she took the path to Apollo's temple, she knew that someone watched her from the shadows, but she wasn't willing to stop her quest now.

At this point, she felt that never knowing would be more painful than a confrontation.

—From *Death at Delphi*

ON MONDAY MORNING I spoke to Camilla on the phone while I scrambled eggs; she was eager to get back to her house and back to work; I agreed. "The distraction might have energized our writing for a day, but now we need our routine again," I said. I was starting to miss my purple chair, where I sat each time Camilla and I worked together.

"Yes. I'll speak to Doug today. I admit I felt a bit intimidated after the break-in and the attack on you," Camilla said. "But we will all be more vigilant now, as will Doug and Cliff, so I think we can resume our normal lives."

"Sam talked to Jake Elliott," I said. "Soon, through him, we'll be taking a stand against Nikon. Asserting ourselves via the press. The story might even come out today."

"It's a good step, I think. Oh, Adam is beckoning to me. We're going to have breakfast on his balcony. He has a lovely little town house; I'll have to bring you by sometime."

"Okay. Go have breakfast, then, and let me know what Doug says."

I hung up and turned to my father, who was on toast duty. Sam and Tabitha were chatting while they set his table and laughing over a chipmunk on the patio who kept looking in Sam's window. "What would you like to do today, Dad? I'm open, except that Sam and I want to talk to Belinda at the library at some point."

My father smiled at me. We had spent the previous day together, going to a movie in town, throwing stones into Blue Lake, and eating a leisurely dinner at Sam's while we watched the sunset from his back patio.

"Well, as you know, Tab and I have to leave tomorrow."

"Now you know you always have at least two second homes in Blue Lake," Sam said cheerfully.

My father nodded. "We would love to come again—maybe in the fall?"

"Oh yes!" I said.

"But meanwhile, there's something you always wrote to me about, but we've never seen."

"And what is that? I thought we hit all the hot spots."

"Not Bick's Hardware!" my dad said, his eyes twinkling. "We saw the outside the other day, but we didn't go in. And now that we met Marge and Horace at your party, I feel we should pay it a visit."

I laughed. I had written all about the eccentricities of Horace Bick and his wife, Marge, and their one-of-a-kind store. It was true: he had not seen Bick's in all its glory. "Of course! We have to take you there. As their sign promises, they have everything, so you might even get a souvenir or two."

"Ohh," Tabitha said, pleased at one last chance to shop.

We sat down together with eggs, toast, and coffee and

spent a hilarious breakfast trying to name our chipmunk friend. Sam ironically said his name should be "Heller," because that was Doug's last name, and for a certain period of his life Sam was always finding Doug at his door, similar to the way the determined chipmunk put his little paws up on the glass and peered in at us. Tabitha said he should be named "Stripey," for obvious reasons, and my father suggested "Eager." Since that described the tiny animal's expression perfectly, we selected that one, and Sam finally took pity on Eager the Chipmunk and tossed some bread crumbs out his way. Eager was soon joined by a friend, and they stuffed their cheeks with bread and darted away.

"Now that Sam has provided the morning's entertainment," I said later as we cleared the table, "I can take you to Bick's for a whole different kind of show."

My father and Tabitha agreed, and the four of us soon left the house and walked down the bluff path until it connected with Wentworth Street. We turned left and walked half a block until we reached the distinctive sign that said "Bick's Hardware." We walked into the foyer, where an inexplicable stuffed grizzly bear held a sign that said "Bick's Is Best!"

"So I've been told," my father said to the bear.

We went inside and stood still so that our visitors could take in the altered reality that was Bick's. It looked like a world bazaar, with shelves that went up to the ceiling, and Horace Bick, as usual, presiding on the floor, asking people what they needed. "Don't use the ladder," I said, holding my breath, and as if in response, a dark-haired man asked Mr. Bick for oil for his tiki torch, at which point Mr. Bick went clambering up a ladder attached to the wall, nimble as a monkey, to retrieve the product.

"Oh my goodness," Tabitha said, clutching her heart.

"It's terrifying every time," I agreed.

Sam sniffed. "The man's been doing it for forty years. He knows his terrain."

I led them through the thematically unconnected departments: kitchenware; beach attire; automotive; stuffed animals; shower curtains; paperback books; and then, against a back wall, Marge's little post office window. Marge spotted us and waved. "Hello, Lena, Sam! How nice. I don't think I've ever seen you in here together."

We looked at each other and nodded in surprise. It was true. "Marge, you remember my father and his wife, Tabitha, from my party, right?"

Marge did. She shook their hands and asked if they needed stamps. "Oh, I would love a book of stamps," Tabitha said obligingly.

Marge rang her up, and on a whim I said, "Marge, have you seen a bearded man in here recently—someone who hasn't been in here before?"

She thought about it, clearly pleased to be consulted. "Well, it's May, and we're starting to get a trickling of tourists. And of course there's always the odd reporter, thanks to this guy." She pointed a thumb at Sam as though she were hitchhiking, and then laughed. "Just kidding," she said.

Sam nodded. Marge had very little tact, but Sam knew, as I did, that she had a good heart.

"He has brownish-red hair and a bushy beard. If he'd been in here, you surely would have noticed him," I said. Marge had an eagle eye.

She shook her head, disappointed. "No, can't say that I've seen him." She noted our expressions and said, "But now I wish I had! What's the scoop?"

I looked around before speaking. "He's—someone the

police are looking for. He's been lurking around town for a few days."

"I'll have my eyes open. I swear, I'm downright paranoid now, with all the stuff that's happened. But everyone in this town is paranoid. You are," she said, pointing at Sam and me. "And I am, and poor Horace is, and that library lady who was in here."

"Belinda?"

"Is that her name? And poor Eddie Stack. He was talking Horace's ear off last time he was in here. Horace figured maybe he was on drugs."

Sam turned a bit paler at the mention of Eddie's name.

Tabitha leaned forward. "Let's change the subject," she said. "We have two little children who live next door to us, and I'd love to get them those lions that I saw in the stuffed animal aisle. They're kind of high up. Can we get them without your husband using the ladder?"

"Oh, that's no problem," Marge said. "Horace! We need you to climb up and get a toy!"

"Oh no," Tabitha murmured, and I touched her arm for consolation.

Mr. Bick came sloping toward us on his long legs, looking like a wind-up toy. "Which ones?" he shouted importantly.

Sam slipped his hand into mine and squeezed it to acknowledge that he, too, thought this was funny, but his face remained expressionless.

WE DROPPED MY father and Tabitha at Sam's house, then started on our own errands. Sam said he needed a few groceries, so we drove out to Dilley's, a big white store on Green Glass Highway about a mile west of the town center.

"Need anything?" Sam said as he grabbed a cart and started piloting it down the first aisle.

"Not really. Maybe I'll get something sweet to feed Dad and Tabby tonight. They both like ice cream."

"Sure. And remind me I need some of those special stickers for my yard waste bags. Otherwise the garbage guy won't pick them up. They have them at the service desk."

"You get your groceries. I'll run and get the stickers. Grab some chocolate ice cream."

"Okay, honey," said Sam.

We grinned at each other, pleased to be sharing domestic chores. I waved and made my way to the service desk, where I found myself face-to-face with Doris Stack, Eddie's widow. Why was she working so soon after his death?

"Hi. What can I do for ya?" Doris asked. She smiled, but I noted the dark circles under her eyes and a general sadness in her expression. She had dark hair and dark eyes; perhaps that was what made her skin seem so pale.

"Um—yard waste stickers, please. Five of them."

"Ten dollars." She opened a drawer behind her counter and counted out the stickers. Then she said, "Can I ask you something?"

This surprised me. "Uh—sure."

"You're Lena, right? I mean, I've seen your picture in the paper a bunch of times. You go out with Sam West."

My face grew hot, but I said, "Yes, that's me."

She leaned forward. "How do you deal with it? The comments from people, the questions? I—my husband recently died, and it was in the paper, and you wouldn't believe the things people have said to me."

"Yes, I would," I said.

"Yeah—I figured you could relate. So what do you do?"

She hadn't yet looked directly at me, except to dart glances at me now and then.

I shrugged. "You ride it out; it dies down eventually. I'm sorry for your loss. I—didn't know your husband, but my friend did. She said—he was a great mailman."

She smiled. "It wasn't his life's dream or anything, but I think he liked his job." A worried expression flitted across her face. "Most of the time, anyway."

"Had he been—threatened, or anything? I'm just wondering what sort of person would harm a mail carrier."

She leaned in, her voice soft, although there was no one else in line. "He told me something a couple of days before he died. I didn't think anything of it, but then later I remembered it, and it gave me the chills."

"What was it?" I asked, nakedly curious.

She reached up to pat her dark hair with nervous hands. "He came home after his route and had a weird expression on his face. I asked what he was thinking about, and he said, 'I think I heard something I wasn't supposed to hear.' I asked if he overheard someone's conversation, and he said no, that he heard a sound that was out of place, or something, and it got him thinking."

"What was the sound?"

"He wouldn't say, but"—her eyes filled with tears—"he said he thought it meant money."

I patted her hand. "I'm really sorry for your loss. I have a friend at the library—Belinda Frailey—and she told me once that there's a support group that meets in the basement of First Methodist. For people who have lost a spouse."

She wiped her eyes. "Yeah? I'll have to look that up. I've been working to keep my mind off things, but it's not really helping, you know? So I'll look into that, for sure."

Now there was someone in line. "Take care, Doris," I

said, and I picked up the stickers and headed back toward Sam.

"We need to talk," I said in a low voice.

He was examining a tomato, but he looked up at me, his handsome face curious. "Not in here?"

"No. Hurry up."

We finished up the last of the shopping and Sam paid the young cashier; then we wheeled quickly out to the car, where Sam stowed several bags in his trunk. He returned the cart and ran back, then tucked into the car and turned to me. "What?"

I told him what Doris Stack had said to me, and he whistled. "So here's what we have," he said eventually. "Eddie Stack hears something he shouldn't hear. He tells his wife it means money. He calls me and tells me he has information about that little girl. So—did he hear a child? Maybe where a child shouldn't have been?"

"It's Athena," I said. "She's here, she's in town!"

He shook his head. "*Why* would she be in town? He has the whole world to hide her in."

I couldn't answer this one. "I'll tell Doug," I said.

"He probably already knows," Sam said. "He's interviewed Doris, right? Isn't that what Allison said?"

"Still," I insisted, dialing our friend's number. I left Doug a message, telling him what I had told Sam, and then hung up. "It's such a letdown," I said. "I feel all riled up with this news, like we should go find Athena right now."

"We're jumping to a lot of conclusions," he said.

"But they make sense!"

"Still. Let the police do this, Lena. They're the experts, and they're not as emotional about it as we are."

With a sigh, I agreed. "Fine. Let's drop off these groceries and go see Belinda." I had called her that morning and she did, indeed, have some more material for both of her research files.

After a quick stop at Sam's, we were back on the road. I stared at the side of his face until he looked at me, smiling. "What's up?"

"I just like you. And I was admiring your noble jawline."

He laughed. "I have never been told about my noble jawline."

"That's what I'm here for."

He slid a hand across the seat and I put mine in it. We continued that way, hand in hand, while Sam steered the car with his left. Finally he said, "You make everything easier."

I looked out the window at the bright landscape, letting a quiet joy seep in.

Moments later Sam pulled into the library lot and we climbed out, then joined hands again. We mounted the steps and opened the door to the "Secret Garden" arbor, and only then did I remember Darla and her obsession with Sam. I darted a glance to the circulation desk and, sure enough, Darla was behind the counter, checking out a book to a dark-haired woman. "Oh shoot," I said under my breath.

"What?"

"The lady there," I said in a low voice. "She's the one I told you about. She's obsessed with you. She asked me once if you'd ever be—"

Suddenly Darla was there in front of us, along with the woman who had checked out the book. They both looked rather starstruck. "Hello, Lena," Darla said. "I don't know if you've met Agatha Wallace? She's one of our regular patrons here."

Sam regarded both women with the blank expression he'd developed over the last year—a form of self-protection.

I looked at the woman with Darla. "Uh—I don't think so, although you look familiar. I've probably seen you in town," I said.

"I think I've seen you at the library before," she said, and I realized that she was right; I had seen her talking to Darla on the steps during one of my last visits.

"Well, nice to meet you," I said. I shook her hand, which was soft and cool.

Both women shifted their gaze to Sam, and I realized it couldn't be avoided. "This is Sam West," I said.

Darla stuck out her hand first. "Sam, it's so great to meet you! I can't tell you how much I admire the way you stood up to adversity and held strong while people oppressed you. I don't know if Lena told you, but I did a paper on you in grad school. It explores the legal ramifications of your situation. I'd love to have you read it at some point."

Her enthusiasm was so great that I could feel Sam recede slightly into himself. He remained polite, however. "It's all a bit too fresh right now. But someday, certainly—I'd be interested to take a look at it."

The woman named Agatha put out her hand again. "Mr. West, I have followed your case on the news for more than a year. It is remarkable, all the twists of fate that brought you to where you are today."

"I agree," Sam said, shaking her hand. "Let's hope fate is finished twisting me."

She laughed, her dark eyes sparkling, and Darla laughed even louder. She was about to say something else, but I quickly interjected, slapping my forehead as if having a sudden realization. "Oh—I just remembered Belinda said she only had a short amount of time to talk with us—I guess she has some visitors coming later?"

Darla drooped slightly. "Members of the library board are stopping by. We're looking for them to fund some renovations."

Sam pounced on this. "Well, we'd better get Belinda's information before she gets too busy."

Darla's face was alert. "Is she researching something for you?"

"Just some vacation destinations," I lied. "I'm planning to take Sam away from it all."

The women digested this for a moment, their mouths parted slightly; they looked oddly like twins.

"Well, it was nice meeting both of you," Sam said. "I'm sure we'll meet again; we seem to share a love of books." He pointed at the volumes clutched in Agatha Wallace's hands.

This broke whatever tension there had been—perhaps I had imagined it—and the women laughed and smiled, waving as we moved to the back of the library.

"Sorry," I whispered. "I forgot to warn you."

"Oh, for the days of boring anonymity," he said.

We found Belinda in her office, studying something with a magnifying glass. She looked up and brightened at the sight of us. "Hi, guys! Good to see you. Pull up a couple of chairs there."

We did, and I said, "Beware. Darla now knows that you're researching something for us, and she didn't seem to believe my 'dream vacation' story. You do lock up those files, right?"

Belinda nodded. "Yup. Or I take them home with me. She can't get her mitts on them, and I would frankly be horrified if she tried."

Sam seemed to be lost in thought, so I said, "Where do we start?"

She nodded, pleased. Belinda was the type who liked to get straight to work. "Okay. Well, let's start with our friend Nikon. You want to close the door, Lena?"

"I do." I got up and shut the office door; I glimpsed the two women, still in conversation near the entrance. Then I returned.

Belinda was enthused about her research, as always. "I got some more Lazos family information. This time it was from a gossip website, of all things, that is published in New York. It came out just after Victoria was found—the date is January second."

She pushed the printed article toward us. "What's weird is that I have tried to locate any other mention of this, and I cannot find a word. Even this article seems to have been wiped off the Internet, but I found it as a screenshot that someone took. Now it's as though it never existed. But here's the evidence."

We looked down at the article, which was a brief blurb with a small picture of two dark-haired people who were both obviously Lazos family members. It read *Georgios Lazos, brother of Nikon Lazos, and Demeter Lazos, his oldest sister, spoke with one of our reporters this week about their notorious brother, currently at large and wanted by authorities. "Nikon has shamed the family,"
Lazos said, "and the way he has treated both of his wives is shameful—his first wife, Grace, ran away from him because of his cruel nature, and now we find out there was a new woman, this Victoria, who we never met because Nikon kept her locked up like a possession. That is not a man. That is not the brother I knew, or a brother I will acknowledge." His sister added that Lazos had always*

been very demanding of his younger siblings, yet had been terribly neglectful of them at the same time, disappearing sometimes for a year or more with no family contact—and often in total control of the family's fortune.

That was all. Sam and I both read it, then looked at each other. "So within five years, at least three of his family members have essentially disowned him—these two, and Demetrius five years earlier. I guess these were two of the siblings that sided with Demetrius in the big rift we read about. Those comments had to hurt—Victoria said Nikon was all about family."

Sam shrugged. "But he was advocating starting a new family with her. Maybe he had ceased to acknowledge his former family. Maybe he disowned them before they disowned him. He's just weird enough to do it."

I thought about this. "I wonder which two were present when they got on the yacht. Victoria said that two of them were there."

Sam shrugged. "We'll have to ask her."

Belinda tapped her desk with a pencil and pushed her glasses up on her nose. "It's weird, though—not just that these family members emerged in the press, but then that they receded again. Does Nikon sue people? Pay them off? Insist upon gag orders?"

"And why?" Sam said. "Who cares? He doesn't seem the type to worry about a little gossip."

"Doesn't he?" I said. "He's this big glamorous tycoon, but he's also weirdly obsessive about details. These would be the little facts that would stick in his craw. And who knows if he's gone back to see those brothers? Maybe to resolve things, maybe to silence them? I don't understand the Lazos family dynamic."

Belinda nodded. "I've been trying to find anything on

either George or Demetrius. They're both still alive, in case you were fearing some sort of primal retribution. But other than that I don't know much. George is married and has two grown sons. Demetrius is married, too, but I haven't determined whether or not he has offspring. I'm working on it."

Sam tipped his chair back and then lowered it again. Belinda seemed relieved when it was back in place. He said, "So this might be important, and it might not. What does it really matter if Nikon is estranged from his family? He's a criminal. He's estranged from the whole world."

"But your family wouldn't have abandoned you," I said. "If they had been here. They would have stayed loyal."

Sam nodded. "They would have. And I'm fairly sure my mother would have told off the press on a regular basis."

I smiled at this image of Sam's mother. Belinda nodded. "I found something about your parents, too, Sam. This one is really sweet."

She opened her other file and held up a printed copy of an old newspaper article. "It's from a newspaper in Saratoga Springs, where I guess you guys lived for a while."

Sam nodded, smiling. "Yeah. When I was a kid. We had a great house there."

"This was published about five years after the story about your parents' engagement. They were married, and you were about three years old." Sam picked up the article and I saw the accompanying picture of his mother, looking almost like a teenager, and little Sam, tucked against her skirt while she posed, smiling shyly, standing in front of a rosebush.

"That's our house," Sam said. "I remember the bush, and that brick wall behind it was our front porch."

"This reporter was doing a follow-up on the earlier human interest story. Apparently it had been one of their most popular stories ever, and so five years later they decided to resurrect it, probably to boost sales. Which I'm guessing it did. It's a great story. Your mom talks about your dad, what a great husband and father he is. But look at the part I highlighted."

Sam held the story between us so that we could both read the part Belinda had marked in yellow:

> *Mrs. West said that motherhood had been a pleasant surprise, and that she could not now imagine life without her son, Sam, three. "Sam is my little companion. When I'm gardening, he holds my watering pail. When I do the dishes, he holds his little towel and dries the unbreakable ones. When we go grocery shopping, he brings his little cart. He's the sweetest boy with the biggest heart. I don't know what I did to deserve him."*
>
> *West adds that she has a special song that she sings to her son at bedtime: Olivia Newton-John's "Sam."*
>
> *"It's our very own mother-son song," she said. "I feel so lucky to have this special guy in my life. I feel like I've been given a second chance."*

Sam stood up suddenly and looked out the glass office window, his back to us. "Give me a minute," he said. Belinda and I sat for moment in silence, not making eye contact.

"Are you okay?" Belinda finally asked. She looked crestfallen. "I thought this would make you happy. I didn't mean to—"

Sam turned and sat back down, wiping at his eyes. "I'm sorry. That came out of nowhere. I had forgotten that song, totally forgotten. But of course. She did sing it to me, for years . . . she had the sweetest voice."

I sprang from my chair and moved to his, hugging him from behind. "I'm glad you got back this memory of her. What a beautiful thing! And it reminds us how much, as you said, your mother loved children. Do you think by 'second chance,' she is referencing her other child?"

Belinda looked thoughtful. "I did wonder about that. And the reporter must have known; I mean, the first story showed her as a pregnant woman. It's not like readers would forget that he rescued her in front of that doctor's office. But it's not referenced here. Almost as though they were told not to ask about it."

Sam was rereading the article, smiling this time. "Saratoga Springs. I wonder if we went there, did some digging, if that would provide us with any information."

"It might. We could certainly contact this newspaper office, see if anyone remembers the story. There have to be some people around who were there at the time. I wonder if they've made the connection to you now—to the Sam West who was wanted for murder. Their hometown boy," Belinda said thoughtfully.

"I'd almost hate to find out," Sam said.

"Meanwhile, I found one other thing. It's a story about your dad getting another decoration. This was in 1988, same newspaper. He was on the scene when a motorcyclist fell off his bike. He gave the guy CPR, did everything in a textbook perfect way, and the cyclist survived because of him. There was a ceremony." Belinda held up a picture of the whole West family: Sam's father in uniform, his mother in a lovely blue dress, little Sam, around six years old, wearing a suit and looking solemn, and tiny Wendy, in her mother's arms with her face half buried in her hair.

Sam shook his head. "I knew my dad was respected.

And I guess I knew he had gotten some commendations. But I never knew this. Why? My mom must have had a scrapbook somewhere. Or did I know it and forget it? I don't know anymore. My memories of them come and go, and sometimes I wonder if I've suppressed some things."

Belinda nodded, her face compassionate. "You've had so much stress, Sam. It can affect memory, did you know?"

"I think I knew, but I forgot," Sam joked.

I pointed at the files. "Thanks, Belinda. You do good work. You shouldn't be buried in Blue Lake. They could use you at the *New York Times*. Or in the government."

She shrugged. "There's really nothing here that could help Doug. And Sam's stuff is just for Sam."

Suddenly a shadow fell over the room, and I turned to find Darla's face in the window; I jumped, and Belinda beckoned her in while closing both of her files in a smooth movement. Sam, who had been holding the article, folded it in half and held it loosely in his hand. "What can I do for you, Darla?"

Darla was so curious I could almost picture her with twitching whiskers. "The board members are here. I said that you'd meet with them in the Stewart Memorial Room."

"Great. Thanks!"

We waited for Darla to leave, but she lingered long enough to say, "So where did you guys choose?"

"I'm sorry?" Belinda said.

"For your vacation getaway. What's the final destination?"

Belinda shrugged. "The jury's still out."

Sam turned and looked Darla in the eye. "I was thinking somewhere in the Caribbean, but Lena likes Rome."

"I want to throw my coins in the fountain," I said, with a helpful smile.

Darla nodded. "We have some books about Rome out here, if you're interested."

"I'd love to check those out. Thanks, Darla!"

She finally left. "She's suspicious," Sam said. "There's something I thought of earlier, when we were talking—"

"What was it?"

"I can't remember. God, maybe I do have a memory problem."

I patted his hand, and we started to gather our things.

Belinda held up a hand. "There's one more thing. Did you know Jake Elliott's article came out today?"

"No!" I said.

"I wasn't sure, but I knew it was coming soon," Sam said.

"Well, I pulled it from the AP. It's a bombshell. Here you go." She turned her chair to retrieve an article that was pinned to her bulletin board. "This one's not in a file; it's right up where I can appreciate it all day long. But you can have that copy and I'll make another."

Sam let me read it first.

NIKON LAZOS EMERGES IN ACTS OF REVENGE

Jake Elliott, Associated Press

Sam West went to Blue Lake, Indiana, more than a year ago to escape the scrutiny he was under in New York City after the disappearance of his wife, Victoria. Instead, Blue Lake became a place of suspicion and persecution, and West realized there was nowhere he could go that his story would not follow him.

After more than a year, West's fortunes changed. It was determined his wife was alive and that she had been kept from the rest of the world by a possessive lover and extremely rich tycoon named Nikon Leandros Lazos. At the time that authorities found Ms. West and her baby daughter, Lazos managed to elude them and disappear.

That might have been the last the world heard of Lazos if it had not been for two things: his daughter and his particularly vengeful personality. First, authorities allege that Lazos had his daughter abducted in broad daylight, hiring a henchman who literally took the child from her mother's arms. Doug Heller of the Blue Lake Police Department is sure that Lazos was behind the abduction. "Lazos had made it clear to his wife that he would never want their family separated. There is no one with a stronger motive than Lazos for kidnapping the baby, and he is number one on our personal most-wanted list and some international most-wanted lists as well."

But Lazos's alleged crimes don't stop there. Blue Lake police also think that Lazos wants revenge not just against his wife, but against her much-maligned ex-husband, Sam West. Heller suggests that Lazos has made certain attempts at revenge against West, although the motive is unclear. Lazos's own brother Demetrius Lazos, now living in Chicago, says this does not surprise him. "Nikon is very competitive—always has been. The moment he chose Victoria West as a love interest he would have seen any other man in her life as the enemy. He has done this since he was a teenager. Despite all Mr. West has been through—yes, I believe my brother would find a way to blame him for the loss of Victoria. Nikon has never been good at taking responsibility."

Authorities could not discuss the initial revenge attempt against West, which involves a recent crime in

Blue Lake, but Heller believes that the other attempts have also been aimed at those West holds dear. Since the discovery that his wife was indeed alive, West has carried on a high-profile romance with Blue Lake resident Lena London, and in the last few days Ms. London has been stalked around town, culminating in an attempt to abduct her. While West and London declined to comment, New York criminal psychologist Sarah Ehrlichman said that it is not uncommon for the guilty to deflect responsibility and to blame their actions on unlikely or undeserving people. "If this man was living his own illusion with his lover, he will see her rescue as a destruction of his world rather than seeing the abduction of the child as a destruction of hers. His actions are narcissistic, and if he is a destructive narcissist, his anger could be significant and intense."

Heller believes that Lazos has at least one contact in Blue Lake or somewhere in the Midwest—someone who keeps a close watch on those Lazos wants to punish. A possible connection to Lazos has already been identified, and an APB has been issued for the suspect's arrest.

In the meantime, Heller wants it made known to those in Blue Lake and beyond: "Lazos was the bad guy when the whole world was pointing fingers at Sam West; and now, even though he's invisible, he continues to be a dangerous man." He encourages anyone who has seen something unusual, or who might have any information about Nikon Lazos, to call the Blue Lake Police Department or the FBI.

For his part, Sam West is philosophical. Thanks to a chance discovery, he was freed from jail last October, and he does not intend to be dragged back because of

*a vendetta. He's grown to like Blue Lake, and he in-
tends to stay there.*

WHEN SAM AND I said our good-byes and walked to the
parking lot (still watched by Darla), I said, "Sam, that
article—did you notice it? That quote from the psychologist?"

"What?" he asked.

"He said Nikon would view it as a destruction of his
world. That's what my note said. About a dream being
destroyed."

"Let's hope this riles him up. That he pokes his nose
out of whatever hole he's dug for himself."

"And let's hope this was the right thing to do," I said.
"There's a chance he could become even more dangerous
once he comes out of hiding."

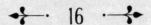

16

The snake is more dangerous when it is threatened.
—From *Death at Delphi*

THAT NIGHT SAM and I took a walk with my father and Tabitha; they were planning to leave early in the morning. My father and I walked ahead while Sam and Tabitha, in an effort to be thoughtful, stayed a few yards behind.

"It's been so great to have you here, Dad," I said. "I waited too long."

He slipped an arm around me. "Which is why we won't wait this long again. Tab and I were talking—we've got a lovely condo near the beach, and after all this, I'm sure Sam especially will want to get away and decompress. You should both come down to Florida."

This sounded wonderful, and I told him so. "Maybe later in the summer, or in September! I don't think I'll have to twist Sam's arm too hard."

"He's a good man," my father said. "We like him."

"I'm glad."

"We like your friends, too. All the people who came to

your party—they were terrific. Even though we're worried about recent events in this town, we're happy to know you're surrounded by caring people."

I nodded. We had walked up toward Camilla's place, and now we moved toward the edge of the bluff to look at the lake. "You don't have to worry, Dad. Doug and Cliff are watching us, and Sam's not going to let me out of his sight."

My father thought about this. "I want you to keep in touch with me. Otherwise Tabby and I will worry anyway."

Tabitha and Sam caught up with us and I smiled at my father's wife. "Tabitha, before we got kicked out of Graham House I hung the framed book cover in my room. It looks amazing."

Her face grew rosy with pleasure. "I was just trying to convince Sam to come and visit us in Florida," Tabitha said. "When you do, I'll show you my little workshop where I do my art and frame prints."

"I would love that. I so admire your creativity," I said, and I was immediately glad that I did, not only because of Tabitha's pleased laugh, but because of the gratified expression on my father's face.

While we stood talking and looking at the lake, Doug Heller appeared and walked over from Camilla's yard. He joined our group and chatted for a while, and then I pulled him aside.

"Camilla wants to come home, and so do I. We need to get back to work," I said.

"I suppose you can. It's been quiet; no, strike that—it's been silent. Which isn't always a good thing. But we can double up on your security, if Camilla wants to come back. I'll talk to her."

I looked behind me; Sam and the visitors were laughing

together about some joke that one of them had told. "And I'd like to know why you need to have a car on both houses. Are you afraid that Lazos will come after us or is it something else? Because Sam has an alarm and a camera, and he feels confident he can protect me."

Doug stared. "What do you mean?"

"I mean Cliff's been parked outside Sam's house every night, and Sam is feeling sensitive about it. Like maybe you guys don't trust him or something."

Doug donned the blank cop face that I found so frustrating. He was quiet for what felt like a full minute. Finally he said, "I'll look into it."

"What does that mean?"

His phone buzzed in his pocket, and he took it out with an apologetic glance at me. "Heller." He turned away slightly, then said, "Hang on." He turned back to me and said, "I've got to take this. I'll talk to Camilla, and I'll let you know about that other issue."

He walked away, his posture tense as he talked to his unknown caller. "That other issue." What did that even mean? No one in this town was making sense to me lately.

Our group headed back to the house for a leisurely dinner. Sam put on some jazz and poured wine while he grilled steaks on his back patio, and my father told us stories about his time in the army. Tabitha leaned her head on his shoulder and smiled at me, and for the first time in a long time I felt some tension ease out of me. Things were good. Things would stay good.

The phone rang, and Sam came in from the patio to pick it up. "Sam West," he said, still clutching his barbecue fork.

He listened for a moment, then turned to us with a triumphant expression.

"They got him!" he said.

"Lazos?" I asked, dumbstruck.

"No. The bearded man."

IN THE MORNING we drove my father and his wife to the airport. Tabitha had a few more bags than she'd had when she arrived, and my father grumbled slightly about how that would make life harder, but his face and his tone never matched the supposedly curmudgeonly words, and Tabitha knew it. She winked at us, and they both waved as they walked through the doors.

Sam looked at me and said, "Now we have an empty nest."

I laughed. "It does sort of feel that way. But all people leave a hole when they go."

"True. You ready to talk to Doug?"

"Yes. The sooner the better."

Sam drove to the Blue Lake police station, located in the north end of town and surrounded by pine trees. There was a circular drive in front and a parking lot behind the building. Sam pulled into the circle drive and parked right in front of the door. "They can ticket me," he said, looking slightly vengeful.

I couldn't blame him. He and the BLPD had a rocky history.

We went inside and found a busy office filled with desks and ringing phones. A receptionist at the front counter asked how he could help us, and we said we were there to speak with Doug Heller.

The young man frowned. "Did you have an appointment? Because Detective Heller is booked all morning, and then I know he has to—"

A door opened at the back of the room, and Doug came

out with Mayor Paul Wilding. I recognized him from newspaper coverage—I had never met the man.

I dug an elbow into Sam's side, and he said, "Wow."

The mayor walked toward us, and I made eye contact with Doug and gave him a wave. He called, "Jim? Let them come on back."

The young man handed us visitor's badges and lifted up part of the counter so that we could go in and the mayor could come out. He was a gray-haired man with a large belly. He was wearing a very expensive-looking suit. "Tell Rusty that I'll talk to him later today," the mayor told the young man named Jim.

Jim nodded and said, "Yes, sir, I will."

Rusty was Bill "Rusty" Baxter, our current chief, who had once had red hair that had earned him his nickname. Now his hair was gray, like the mayor's.

The mayor seemed to notice us for the first time. He raised his brows and held out a hand. "Mr. West," he said. "I know Blue Lake has issued you some apologies, and I once made one on television, but I have never made one to your face. Please do accept my regrets."

"Of course," said Sam, ever gracious.

"And to you, too, young woman. Every man should have a woman in his life as loyal as you, I must say."

I didn't know what to say to that; I merely smiled.

"What brings you here?" the mayor asked, suddenly alert. Perhaps he feared that the police were tormenting Sam again.

Sam slipped an arm around me. "We received word that the police have apprehended a man who accosted Lena. We would like to know some details."

The mayor moved closer, and I could smell his aftershave, which was clearly expensive. "I would like to know about this, as well. I'll ask Douglas to keep me apprised. Whatever you need from us, Mr. West, you say the word. I read that article about that crazy Greek man who's been going after you. It boggles the imagination, wouldn't you say?"

He looked at me with some piercing gray eyes, and I nodded. I realized the mayor was quite charismatic.

He shook our hands again and said, "Whatever you need." He pointed a finger at Sam, handed him a business card that he pulled out of his suit pocket, then marched out the front door.

"Wow," I said.

Sam laughed a little as we made our way back to Doug's office. He had left the door ajar, so we walked in to find a cluttered desk, a window view (more trees—a Blue Lake staple), and a framed map of Blue Lake on the east wall. On the west wall was a giant bulletin board filled with various notices and wanted posters. At the center of this was the smiling face of Nikon Lazos.

Doug, who was already seated at his desk and looking at a file, glanced up and smiled at us. "I'm glad you came in. Take a seat." He gestured to two brown chairs that sat across from his desk. We sat down, waiting for him.

He didn't waste our time. "We were right; it is Wally Kallis. We've got him in lockup and we've advised him that he can make a phone call, but he hasn't asked to talk with anyone. In fact, he hasn't talked at all."

"Not even to tell you why he grabbed Lena?" Sam asked.

"Not even to verify his identity. The guy is a clam." Doug smiled at us. "But here's some interesting news. About half an hour ago, a lawyer showed up. He said he is representing Mr. Kallis, and that there has been a misunderstanding. I asked how this guy happened to know that

Mr. Kallis was in custody, since he had not made a phone call. He said that he heard of the arrest on a police radio."

"Bull," Sam said.

Doug nodded. "Yeah, this one smells bad, but right now all we can do is wait them out. Neither one of them is saying much, but Mr. Kallis isn't going anywhere until he does. Lena, if you'll just verify that this is the man who grabbed you?" He pulled a mug shot out of the file in his hand and showed it to me.

"That is absolutely the man. I get chills just looking at him. And why is he smiling?" I asked, horrified.

"He doesn't seem to be playing with a full deck," Doug said thoughtfully. "Which makes you wonder why someone would take the risk of hiring him. He could mess things up, as he in fact did."

I pushed the picture back toward Doug. "Put that away. You're not going to let him go, are you?"

"No way. He tried to abduct you and he physically assaulted you. We'll be charging him presently. The lawyer is waiting for that, so he can figure out his next move."

Sam nodded. "Thanks for filling us in. You got this guy—now just get Nikon. One down, one to go, right?"

"At least one. We'll want to catch any other creepy little minions that Nikon has working for him. Who broke into your house, for example? It wasn't this Wally, because he's very tall, and the ninja was of medium height."

"I temporarily forgot about the ninja," Sam said, frowning.

Doug's phone rang. His phone was always ringing. "Heller," he said. His face looked tired again. I touched Sam's arm, signaling that we should leave, and we stood up.

Doug held the phone away from his head and said, "I'll talk with you guys soon."

I paused. "Where's Cliff today?"

"He's on afternoon shift," Doug said, and went back to his call.

We moved through the mass of people taking calls, typing reports, filling out forms. It was nice to see the people who kept Blue Lake safe every day.

Sam and I turned in our badges and walked back to our car. I climbed into the passenger seat. "I've got to call Camilla. She must be chomping at the bit to get back to Graham House."

"I'll bet Adam is trying to think of a million ways to stall her," Sam said, grinning. "That's how I feel about you leaving Sam House."

I laughed. "Is that what it's called? Well, I love Sam House. But Camilla's place is currently my home. And I miss my cat. You and I can always visit back and forth, but poor Lestrade needs his attention."

"Right. Hey, do you mind if I stop at Bick's? I want to make sure I have backup batteries for my security camera."

"Sure. I could use a new book to read. And I want to get some stamps so I can send a thank-you card to Dad and Tabby."

Sam was quiet for a moment. "Do you think they liked me?" he finally said.

I turned in my seat, surprised. "I know they did. My father told me so, in fact. He likes you and trusts you, which is why he was able to leave."

He nodded. "Good." Then he smiled at me. "That's really good. Everything is going according to plan." He took his hands off the wheel and rubbed them together like an evil genius, and I laughed.

* * *

WE SEPARATED IN Bick's, and I wandered back to the post office counter, where Marge was telling a story to some tourists. She loved sharing horrifying true crime tales that she watched on *Dateline*. "And the bride's body was never found," she intoned as she handed them their receipt.

"That's terrible," said the woman, who wore an Ohio sweatshirt. "What a horrible story."

Marge shrugged. "Oh, every week it's a different one. Makes you wonder how many murderers you walk past on a given day."

The tourists thanked her and walked away, looking demoralized. I gave Marge a stern look. "You shouldn't scare the visitors," I said.

She grinned. "Got to do something for entertainment, stuck behind this dusty counter all day."

Shaking my head, I said, "I need a book of stamps."

"Will do. Did your dad enjoy his trip?"

"He did. They promised to visit again before the end of the year."

"That's nice, that's nice." She busied herself getting the stamps and ringing them up.

"Marge?"

"Hmm?"

"Yesterday when we were here, you were talking about how paranoid everyone is. Or was."

"That's for sure. Why, just yesterday I was convinced there was a shadow on that wall, and—"

"You also said that Eddie Stack was paranoid."

"Oh yeah. Him and his wife both. You ever met Doris?"

"Yes. So how was he paranoid?"

"Oh, he was always suspicious of the people he brought the mail to. This guy looks like a terrorist. That lady looks like a mug shot. But he also had bad dreams. He told Horace all kinds of whatnot. Let me call him. Horace!"

Horace appeared, looking ready as always to climb his ladder. He wore green overalls today and resembled a large blade of grass. "What do you need?" he asked. Sam approached the counter, too, with a bag that said "Bick's Is Best!"

Marge greeted him and then pointed at her husband. "Horace, tell them what that Eddie Stack was telling you. You said he was acting paranoid and like a drug addict or something."

Horace nodded. "Oh, the crazy stuff some of these people tell me when they're here shopping for this and that. I just take it all in, I don't judge, mind you. Oh, there's that box of nails," he said absently, pulling it from his pocket and setting it on Marge's counter.

"Eddie Stack?"

"Oh, sure. He told me he dreamed things that made him feel weird while he was awake. He dreamed that the kidnapped baby was chasing him, but she was all grown up."

"Athena?" I asked.

"Yes, the little girl of Victoria West."

"Well, I suppose that baby is on everyone's mind. And her picture is in the paper almost every day," Sam said.

"Yeah. And so is the bad guy—the Kodak guy," Mr. Bick said, rocking back on his shoes.

"Nikon?" Sam asked sharply.

"Yeah, right. I knew it was a camera." Mr. Bick nodded at us, pleased with his attempt.

"And why is that notable, that Nikon is in the paper?" I persisted.

"Because Eddie swore he saw him, too. He was like that—suggestible, I guess. Saw a picture of someone on one of his mailers and then that person was on his mind. He was seeing everyone."

My hands froze, the stamps still in them. Marge Bick stared at her husband, her mouth open in surprise. I said, "Mr. Bick. Horace. Eddie told you that he had seen Nikon Lazos?"

He peered at me over his glasses. "Well, sure, but like I said . . ."

"How long before he died did he tell you this?" Sam asked.

His face grew red with some unclear emotion. "I—maybe one or two days."

Marge clapped her hands. "Horace! Didn't you think that might be important?"

"Well—you had to know Eddie. He was a conspiracy theorist. You took what he said with a grain of salt."

I leaned forward. "But the timing—don't you think it sounds suspicious?"

He looked uncomfortable. "Well, I do *now*!"

Sam's eyes met mine. He looked as shocked as I felt. Could Nikon actually be in Blue Lake? "We need to tell this to Doug," he said.

"Should I call him?" Marge asked.

"We'll go there," Sam said.

We ran out of the store and back to Sam's car.

"LET'S JUST GET this straight in our minds," Sam said. "Eddie Stack was in Bick's Hardware a day or two before he died. He seemed paranoid, and told Marge that the Lazos baby had grown up and was chasing him in his dreams.

Then he said that he had seen Nikon Lazos himself. And he told his wife that he heard something he shouldn't have heard."

"If he recognized Nikon, and Nikon found out that he did, that would explain why he killed him. What about the grown-up baby? Doesn't that make Eddie sound crazy, like the Bicks said?"

Sam shrugged. "He could have just seen a woman who looked like the Lazos child, and it put the baby in his consciousness. Then he dreamed about her."

I thought about this. "It's funny—I've seen some women lately who looked familiar to me, and then I realized that they reminded me of that Lazos family picture, with all the brothers and sisters. They all look so distinctive, the Lazos family, with very distinct features. And yet it seems like everyone with dark hair reminds me of them."

"Who in particular?" asked Sam.

"Well—the new library woman. Darla. She has dark hair and blue eyes, and she looks sort of like that Demeter from the photo. Or she would without her glasses. And then yesterday she was talking to the patron named Agatha, who looked like her dark-haired twin. And even Eddie Stack's wife, Doris, looks kind of like the Lazos women. It's as though Blue Lake is just filled with the resemblance. So yeah, I guess Eddie could have seen one of them and juxtaposed the image of the baby."

"It's all pretty nebulous," Sam said. "And yet it feels like something is at the outer edges—something I should remember."

I was on the outskirts of a thought, and I tried to put it into words. "So wait—if there are women in town who look like his sisters—I suppose one or more of them could *be* his sisters, right? Or maybe the man Eddie saw wasn't Nikon, but one of his brothers."

"They all do look similar," Sam said. "But why would they *be* here? Why here, of all places? That doesn't make sense."

I sighed. "Can we even take what Mr. Bick said to Doug? I mean, what could we do with it?"

"We should tell Doug regard—"

My phone rang, and I clicked it on. "Hello?"

"Hi, Lena!" Allison's voice was bright again, the way that I liked to hear it.

"Hey. What's up?" I asked, distracted.

"I have late shift today, so I'm just having lunch with a neighbor," she said. This was good news; Allison was so worried that her neighbors hated her, and clearly that was not true.

"Well, that's nice."

"She found out that I know you, and she said you should join us. Agatha said after lunch she could show us the renovations she made to her basement. Remember I said a bunch of people renovated? But first we're just having a lovely salad and some tea cakes. I can't believe we waited a year to visit each other!"

"I'll try to stop by," I said. "Sam and I just have to finish something up."

"Tell Sam to come, too. Agatha says she is a fan," Allison joked. A voice sounded in the background; Allison laughed and said, "She said she insists that you come. Otherwise she's going to hold me hostage until you do!" The woman in the background was laughing with Allison.

I said good-bye and stared at the phone. "That's weird."

"What?"

"Allison has a neighbor over, and she called her Agatha. And we just met that Agatha at the library—oh my gosh."

"What?"

"It was on the edge of my mind, all this time, and now I remember why I know her. I went to Allison's before she found Eddie Stack, and there was a woman gardening across the street. She waved to me. And I remember thinking that she looked so familiar, maybe like someone I had seen in a movie. But it wasn't that—she had looked like a Lazos. In that picture Belinda showed us, several of the women had those scarves tied into their hair, and she had one, too. Her dark hair tied back while she tended her garden."

"Agatha is a Greek name," Sam said, his expression thoughtful.

"Like you said, it couldn't be, right? Nikon's sister, living right here in town? Why wouldn't the authorities know? She would have to be registered somewhere, be known to someone . . ."

"Unless she's here under a different identity."

"But her name is Agatha, right? Could that be a Lazos sister? It's not a common name."

Sam leaned toward me. "How long has she lived there?"

"I don't know, but Allison's been here a year, and she just implied that this Agatha has been there at least that long."

"Why would she be in Blue Lake? Did he plant her here to keep an eye on me?"

My hands were tense in my lap. "Nikon's brother said he would have seen you as the enemy. Maybe from the very beginning. So why not send his sister here to live so that she could give him reports about you? Especially if he feared you would take steps to find Victoria. It was only

Victoria who had no contact with the outside world. Nikon could have been keeping track of you all this time, from his yacht."

"Why would his sister do that? Give up her life, her home, to come and live out here by herself?"

"Family loyalty?"

Sam drummed his fingers on the steering wheel. "If she traveled from Greece, they should have known—"

"She didn't," I said suddenly. "Remember? Victoria told me that when they boarded the yacht, he had a brother and a sister already in New York to see them off. She was already in the States—who knows how long? Maybe they lost track of her."

"We need to call Doug."

"Wait—there's something else. Allison had mentioned that everyone had done renovations. Now she just said that Agatha wanted to show us her renovated basement. What does that mean? What could that mean? Sam—she said that Agatha *insisted we come.* What if that was a threat? What if she's using Allison as some kind of pawn?"

Sam held up a hand; he was still thinking. "Yesterday," he said. "There was something yesterday, when I met the two women."

"What?"

"How did she introduce herself?"

"Well, she didn't say Agatha Lazos."

"No!" Sam looked shocked, and he leaned toward me. "She said Agatha *Wallace.*"

"So?"

"That's Victoria's maiden name," he said.

 **17**

*In the same moment that she realized the danger she
also saw the impossibility of her escape. The gods
were not protecting her now; they were laughing.*

—From *Death at Delphi*

WE CALLED DOUG on the way to Allison's house. He wasn't
there, and I insisted that they contact him immediately.
"It's an emergency," I shouted. "Tell him Lena London has
an emergency!"

I also tried dialing Doug's cell, which went to voice
mail. I left a similar message, then sent him a text: *Emergency at Allison's. Might be a Lazos sighting.*

Sam seemed to settle down as he drove. "We have to
consider that we might be wrong. If so, we can't go in guns
blazing. Just act as though you're responding to Allison's
invitation, and we'll get the lay of the land."

"I know. This is all speculation, and she could just be a
nice neighbor lady who takes out books at the library. It
could be nothing. Nikon's family hates him anyway, right?
So they wouldn't be helping him with such a terrible crime.
But Sam—Allison said that *Agatha* said we should come.

She said 'Tell Sam to come, too.' What if that's a threat? What if she's threatening Allison to get to us?"

"Lena—look in my briefcase in the backseat. I think the picture Belinda gave us is in there."

I unbuckled my belt and leaned into the back; Sam was pulling off of Green Glass Highway and heading toward Allison's subdivision. I removed a file from Sam's briefcase and riffled through it. "Wait—pull over somewhere. I don't want to look at this right outside her house."

He tucked the car under a shady elm in someone's driveway, and I located the picture. There again were the Lazos children grouped around their parents. "There are the two brothers, George and Demetrius. They've both disowned him," I said. "And so has the sister named Demeter. That leaves four sisters."

"Can you read that caption?" Sam said. "It's kind of blurry."

"Something about the Lazos patriarch and matriarch. Sons—I can see their names. Then daughters: Demeter, Gaia, Adoni, Korinna"—I turned to Sam, my eyes wide—"and Agatha. The youngest."

"Little sister. Maybe a case of hero worship?"

"Oh God. Why is she at Allison's? Why does she suddenly want Allison to come over? Is Nikon going after my friends now?"

"Be calm. Let's go and see. Doug has the information. Try calling Cliff."

"I don't know if I have a cell number for him. No wait—I do. I called him once before, when I got the note on my car."

I found Cliff's number and dialed it, but it, too, went to voice mail. "Damn it! Cliff, this is Lena! We're at my friend Allison's house. She lives in the Elm Park subdivision on the corner of Willow and Grace. There's a rock on her lawn that says 'Branch House.' We think she's dining with Nikon's sister Agatha, and she doesn't know who she has in the house. We're going there now."

I hung up, and Sam pulled away from the curb. There was no traffic to speak of, and the subdivision was as quiet as always, except for the happy birds.

Sam pulled up in front of Branch House, and we got out. I didn't look at Sam because I knew my expression would betray something; she could be looking out the window. I focused on the door, and I rang the bell, feeling stiff as a rod until I heard Allison's laughter on the other side. She swung the door open and said, "Oh, I'm so glad you could make it! I guess you guys met the other day?"

"Just yesterday," I said, as Agatha Lazos came around the corner and smiled at me. And surely this was Nikon's sister. The miracle was that we had not seen it before. She had his eyes, and Athena's eyes, and, like the woman in the picture we had studied in Sam's car, she had an unusually long and graceful neck. Today she had knotted a blue silk scarf around her throat; she wore a white blouse and capri jeans, with a pair of jeweled sandals on her feet. "Nice to see you again," I said. It was so hard to be friendly that I was sweating with the effort. I reached out to take her hand, and she shook mine. Her hand was cool and dry, just as it had been before.

"My pleasure," she said. "I only realized later that I had seen you here, at Allison's. You had come out of her house once, and we waved at each other. And of course on the day that all those terrible emergency vehicles were here— I saw you then, too." She spared a cool glance for Sam. "I saw you both."

"Yes," Sam said. "Funny how we don't make those little connections."

"Would you like some salad?" Allison asked. "I got the recipe from the chef at Wheat Grass, and it turned out really well. Agatha loved it."

Agatha inclined her head. "I did. Salad is my favorite food, and this one is so flavorful." I detected it now—the hint of an accent that came out with some of her vowels. Slight, but there.

"I heard you were going to give a tour of your house," Sam said. "We would love to see it, because Lena and I are going to do some renovating, too."

"Are you? So you are—a couple? You live together?" Her words were light, friendly, but her eyes were watchful and untouched by the smile on her lips.

"We are a couple. We live together when we can. Lena has another residence, as well."

"Ah yes. Allison tells me that you work with a very famous novelist. This is so exciting."

"It is. But Sam and I are both tired of being in the public eye. We never wanted to be famous, but the newspapers have made us that way. I suppose you've seen us in the news," I said.

Something flashed in her dark eyes, and then she shrugged. "Of course. As I mentioned to Mr. West at the library, I have followed his case with interest. Like the rest of the country, I suppose. How difficult for you both, but in any case, these things happen. We must accept them with grace."

This made me angry. "I'm curious," I said. "Did you know the mailman Eddie Stack? The one who was murdered?"

Allison looked shocked. "Lena, I don't think—"

"I did not know him well, but of course I knew his face. He came by each day with our mail," she said. Her eyes narrowed slightly.

"Sometimes he messed up Allison's mail," I said. "Even though Branch is a simple name. And I suppose Wallace is a simple name, too."

"It is. Very easy to spell and say. No, I didn't have much trouble with mail. It was on time, it was not torn. A nice enough mailman."

Allison was staring at us with wide eyes; she had lost track of the conversation, and even my sunny friend must have sensed some undertones in our dialogue.

"Wallace is apparently quite a common name," Sam said. "It was actually my wife's maiden name. Hers is another name I'm sure you know from the news. Victoria West? She lives here in Blue Lake some of the time?"

"Oh yes. I see her on television often. She is a lovely woman. Although her pretty face is always marred by her tears. It is sad."

"Yes. It is sad." Sam, too, was wearing a fake smile and seeming to have a hard time of it. "Excuse me for one moment. I left something in the car. Allison, will you dish me up some of that salad?"

This Allison could understand. "Of course! Lena, Agatha, can I get you some?"

Agatha brightened. "I would love some more. Come and taste it, Lena—it is splendid."

I went with the two women into Allison's kitchen, trying not to worry over what Sam was up to. He had slipped out the front door, and I strained my ears, listening for the car door.

We sat and I pretended at sociability; I think I ate the salad, although I tasted and saw nothing. Allison chattered happily, oblivious to the growing tension. I couldn't stop looking at Agatha's dark eyes, so flat and cool as they looked back at me.

After a few minutes, she showed her white teeth in a smile. "We seem to have lost your Sam."

"I should go see what he's up to," I said, standing up.

She stood, as well. "Let's all go. I'll show you my house."

Allison perked up at this. She loved house tours. "Great! Let me just cover this food, in case there's a fly in here."

We made our way to the front door. Allison opened it, and I peered past her, looking for Sam.

He wasn't near the car. I looked across the street, at the house where I had seen Agatha gardening. He wasn't there, either.

Agatha looked amused. "What a strange time to take a walk," she said. "Your lover is unpredictable."

Terrified, I did a quick scan. What if someone had killed him? What if he were somehow lying out in the woods now, where Eddie Stack had ended up? What if the Lazos clan was like a group of terrible spiders, luring people to their doom?

What if there were more Lazos sisters in this town? What if Eddie Stack's wife was a Lazos, and she had killed him because he told her about something he saw? What if Darla was a Lazos, and she had told Agatha about our research with Belinda?

Panicked thoughts bounced around my mind, but there was only one clear reality shining through: I was following Allison and Agatha across the street. Agatha was smiling serenely as she glided along on her jeweled slippers.

She turned once, to beckon us forward, and her ring flashed in the sunshine: a silver ring with an embedded jade snake. *The snake lady.*

"Come, sweetheart," she said, clasping my hand in a tight grip.

18

"Run!" he cried as a bullet whizzed past them. "Don't look back! I'll be right behind you."

She no longer trusted the gods, but she did trust him.

She ran; soon enough she realized that his footsteps had ceased pounding behind her, and she feared the worst.

In this place of sacrifices, she was highly conscious of what she could not bear to sacrifice.

—From Death at Delphi

I FORCED MYSELF to be calm. She had called me "sweetheart." She wore Nikon's ring. Did that mean Nikon was here? Perhaps it was a family ring, and they all wore one. Perhaps the snake was from the family crest, identifying them as a clan of betrayers . . .

So what did I do? Go into the house of this bizarre woman in hopes of finding Sam? Perhaps I was still misunderstanding the situation. Perhaps she just wanted to get a sense of what, if anything, we knew. What if she had not intended for Allison to call me at all? If that were the case, then she, too, might be trying to plan her next move.

If Sam were with me, I would have simply refused to go to her house; I would have made an excuse and kept Allison away, as well. But now Sam had disappeared, and

I knew he wouldn't have left my side without good reason. If he were now in danger, who was there to help him but me? Surely Doug and Cliff would be here soon to back me up, but for right now I was on my own.

Allison said something to Agatha, and the latter let go of my hand as she turned to answer my friend. We followed her up a well-tended walkway and through a large wooden door. Her foyer was wide and stone tiled, with bright white walls and a central glass-topped table that held a huge bowl of white peonies. We filed past this, heading for a doorway at the end of the hall, and my gaze fell on the table, where an ant who had obviously escaped one of the flowers was now marching across the glass surface. Agatha sniffed and crushed it with her thumb.

My phone vibrated in my pocket; I had turned off the sound, a fact for which I was most glad. Waiting until Agatha turned the corner, I glanced quickly down and saw a text from Doug: *I'm here. Saw you go in. Where's Sam?*

I wrote back *Don't know*, and, on pure instinct, slid the phone inside my bra, between my breasts. Then I turned the corner into a spacious room, designed with a decorator's flair and what seemed to my heightened imagination a distinctly Greek look.

"Oooh, this is lovely!" Allison said. "That color of blue on the back wall—I can never find colors like that in the paint palettes."

Agatha shrugged her elegant shoulders. "I had it imported," she said. "I wanted something that looked like the deepest blue sky, day turning to evening."

Allison strolled around, occasionally touching things. Agatha was watching me and pretending not to, and I was pretending to be fascinated by some elaborate border at the place where the walls met the ceiling. There seemed to be mythological characters on it. "Do I see Zeus and Hera up there?" I asked.

"Yes, of course." Agatha smiled with her white teeth. "The gods in my personal temple."

"That's cool. What were some of the other gods? I can't remember from school. I know there was Apollo and Zeus and Athena and Poseidon. Wasn't there a Nikon?" I asked, my eyes on her.

Her brows rose and something changed in her eyes. "Not a god, no. There was a sea spirit called Nikon. He was unfairly killed by the gods."

"Oh, okay. I knew I heard that name somewhere."

Allison put her hands on her hips. "Well, you also know it from the papers! The guy is in the headlines every day. And I'm sure you saw that latest article by Jake Elliott, right? Didn't you and Sam ask him to write it?"

This brought Agatha a little closer. "Is that so? You mean that article that suggests the man who lived with Victoria West and fathered her child is somehow seeking revenge on everyone?"

"Yes. The guy seems totally nuts," Allison said.

Agatha's hand came up, gracefully, and tucked a strand of her dark hair behind her ear. "Before our tour begins, I need my sweater. Allison, it's in the room just behind you— would you get it for me? A white knit thing, slung over a chair."

Allison straightened, her friendly face bright. "Sure!"

She moved curiously into the next room, and Agatha glided silently after her, shutting the door to the room and then locking it with a key she pulled from her pocket. "What—?" I began.

Her smile was wide and disturbing. "There's no need to involve her yet, is there? Not in our private conversation." This was it: the confrontation. And in a weird, surreal way, I wanted to know what was about to happen. I felt that, if it came down to me grappling with her, I could potentially win. I was fit from my daily walks around Blue Lake, and I routinely picked up the German shepherds to put them in the bathtub. I could take this woman. If I couldn't, it didn't matter. I had Doug outside, and soon he would be inside.

"She shouldn't have come here at all. Why did you make her a part of this?"

"I needed her help. She is a nice girl. A sweet neighbor." She folded her arms. "You are something else."

"You're assuming I know what you're talking about."

She laughed. "Don't bother. I saw it in your face the moment you walked in Allison's door. And your lover is an even worse liar."

"Sam?"

"His hatred was like a book written on his face."

"So is yours. Except there's no reason for you to hate Sam, or me. What did either of us ever do to your family?"

Her smile vanished. "You defended that man from the start."

"Because he is innocent. You backed the wrong horse, Agatha. Nikon is a murderer. He killed Eddie Stack, or had him killed."

She moved closer to me. "My brother is not a murderer. He is a sweet soul, and loyal. I am the youngest, but I have always been his protector. The mailman was unfortunate. He—learned something, and in that instant I knew that he knew. I couldn't have my brother threatened again. He is a free spirit. I will not let them put him in a cage."

Now the fear I should have felt earlier kicked in. "*You* killed him."

I heard a tentative knocking, and Allison's voice. "Agatha? Lena? This door is stuck."

Agatha shrugged, her expression blank. "He did not feel it. He did not even know he was about to die. He had been about to start his mail delivery. We were talking in a friendly way; I asked him to help me find something I had dropped on the forest path. He was very accommodating. The gun was hidden. It was a painless death."

"God," I said.

"Yes, blame me if you will. But you killed, as well."

"I'm sorry?"

"Everything my brother loved, everything he worked and slaved for. You worked and worked until you ruined it. And then you freed the man who would ruin my brother's reputation."

Poor Allison tried again. "Agatha? Lena?"

My eyes moved to the door, which shook slightly as Allison tried to open it with more force.

"You're all turned around. Your brother tried to frame Sam for murder! That's evil, Agatha. And so are you. You killed an innocent man."

She nodded. "I am a guardian. I cannot always think of the feelings of others. He knew things, and he was going to expose us."

A burst of fury blotted out my fear. "I'm letting Allison out," I said, walking boldly toward the room where my friend was imprisoned. I yelled, "Allison, she locked the door. Call for help—"

"I took the liberty of hiding her phone at her house. She was looking for it; calling herself absentminded." Agatha laughed. "Meanwhile, don't you want to talk with your lover?"

I turned back. "Sam? Where is he? You have him here? How? You were with us! How did—?"

A shadow loomed on the white wall of the foyer, and then a man stood in the entranceway. "He happened to meet up with me," said a charming voice, slightly accented and full of what almost seemed like humor. "I am pleased to meet you at last."

I started to scream, but he held up a hand.

"We have soundproofed the house in our recent renovations. Please save your voice," said Nikon Lazos with a gentlemanly bow of his head.

I WASN'T ABLE to say anything more to Allison, who had gone silent. I couldn't try to text her, so all communication was effectively blocked. Doug was here, I told myself. Doug would let her out soon. Nikon and Agatha led me down some stairs to a lower level with several doors on both sides of a long, carpeted hallway. Nikon opened the first door and we entered what looked like a small apartment, with a couch, some chairs, a television and stereo, even a small refrigerator in one corner. Sam had been sitting on the couch, but he rose when we walked in.

"Lena," he said. "I'm sorry."

I shook my head. I wasn't going to discuss anything in front of the Lazos family. Where was Doug? My hand was itching to take my phone and attempt to send a text. Wouldn't I have to tell Doug we were in danger in order for him to break in?

"She's plotting," said Agatha, pointing at me.

Nikon smiled at me. I remembered what his first wife, Grace, and then Victoria, had told us about his charisma.

I could sense it, even now, but his endless smiling made him seem sociopathic. He was as handsome as his pictures, with tanned, healthy skin and a white-toothed smile like his sister's. His famous silver hair was gone, however— dyed to its original black, and the mustache and beard he had grown were dyed black, as well. It was a fairly good disguise. He studied me with compelling gray eyes.

"Miss London, I will need to check for cell phones. Mr. West has already kindly given me his." In front of Sam's pale and furious face, Nikon Lazos patted me down. At one point his eyes were only two inches away from mine, and I feared my phone would buzz and give me away.

He nodded, satisfied, and said, "And now if you could have a seat on the couch? Right next to your Mr. West. That is where you've chosen to be, yes? So you have both se- lected your paths. We all do."

"I would like to leave, actually. So kindly get out of my way." I tried to push past him and was immediately re- strained by an arm like iron. "The couch, Miss London. We will have a nice talk. Would you care for something to drink?"

Would this get them both out of the room? "Perhaps some tea."

He waved a hand and said something to Agatha in Greek. She glided out of the room without another word. He stayed.

He pulled a chair across from Sam and me. "My friends. We are intimately connected, are we not? For so long, we thought of each other."

"You thought of sending Sam to jail. Of ruining the life of an innocent man," I said.

Nikon smiled at Sam. "Your woman is spirited. My

Victoria was, as well. Alas, she chose to leave me. And now she lives here, in your town. To be closer to you."

"Because a cruel man stole her child," I said.

Sam put a calming hand on mine. With a slight movement, he shook his head. Perhaps he knew something I did not?

Nikon sighed. "The child is happy. I would never allow otherwise. Victoria—well, she chose her unhappiness."

I wriggled in my seat. "I would like to use the bathroom."

He nodded. "In a moment, perhaps. Agatha tells me that the two of you will soon be leaving. Making your own escape, yes?"

Sam and I stared at him, uncomprehending.

"To Rome, I believe? Perhaps you were finding life here too difficult." He smiled, pleased at the thought, and I recalled what we had told Darla at the library—our fictional vacation to Rome or the Caribbean. "Agatha was alarmed when she learned you would be leaving town. She feared you would not return. She has spent a year of her life investing in you, keeping you in her sights." He sighed with some theatricality. "My sister—she is spontaneous. I like to plan, plan. Even if it takes years. I had time, here in our snug house. But Agatha has taken steps, and now I must adapt."

"She killed someone, you mean," I said.

He shrugged. "She feared he knew the truth. For a year no one looked twice at this quiet little house. We could not risk this exposure—I understand her actions. But she also made an imprudent connection with this other local man, this fool, and he has also put us in some danger. Even now he sits in the police station, on the verge of implicating us."

"What did she want him to do?" Sam asked in spite of himself.

"Agatha is imaginative. She liked to keep apprised of Victoria's actions, and both of yours, and the man supplied her with photographs, information. She shared this with me. It helped us pass the time and focus our thoughts."

Sam and Nikon studied each other across the small space: gray eyes and blue eyes locked in a battle of wills. Then Nikon broke the stare and slapped his knees. "In any case, Agatha was hasty, and she has forced my hand. We will have to leave our little home in Blue Lake. We have enjoyed our time here. It is a pretty town. We were a happy little family."

"Where is the baby?" I asked.

Nikon's face was like stone. "You will not speak of my child."

Sam looked impatient. "Lena and I would like to leave now."

Nikon laughed. "Of course you would. That is natural. However, here is the situation. I was taking my time in deciding what to do with you, and your clever Lena who found my ship and my family. With my dear Victoria, who once so passionately loved me."

"Until she found out what you were," Sam said. I feared that he would antagonize Nikon into a temper, but the older man continued to smile.

"In the end, all of my plans involved taking Victoria away with me. I wanted it to look natural, as though she simply tired of Blue Lake and her giant, that bodyguard. She just packed her bags and left. Now, though, I must leave quickly, so I cannot use finesse. You will call her for me and ask her to come here. I can subdue her quickly and prepare her for travel. This is the quickest way for this to happen."

"You'll never get her across a border," I said. "You need a passport for her, for the baby."

Nikon smiled. "There are many places to cross borders, and many people who want money. I have enough money to buy my future. And to destroy yours, if I wish. Or if Agatha wishes." His smile vanished. "Enough talk now. My friend Sam will make a phone call, and we will begin."

Sam's face was grim. "I'm not your friend."

"It is in your best interest to do what I ask. Call her, be friendly, tell her you need to talk to her about her lost child. Tell her she should meet you here for reasons you will explain. I will handle the rest."

Sam shook his head. "I won't do it. I won't put her in danger."

"You're putting Lena in danger if you refuse."

"I have to go to the bathroom," I yelled. "Right now. Or I'll make a mess in your nice little apartment."

Nikon's gray eyes studied me, suspicious yet concerned. Ultimately he was too much of a gentleman to refuse my request. He shrugged. "Across the hall. I will accompany you. We will leave Sam in here." He escorted me out the door and locked Sam in the room. He pointed out a small bathroom a few feet down the hall, and I went in. When I shut the door I realized that he intended to stand right outside. I turned and saw a little modern bathroom. It was beautifully decorated; I found it absurd that the whole house was so up-to-date, so attractive, as the backdrop to such primitive minds.

I took out my phone with trembling hands. At first I couldn't get a signal, but then, in one corner, I did. Desperate, I texted Doug. "Nikon here. Threatening Sam and me in soundproof basement. Wants to lure Victoria, probably kill us. Can't write anymore after this."

I slipped the phone back into my bosom, flushed the toilet, and turned on the faucet, making some splashing sounds. Then I went back out into the hall, where Nikon Lazos stood waiting for me like some medieval knight.

"Better?" he asked.

"Much," I said.

We went back into the room where Sam sat. Before Nikon shut the door, I heard the tinkle of breaking glass. Perhaps Agatha was not as calm as she seemed? Dropping the tea things suggested that she was nervous. Would we be able to use that to our advantage?

I joined Sam on the couch, and he took my hand. Nikon took something out of his pocket; it was Sam's phone. "Time to make the call. Remember to sound friendly. Think of a plausible reason to bring her here."

Sam took the phone, but shook his head. "I won't do it. Find her yourself."

Nikon Lazos went back to the table, opened a drawer, and pulled out a gun. "You'll do as I ask," he said, pointing it at Sam.

I stifled a scream. Sam was about to refuse, I saw that, and I said, "Do it, Sam." I tried to convey, with my tone alone, that help was on the way, and he didn't need to battle with Lazos. He looked at me and I nodded ever so slightly.

Sam studied his phone. "Her bodyguard will look up the address. He'll want to know who Agatha is before he comes here."

"Then tell her to come to your friend Allison's house. I can easily intercept them there, and—" Suddenly the door banged open, and Doug Heller stood there, one side of his face covered in blood, his gun pointed at Lazos.

I screamed without thinking, and Lazos turned in surprise.

"Drop it," Doug said, wiping at his face with his free hand.

Lazos said nothing, but lunged suddenly at Doug and began grappling with him like a gladiator. Both men still held their guns, and I felt terrified that one of the weapons would go off.

"Get out, you two," Doug managed. "Lazos, drop your weapon—and—surrender." He pushed out the words with great difficulty as he wrestled the Greek man.

With a sudden burst of inhuman energy, Lazos reared back like a lion and fired his gun. A moment of shock followed, in which Doug dropped his weapon and Lazos kicked it into a corner.

A bloom of red appeared in the upper left corner of Doug's shirt, and he crumpled, his face white. "Lazos, you're a dead man," Sam said. He stood up, furious, and Lazos turned with an almost triumphant expression.

"No, not me. And I will not wrestle this time." He aimed his gun at Sam. "You should have stayed in jail," he said, his expression half angry and half regretful.

In a moment of pure insanity that was the product of fury, Sam curled his lips. "Take your best shot," he yelled, poised to jump on Lazos.

"Sam, no!" cried a voice, and Cliff barreled into the room, hurling himself between the two men just as the gun went off. I screamed as Cliff fell, and in that short moment that Lazos stared down, disoriented by the new arrival, Sam lunged forward and punched him so hard in the face that he staggered and fell, dropping his gun. Sam was on it in an instant, and I was on the floor, trying to remember a long-ago first aid class as I contemplated two bleeding men.

Doug caught my gaze and shook his head at me. "It's under my shoulder; I won't die. Look at Cliff."

Cliff was not conscious. I ripped open his shirt and saw that the bullet had pierced his chest; I prayed that it had not gone through his heart. He was breathing, but in a ragged way. I tore at his shirt so that I could use a strip of the fabric to put pressure on his wound. Instinctively I stroked his hair. "It's okay, Cliff. It will be okay." I had the same déjà vu that I had experienced when I saw Cliff climbing the stairs in Camilla's house. I stared at a gray stripe in Cliff's brown hair and saw, in an instant of clarity, why that feeling kept returning.

Why Cliff had been watching us at Sam's house, even though Doug had known nothing about it.

Why Cliff had been nearby when I was attacked.

Why Cliff had looked so gratified when Sam had paused to shake his hand.

Why Doug had said that Cliff took the job in Blue Lake because he had "family in Indiana."

And why Cliff, like Sam, had one single silver stripe growing in the bangs of his thick brown hair.

I looked up at Sam, who wore a murderous expression as he stood over Nikon Lazos, pinning him down on the ground with the threat of his own gun.

Sam had no idea, in that chaotic moment, that he was guarding the brother who had been guarding him.

The brother who might now die.

Doug had been speaking quietly into his cell phone, and moments later the tiny room was filled with police and emergency people. They took Cliff first. Despite my efforts, he had grown deathly pale, and the carpet beneath him was soaked with blood. Doug was still conscious and giving directions to a deputy when they put him on a stretcher. I touched his good shoulder. "Thanks for being there," I said.

He squeezed my hand briefly and said, "You bet." He was pale but conscious when they carried him out.

Sam pointed out both guns to the police, and they took them away in evidence bags right after they cuffed Nikon Lazos, who watched Sam and me with a calm expression. His eyes were chilling, though. They were full of hate and something else—something smug, as though he knew a secret.

I felt months of stress building up inside me, and suddenly I was yelling. "You could have stayed away forever, I'll bet, if you had just left Sam alone. You and your insane sister. Now look what you've done to yourself!"

Lazos smiled at me. "I'll be back," he said. "I'll finish this."

Before I knew it I had slapped him hard across the face, leaving a red mark. "How dare you threaten the people I love? How dare you hurt them? I hope they put you away for a thousand years! I hope you realize the pain you've caused so many other people! If Cliff dies, I think I'll find you and kill you myself!"

Nikon Lazos smiled at me; he seemed weirdly pleased by my agitation. Before Sam or I knew what he was doing, he had leaned forward and kissed me on the cheek. "Sleep tight, Lena," he said.

That's when Sam punched him again, and a harried police officer, sending Sam a disapproving glance, pulled Nikon away from us.

Then we were left alone in the strange space, now silent as the void.

"That felt good," I said. "I've wanted to scream in his face for a long time. I'm glad I got to do it."

"It did feel good," said Sam. "But I couldn't stand that look on his face. Like he has a million secrets."

"He has nothing," I said. "He's just crazy. His money makes him feel invulnerable."

"Cliff saved my life," Sam said blankly. "He just jumped right in front of me. Where was his gun? Why would he do something like that?"

I took his hand. "Let's go. I hate it here."

We moved into the silent hall, and as we walked toward the stairs I heard a tiny sound, almost like the mewing of a cat.

I stared at Sam and he looked back for a full five seconds. Then we heard it again.

"I heard something I wasn't supposed to hear."

"Oh God! How could we forget?" I cried. We ran, following the sound to the second door on the right, which was slightly ajar. I pushed it open, desperate, fearful, and saw the most beautiful sight of my life.

Little Athena Lazos stood in her crib, smiling and reaching for me.

SAM CALLED VICTORIA after all. He told her he needed her to come to Allison's subdivision. He would not tell her why, but said he needed to talk to her immediately. He hung up and turned to me. "I can't have her crashing her car because she's half crazed with excitement. Although that giant bodyguard will probably drive."

"Right." I took his hand. "Are you okay?"

He shook his head. "No. I put you in danger. I made stupid mistakes. I got Doug and Cliff shot!"

"That wasn't you; they both came running in like wild men. I'm not sure anyone was thinking clearly. It—it could have been much worse."

My eyes strayed to Allison, who was still giving her statement to a police officer on Agatha's front lawn. They had already talked to Sam and me. Now we had to return a baby to her mother.

Sam looked at his watch. "I need to get to the hospital, see how they're doing. I'm not going to be able to rest until I know . . ."

"Here she is," I said as I saw a car pull up. "You talk to her." I went inside, where a female officer sat playing with Athena, who was newly diapered and in fresh clothes. Her hair had been brushed into a gleaming silken skein and she had made quick work of the bottle we had found in the refrigerator.

"May I take her?" I said. "Her mother is here."

The officer gave Athena a kiss on her pretty head and handed her to me. I tucked her against me, enjoying the surprising solid weight of her, the scent of her baby skin, the sweet sounds she made as she murmured in my ear.

Eddie Stack must have heard her when he delivered the mail. I tried to imagine it. Perhaps he had a letter or package that wouldn't fit through the slot. Perhaps Agatha had to sign for something. But she opened the door, and the baby was out of her soundproof basement nursery—playing upstairs with her aunt. Then the baby laughed or cried, and Eddie Stack must have looked surprised, because Agatha Wallace lived alone. Maybe it dawned on him slowly—her resemblance to the missing Nikon, and to the baby whose picture was in all the papers. He saw the truth, and Agatha knew that he saw. Unfortunately, Eddie hadn't seen Agatha as a threat, but as his little secret.

I shook away these thoughts and looked into the baby's little face. "Your mother missed you very much. Do not pretend you don't recognize her, okay? When you see her, you say 'Mama.'" I wasn't sure the baby would remember Victoria after all this time; it didn't seem likely that she would, so I wanted to plant the idea.

Athena giggled; it gave her two fat chins and made her irresistible. "Oh my goodness, I see why she missed you so very much. You are an angel. Okay, look through the window. I can see your mommy talking to her friend Sam. And he's gently explaining about you. See her face? She looks disbelieving. Now she's looking around. So here we go."

I opened the front door of Agatha Lazos's house and Nikon Lazos's lair. We moved toward Victoria, who did not spot us until we had taken three steps or so. Then she looked right at us and with some uncertainty said, "Athena?"

Then, "ATHENA?" She screamed it, and cried, "My baby!" as she ran toward us as though she was floating above the cobbled walk.

Athena was still smiling, and I was still murmuring calmly in her ear. "Your mama missed you," I reminded her.

"Mama?" she asked. Then she looked at Victoria, who stood before us with huge green eyes that were rapidly filling with tears. "Mama," she said.

I handed her over to her mother, who kissed her on every available inch of skin and made the baby giggle some more. "Thank you, Lena," she said breathlessly. Sam joined us, and Victoria gave him a half hug with her free arm. Tears flowed freely down her face, but she was smiling. "Thank you, Sam. Oh God, I will never ask for another thing in my life. All of my prayers are answered."

She held the baby up and laughed into her face, and Timothy, her bodyguard, walked toward her, his face creased by a huge smile.

Sam kissed her cheek. "I'm so happy for you, Vic. I hate to run, but I have to get to the hospital. Lena, are you coming?"

"Give me one minute. I have to talk to Allison."

I left Victoria and the baby in Tim's arms, and walked across the street, where Allison stood with John, still trembling slightly as she finished speaking with a police officer. The cop thanked her and moved away, and she looked at me with wide, disbelieving eyes. "They were across the street from me, Lena! I can't believe that your enemies were right across the street, and I never saw anything, never noticed . . . I'm so sorry!" John slung a big arm around her.

"How could you have known?" I said. "She was just a pretty, friendly woman who kept to herself and had a nice garden. What would make anyone think she was Nikon's sister? That was the beauty of their setup."

Allison looked at me uncertainly, and then at John. "But when she moved in, we should have noticed—oh, except she was here first, wasn't she, John? She lived here when we moved to this block."

I nodded, patting her arm. "She's been here for more than a year, keeping tabs on Sam. I hate to think how many times she must have walked or driven up our bluff, like some spider surveying her web." I folded my arms against myself. "Agatha Lazos didn't move into your territory," I said. "You moved into hers."

Allison shivered. "That's even worse, somehow. Oh, God."

John gave her shoulders a squeeze. "Babe, it has nothing to do with us. All murderers live somewhere. She just happened to live there. Poor Eddie," he said, his expression sad.

I nodded my agreement. "You guys will be okay, right? I have to run to the hospital with Sam. Doug is there, and Cliff—" To my surprise, I felt tears building, and something caught in my throat.

"We'll be okay. You go, Lena!" Allison said. "Please tell us how they're doing."

I waved and jogged toward Sam, who had pulled his car up and waited with the engine running.

I looked back once to see Victoria West leaning against Timothy, a man as solid as a tree trunk, and singing to her baby, who laughed. They all seemed to sparkle in the spring sun.

Back in Sam's car, I realized that only about three hours had gone by since we'd arrived at Allison's, but it felt as though it had been two days. Exhaustion hit me like an anvil, and I leaned back against the passenger seat with my eyes closed. "What happened to Agatha?"

"I don't know. It's one of many things we need to ask Doug and Cliff. Lena, do you think Cliff will be okay?"

"I hope so," I said. I opened my eyes and turned to him. "Sam—listen, I might be wrong about this, but—I think I figured something out back there, in that instant after all the guns went off, when I was kneeling next to Cliff."

"What's that?" His eyes were on the road. His body was alert, stiff, but he was clearly as spent as I was. He had looked death in the face, and now, his adrenaline gone, he was fading.

"I don't know—I'm not sure if it's the best time to tell you."

He stopped at a red light at the intersection of Rowland and Green Glass Highway. "Lena, please. We can't have any more secrets. Just tell me, and we'll deal with whatever it is."

"Okay. It dawned on me, while I was stroking his hair— I mean, not just that, but I was thinking about all the weird pieces that didn't make sense until I put them together, and then suddenly this picture just emerged."

"Just say it."

"I think Cliff is your brother."

Sam's eyes grew so wide he almost looked like a different person. He sat through two more red lights, silently processing what I had said. Luckily, there was no traffic behind us on this relatively secluded road.

Then, in a *very* delayed reaction, he began to laugh. At first I was worried, thinking he was hysterical, but he was merely amused. Finally he wiped his eyes and said, "You know what's funny? I think you're right. And I can't believe I didn't see it before."

"Why?"

He sighed. "On two different occasions, when I was at Doug's office, he absently called me 'Cliff.' Then he would apologize and say he didn't know why he did it. And two different times Cliff asked me something about my mother. I thought he was just being sympathetic, but he was being curious! And the other thing is—he looks like me. I see it now, but I didn't before."

I smiled at him. "I used to think he was disapproving of you, or us, or both. But now that I think back, it was a totally different expression on his face. He was proud of you."

Sam stiffened in his seat. "What if he dies? What if he's dead now?"

"He's not. He won't. We won't let him, Sam."

He nodded and pulled onto the highway.

19

*She feared he would never wake to learn the truth
that she had only just discovered herself, sitting bereft at his bedside: she loved him.*

—From *Death at Delphi*

THE NEXT MORNING Doug Heller spoke to us from his hospital bed, looking impatient. "They found Sam's stationery
in a drawer in her house. She was your note writer and our
ninja, too. Back when she was a kid, it turns out, her wonderful eldest brother taught her a bunch of lock-picking
tricks, and she got really good—the student exceeded the
master. So Nikon hired a former thief to train her. They
would go to the parties of wealthy friends just so that little
Agatha could try out her skills on their house safes. She
had the perfect cover because she was literally a child—
only twelve or so when they started. The two of them, richer
than the gods, pilfering from friends just for the thrill of
it all. And they never got caught. She was particularly proud
of that part, they tell me."

"So that English reporter was right. He had an accomplice, and it was Agatha. She's caught now," I said with

deep satisfaction. "They both are. Tell me they're in really tiny cages."

Doug grinned. "They're safely locked up, with about six agents on each one of them. Agatha has been charged with the murder of Eddie Stack, but soon they'll both be flown to New York to face a bunch of charges there. Little Agatha has been busy with her false identity, traveling around and doing misdeeds for her big brother."

"Why?" Sam asked, shaking his head.

Doug took a sip of the water in his hospital mug. "My guess? Rich and bored."

"They're disgusting, the two of them. Why was she even in Blue Lake?"

Doug pointed at Sam. "To keep tabs on him. Weird, right? This was way at the beginning, after Nikon boarded a yacht with Victoria and all was well with the world. He wanted Sam watched, because Victoria had loved him."

Sam still looked pale; he leaned his head back on the little armchair he had pulled close to Doug's bed. "I can't take it all in."

Doug sighed and adjusted his covers, then touched his forehead gingerly. "Ouch. Sometimes I forget it's there. I've mostly been distracted by the bullet wound."

"God, don't remind me," I said. "Are you in terrible pain?"

He smiled. "Nope. I'm on some drug that erases pain. I wonder how long they'll let me stay on it."

I pointed to his forehead. "So what happened there? You were gushing blood when you burst in on Sam and me in that basement."

"I got your text and realized I had very little time. I didn't want to ring the bell and alert them to my presence.

My best way in was through those big picture windows in the living room. I broke one of them with a rock, and when Agatha came running I held up my gun and told her to be quiet. She was so submissive I guess I assumed she had given up. Then she pointed me toward the basement and whacked me with some big ol' bottle of wine or ouzo or whatever the hell those two drink. Blood? Souls, maybe?"

Sam laughed rather bitterly.

"That's attempted murder!" I yelled.

Doug nodded. "With which she has been charged. They read quite a list to her."

"So what happened after she hit you?"

Doug pursed his lips. "I got rough with her. I had to wrangle her hands together to cuff them before I ran down the stairs."

I shook my head. "Can you believe that insane plan? Like that ever would have worked!"

Doug looked troubled. "I'd like to say it wouldn't have worked. But we didn't know he was there, and somehow Agatha Lazos was under the radar. That's on the FBI. The fact is that, hard as we try, people get past us. And Lazos has a lot of money and connections." His face brightened. "But they're in custody now. I only wish Cliff hadn't been hurt."

Cliff's name had us all feeling bad again. He had spent most of the night in surgery, and his prognosis was unknown; he currently lay unconscious in intensive care. We had been avoiding talking about him.

Doug shook his head. "I still can't believe that guy. I had called him with my location, but I didn't know where he was. Then he just leaped out of nowhere and took a bullet. Saved all our butts."

"He's a hero, and so are you," I said.

Doug shook his head. "I underestimated Lazos, and it almost cost us all our lives. I can't believe how strong that guy was."

Belinda came in, holding an overnight bag. "Hi, guys," she said. She smiled at Doug, who was looking at her with a longing expression.

"Hey, cutie," she said.

"Hey. Did you ask them when I can get out of this place?"

Belinda frowned. "*This place* took very good care of you. But they said tomorrow."

Doug sighed noisily, and Belinda bent to kiss his forehead; she did this very tenderly, and suddenly I wanted to cry. "You two are so sweet," I said.

Sam reached across to hold my hand. "Lena's been through a lot."

I shook my head. "*You've* been through a lot. And now this. Sam, I know you're worried about Cliff, but I just know he'll be okay. You guys will have plenty of time to spend together, and—" Too late I realized that I had said too much.

"What the hell are you talking about?" Doug said, looking irritable. "Why do Sam and Cliff need to spend time together?" It seemed almost as though Doug were jealous at the thought that Sam might prefer Cliff's company to his.

Belinda, too, looked curious. "Sam is worried about Cliff?"

"Yes—well—he was shot. He took a bullet for Sam and saved his life."

Belinda was far too smart to be in the dark for long. "Oh my God!" she said. "Why did I not see it sooner? I've had *meals* with the man. It's as plain as the nose on Sam's face."

Now Doug looked downright thunderous. "If someone doesn't fill me in I will arrest everyone in this room."

I looked at Sam, who still wasn't feeling very talkative. He nodded at me. I turned to Doug and said, "Belinda did some research for us about Sam's family. She found out that his mother had given birth to a child years before Sam was born. With another man. So we knew that Sam had a sibling somewhere in the world."

Doug nodded, and then his eyes widened. "Cliff!"

"I think so. Apparently we all think so. But I didn't realize it until he leaped in front of that gun. He yelled 'Sam, no!' and there was something about his tone, and then about his face as he lay there, and about the gray stripe in his hair. Sam is starting to get one, too, in the same place. His mother's father had the same stripe."

"I am the worst detective in the world," Doug said, looking depressed.

"No, you're not. You've been amazing ever since I came to this town."

"Cliff even told me that he had family in the area he hoped to reconnect with. But people say stuff like that all the time. I didn't know he meant that his long-lost brother was Sam West!"

We all looked at Sam, who had not really been himself since we arrived at the hospital. "If he dies, it's my fault," he said.

We all talked at once, assuring him that this was not true, and a nurse appeared in the door. She frowned at Doug. "Detective Heller, you should not have this many people in the room. Your doctor instructed you to rest."

"I am resting," Doug said. "They're helping me rest."

The nurse frowned again, then turned to Sam. "Mr. West, you asked for an update on Mr. Blake's condition."

"Yes?"

"He is awake now and asking after his friends." She consulted a piece of paper in her hand. "He said we should not let Nikon hurt Sam."

Sam stood up. "Can I see him?"

"Yes," she said. "For a few minutes."

He exchanged a hopeful glance with Doug and Belinda; then he took my hand and pulled me with him out of the room.

CLIFF WAS SITTING up in his bed; he was white with pain, but alert and alive. His eyes widened when he saw Sam. "Oh God. I'm so glad you're all right," he said.

Sam moved closer to him, pulling a chair up next to his bed. I sat down near the door. "I should be saying that to you," Sam said. "I've been worried out of my mind. You took a bullet for me, Cliff. Where was your gun?"

He shook his head, almost smiling in his disbelief. "I came in the broken window and heard Allison calling. I went to the room where she was and let her out, and then that lunatic woman attacked me from behind. Doug had started to cuff her, or had cuffed her, but somehow she only had a cuff on one hand. I pinned her down and redid the cuffs, but she was crazy, spitting threats at Allison and saying wild things. I had cuffed her hands in front, and she got my gun out of the holster. Not my best moment. I struggled with her and got it out of her hands, but then she kicked it away and I couldn't find it. I saw the open basement door, and then I heard a gunshot. Thank God Doug had left the door ajar, so I could follow the sound. But then I got there in time to see you taunting an armed man. I couldn't believe it! I just jumped without thinking. I didn't come all this way to—" He stopped and coughed. "I didn't spend all this time trying to find this guy just to have him kill innocent people."

Sam leaned in. "Where was it you came from, Cliff?"

"Saint Louis."

"Did you grow up there?"

Cliff looked startled. "Thereabouts."

"Doug said you had a good job out there."

He fiddled with his IV, not looking at Sam. "It was a good fit. But then I heard about an opening in Blue Lake."

"And you left Saint Louis? I can't imagine Blue Lake pays you more. And it's a pretty small town, Cliff."

"I had always been interested in the place. Ever since I followed your case, to be honest. You moved here from New York, and I always wondered why. What would make a guy like Sam West choose this little town?"

"So you relocated here?" Sam sounded dubious. But if he was trying to force an admission from Cliff, it was going to be slow going. The brothers were equally reticent.

"Cliff," I said. "Should we call your parents? Are they in Saint Louis?"

Cliff looked at me, surprised. "They are, yeah. But don't call them. I think I'm going to beat the Grim Reaper this time, and I don't want them getting all upset over nothing."

"It wasn't nothing," I said. "You almost died, Cliff. And I'm guessing you're their only child."

He frowned. "Why do you think that?"

"Because people who adopt often have only one child."

Now he looked secretive. "Did I mention that I was adopted?"

"No," I said. "I guessed."

"How did you guess?" he asked.

"Because I found out that Sam had a long-lost sibling,

a child of his mother that he never knew about. And yesterday I started to suspect that long-lost sibling was you. Am I right, Cliff?"

He wouldn't look at me, or at Sam. His white face grew a bit redder. "I wasn't going to bother you with it. I just wanted to see you. Maybe get to know you. The thing was—I talked to her, way back when. I had written her a letter, and she called me. She was real sweet on the phone, and she said she would love to meet me. Said she never wanted to give me up, in fact. I guess she was pressured pretty heavily by her parents, who didn't like my dad. They were both kids, really. Anyway, when I talked to her, she said she wanted to tell her family first, and then we would all meet together—a big reunion, she called it. Once she told her daughter and her son, she would call me back, and we'd all get together. She said—she told me she loved me the moment I was born, and she always had me in her heart."

The room was silent for a moment. Cliff's eyes were on the window, through which we could see a pigeon on the gutter, sunning himself and blinking his eyes.

Cliff stole a look at Sam. "I saw the crash story on the news. They started listing victims, and I saw that it was all of them but you. I couldn't bother you then. I didn't know if she had told you or not, and even if she had, you had just lost your whole world. You didn't need me to come barging in and making demands. So I just waited, and once in a while I tried to find out what was happening with you. When you ended up in the news, too, after Victoria disappeared—well, I followed that very closely. I tried to think of every scenario in which you could be innocent, and I thought of quite a few. I sent a letter to the DA in New York, outlining them all."

"What?" Sam said, shocked.

"He never even responded. They were good points. And one of them was the possibility that Victoria had been abducted by someone who was not giving her access to communication with the outside world."

"That's amazing," said Sam. His eyes had not really left Cliff's face since we had entered the room.

"Anyway," Cliff said, "I can't tell you how great it was to see you in person. When Lena introduced us at Allison's house, that day she found the body in the woods—Lena was so casual, saying 'this is Sam West.' She couldn't have known how wonderful those words were to me. But like I said, I never meant to be a bother."

Sam waited until Cliff looked at him and then said, "How could it be a bother, Cliff? You're the only family I have in the world. You're my brother!" He smiled so widely that Cliff couldn't help but smile back. "Not to mention the fact that you saved my life!"

Cliff looked dazed by the turn of events. "I did not expect to tell you all this today. I guess Lena got it out of me. I just felt happy to be able to be close to you. Hang out with you sometimes. Get to know you—and Lena. I saw you both in the papers back in winter, and I was happy for you. That you had someone in your life again. I remember way back when I read about your marriage to Victoria. That seems like a long time ago.

"Anyway, I thought maybe, someday, there'd be a good time to mention the connection to you."

"Oh God, *men*!" I yelled. "You never would have told him! You're two of a kind."

They grinned at this, and Sam pulled his chair closer to his brother's bed. "Is that why you watched my house at night? Because you were protecting me?"

Cliff nodded. "Ever since that dead body turned up I've had a bad feeling. Nikon Lazos had it out for you; Doug and I talked about it a lot, and Doug said this had his fingerprints all over it. Metaphorically, anyway. I just—I'd get nervous when I didn't have you guys in my sights. So I figured I'd just sort of camp out there, see what I could see. Doug ended up asking me about it—all the extra time I was spending. I told him I just had a bad feeling, and that I wanted to do what I could. He probably thought I was bucking for a promotion."

"That's why you were right there when the bearded man attacked me," I said.

"And why you sat outside my house when you were off duty," Sam said. "When did you sleep, Cliff?"

He shrugged. "Here and there. It's a good thing we were all vigilant. Especially after your break-in, and Lena's notes—I knew we were dealing with someone who wasn't quite right. Have they got her under lock and key, by the way? Because she is nuts."

"Agatha's in jail."

"Did they find the baby?" Cliff asked, pale and concerned.

"Yes!" I said. "In Agatha's house. Right down the hall from where Nikon shot you. But it was Agatha who murdered Eddie Stack. He knew about her, and Nikon, and probably the baby. She said she shot him."

Cliff nodded. "That doesn't surprise me. Lazos didn't strike me as the kind of guy who does his own dirty work. But it is surprising that he delegated it to his little sister!" He shook his head. "So—Nikon?"

"In custody," said Sam.

"And what about the poor baby?"

"Back with her mother," I said.

"Really? Wow, that's great!" This made Cliff smile, then laugh, until he clutched his stomach in pain. Sam leaned forward, solicitous.

"You need to take it easy," Sam said. "We should leave so you can rest."

"I'd prefer it if you stayed," Cliff said. "I like to keep my eye on you, little brother."

The words had the same effect on all of us, and it was through my tears that I saw Sam lean forward and take his brother's hand. "Then I'll be right here," he said.

20

*They boarded the plane together, but it was hard
for them to leave this land, ancient and profound,
where they had sought adventure and found each
other. Despite their fear and the danger they had
faced in the country, Greece and its people had stayed
in their hearts.*

*They watched the sun go down over Delphi, and
he kissed her—a promise of a new dawn.*

—From *Death at Delphi*

ONE WEEK LATER I sat in the kitchen with Camilla, drink-
ing tea. We had been chatting about the book, and about
Adam and Sam, and Nikon and Agatha, and about Clifford
Blake.

Jake Elliott had written a follow-up article in which he
had detailed some of the misdeeds of the Lazos siblings,
but in which he had also covered the unexpected revelation
that Sam West was not alone in the world. He had included
a photo of Sam and Cliff talking together in Cliff's hospital
room, and somehow he had captured the resemblance that
none of us had seen until the day that Cliff saved Sam's life.

The article had been picked up by every major media
outlet, and Sam West led the headlines once again. We
heard his name on the television news and on the car radio.
We saw his face in newspapers and magazines. He and Cliff

received endless calls to appear on television and tell their story. The only thing in the news that got more attention than the reunited brothers was the even more dramatic (and photogenic) reunion of Victoria West and her lovely baby.

Unlike Sam, Victoria was eager to tell her story to the press who had been so accommodating while she was looking for her daughter, and she, Athena, and Tim (who seemed to be functioning now more as boyfriend than bodyguard) had stopped by to thank us before flying out to New York to appear on the *Today* show and to reunite with her family out there.

"But we'll always keep our place in Blue Lake, and we'll come here on vacations," Victoria promised in a final visit to us before she left. She intended to move to New York permanently with her child and her new boyfriend to be close to her family and start a new life. "I'll never stop being grateful to you all. And don't forget that you have a reward coming. I offered one hundred thousand, remember? And you found my baby, the two of you."

Sam and I stared at each other; I saw what I was thinking in his eyes. He nodded at me and said, "Vic, we don't want your money. Save it for Athena's college account, or as seed money for her future career, or maybe a future wedding. We have everything we need, and you don't have that kind of money to throw around, do you?"

Victoria smiled at us, a smug and secret smile. "Nikon considered us married. He never signed any documents over to me, but he said that everything of his was also mine. I took him at his word on the day I left the yacht. He liked to have portable money, usable in any country, so he had some gold on the ship. Can you believe it? Some gold pieces and bits of jewelry, and some plain old bars of gold. I helped myself before I left. I had some in my purse, and some in a bag that I asked one of the nice Federal men to carry for me. Now it's all safely in a bank under my name. I'm not as rich as Nikon, but I'm rich."

I laughed. "Victoria, I'm so happy for you. They say living well is the best revenge. I think you and Athena will live very well."

She pulled me into an almost fierce embrace. "Thank you, Lena. For everything. And you take care of our dear Sam."

"I will," I said. She turned to hug Sam, and then Camilla, and Adam. Tim, less demonstrative but surprisingly earnest, shook everyone's hand. Victoria allowed us all to hug and kiss the smiling baby before they swept out of Camilla's house and out of Blue Lake. A part of me was sad to see them go, while another part was highly relieved.

And so we had reached this placid day, on which it seemed the drama was behind us. Sam had gone to the hospital to pick up Cliff, who was being released and was planning to convalesce at Sam's house for a while. We were waiting for their arrival; Camilla had asked if she could make lunch for them (or, more specifically, if Rhonda could).

When someone knocked at the door, I ran to answer it, finding not Sam and Cliff, but Belinda and Darla. Belinda wore a stern expression, and Darla looked at the ground with downcast eyes.

"Do you have a minute, Lena?"

"Sure. Come on in," I said. I introduced Darla to Camilla, who had come out of the kitchen to see who was at the door.

Camilla shook Darla's hand, and Belinda said, "I persuaded Darla to come here with me today to make a little confession to you."

Camilla's look was shrewd. "Why don't we all sit down?"

We did so; Belinda and Darla sat on a couch facing the chairs that Camilla and I chose. Belinda said, "Darla waited a week because she was very upset. She found out about Agatha when the rest of us did. She didn't know anything about her except that they both liked books and they were both fascinated with Sam West."

Darla really did look miserable, and I felt a burst of pity for her. "Is this about the paper you wrote about Sam?" I asked gently.

She shook her head miserably. "No. Although I really did write that paper. But I mentioned it to Agatha once, in passing, while we were talking about law school and how expensive it is. I guess I was feeling sorry for myself, thinking about all my debt, and the next thing I knew she was offering me money. Anything I could find out about Sam West, she would pay me—and I mean lots of money. In cash. So I told her I would do it."

I wasn't surprised. I had expected something like this the moment I had seen them on the steps. "That's unfortunate," I said.

Darla looked up, her eyes wide. "I didn't find that much. I took a picture of you once, which wasn't okay, but that was really the extent of it. I tried to get information from you and Sam, but you just didn't give me anything."

I stiffened. "Are you Joseph Williams?"

She shrugged. "No—that's just a name one of the editors of the *Indiana News X-press* made up. But I did supply the picture and a few statements about you two that I had learned from Belinda."

"Sorry," Belinda said, still looking stern.

We all thought about this in silence for a while, and

Darla finally said, "I'm really sorry. I hope you'll forgive me. I was just blinded by the amount of money she was offering."

"How much money did you get out of her?" I asked. "I hope it was a lot."

Darla's eyes widened. "Well, like I said, I didn't get that far. But after the Joseph Williams article, she told me to keep it coming, and to send her my latest tuition bill. She paid it, and my outstanding tuition balance, too. I guess it was an act of faith for what she figured would be a long-standing agreement. I'm really sorry," she said again.

I sniffed. "Be sorry about lying and misleading us. But don't be sorry about taking her money. They're filthy rich, and they're criminals. Hopefully, when you get your law degree you'll help people and it will balance things out."

Darla wiped at her eyes. "That's a generous way of looking at it."

Camilla spoke from her chair. "You clearly were led astray by a bad woman with a certain charisma that she shared with her brother. Those two were very good at getting people to do their bidding."

Darla was starting to look like a woman reprieved. It seemed she had feared a very different response to her confession.

I looked at Belinda, who also seemed pleased with our response. "The fact is, though, that you have to make these apologies to Sam, not Camilla and me."

The misery came back to Darla's face. "I know. I—I'll do it today. Do you know when he might be by?"

I shook my head. "You can't do it today, because he'll be busy with his brother, and the two of them have a lot of catching up to do. I don't want this upsetting him while he's enjoying getting to know Cliff. When the time is right,

I'll mention what happened with Agatha, and I'll tell Sam you'd like to apologize. And then he can decide when he wants that to happen."

"Okay." Darla looked uncertain.

Belinda nodded. "That will give him lots of time to come to terms with it. Then maybe he won't feel as upset when you finally do talk to him."

"Okay," Darla said again. "I hope he won't want me fired from the library. I need the money."

"Sam would never try to deprive you of your job," I assured her.

Camilla stood up. "Thank you so much for coming by, Belinda and Darla."

Belinda stood up, too, tapping Darla on the shoulder. "I'm glad we could get this out in the open," Belinda said. "Now I'm going to take Darla back and check on Doug."

"Hey," I said. "He never told us what he decided—about the chief thing."

"I'll let Doug tell you. That's his news to share, not mine."

Darla had thanked us and made her way down the steps when I stopped Belinda. "You guys are back together, right?"

Belinda smiled. "We are. Thanks for nudging me in that direction. We're—really happy."

"I'm so glad."

I gave her a quick hug and she went down the stairs to her car; she and Darla pulled out of the driveway and disappeared down the gravel road.

While I watched, another car pulled in. I saw Sam's familiar profile at the wheel, and Cliff's dark head in the passenger seat. I could see, even from this distance, that they were in the middle of a discussion. Sam parked near the porch, but they sat there for a while, finishing their chat. Then Sam got out and came around the side to help Cliff out.

Cliff looked far better than he had a week ago; his coloring had improved, and he was smiling, but he still moved gingerly.

I greeted them and welcomed them into Camilla's house. Soon after we had seated both men at Camilla's table, Doug showed up and joined us. The five of us chatted and laughed, dining on sandwiches that Rhonda had made for the occasion.

"How long do you think you'll stay at Sam's, Cliff?" Camilla asked.

Cliff shrugged. "The doctors are already impressed with my recovery, so it should be all downhill from here. I'd like to be back on the job soon."

Doug shook his head. "We're covered. Don't hurry back on our account. We've got a guy from Meridien covering your shifts; he'll do fine until you're back on your feet."

Sam grabbed a chicken salad sandwich and put it on his plate. "He'll stay as long as it takes him to recuperate. That was a life-threatening wound, and he needs to rest and relax. We're going to investigate the local scene known as Blue Lake fishing. What's more relaxing than that? And I've never done it. I went out and bought us some new poles."

"Do you have a boat?" Doug asked.

"I figured I'd rent one," Sam said.

"You can borrow mine. Assuming that you go out while I'm on duty. If not, I'm thinking I should be in the boat, too."

Sam grinned. "You're more than welcome."

Camilla smiled at Cliff. "Have you and Sam had time this last week to do some catching up?"

Cliff nodded. "Nothing to catch up on in terms of shared memories, but Sam told me a lot about our mom, which I appreciate. And soon I'm going to take him to Saint Louis to meet my adoptive mom and dad, who want to adopt him, too." He said this with a grin, and Sam punched his arm with an affectionate expression. "And we found out we have a lot in common. We're pretty much on the same page philosophically, I guess you'd say. We both appreciate art. We like similar music. And we have the same middle name, isn't that wild?"

Doug raised his eyebrows. "What's your middle name?"

"Edward," the brothers said in unison, and we laughed.

Camilla speared a strawberry with a toothpick and said, "Cliff, I am a mystery writer, and I have plotted many books. But in this real-life story, I never saw you coming."

"None of us did," Sam said. "But I sure am glad he showed up."

Cliff put a brotherly arm around Sam, and I smiled, then spied Doug, who was stealing a glance at his watch.

"Do you have another meeting with the mayor?" I asked.

"Not exactly."

Camilla turned her gaze on him. "Lena tells me you are faced with a decision."

"I was. I made it." Doug's face was suddenly shy.

"And?"

"Bill Baxter has two years till retirement, and he is highly qualified. He's going to be chief until he retires, at which point I will once again be offered the position. Gives me some time to think about it, right?"

A flood of relief washed through me. I realized for the first time that I had not wanted Doug to take the position because I had not thought it would make him happy. "I'm glad, Doug. I think you're great at doing what you do right now."

"Me, too," Sam said. "Except for your early work on the Sam West investigation, which you botched horribly."

Doug laughed. "That West guy was a pain in the butt from day one. Thank God that whole case is closed for good. Wife found, baby found, perpetrator found."

"Sam West exonerated," I said.

Doug took a sip of his coffee and leaned back with a satisfied expression. "I've got to tell you—I am sleeping better at night knowing Nikon is in a cell."

"It's all over now, for good!" I said. "No more enemies can crawl out from under rocks. No more mysterious antagonists from distant Greek islands with ancient vendettas. No more missing wives or babies, no more tabloids chasing Sam wherever he goes. Right?"

Camilla was gazing out her kitchen window at the lake, which tossed in the summer wind. "How could there be anything else, Lena? Blue Lake is just a quiet little town. What possible secrets could people be hiding here?"

She looked back at us and we all burst out laughing.

Doug held up his cup. "To Blue Lake!" he said.

Outside the sun dimmed slightly as a silvery cloud partially obscured its light. "To Blue Lake!" we said, clinking our glasses against his.

Keep reading for a preview of the next
Writer's Apprentice mystery!
Coming soon from Berkley Prime Crime.

> *"At the risk of appearing forward, I must tell you this:*
> *when I met you,*
> *I realized there were no other women in the world.*
> *Not for me."*
> —from the correspondence of James Graham and
> Camilla Easton, 1970

GRAHAM HOUSE WAS a respite from the July heat, especially in the air-conditioned office of my collaborator and hero, Camilla Graham. I was there now, sitting on the floor and telling an amused Camilla the story of my first date, which had involved much awkward conversation and an even more awkward attempt at a kiss, and I had reduced Camilla to a giggling fit more than once as the story progressed. It was amusing to both of us to contemplate my fifteen-year-old self, pretending to be a sophisticated woman while being scared to death. Camilla's German shepherds, pleased to see me at floor level, had immediately demanded petting, and Heathcliff was starting to lean on me as he relaxed into my massage. "Heathcliff, get off! You giant rug. You're making me hot. You too, Rochester." They smiled at me with open, panting mouths, remaining exactly where they were.

Camilla laughed. "You've spoiled them, Lena. They get

much more attention now that there are two of us in the house—double the walks and the petting. Clearly they are smug about it."

I sniffed and looked into the brown eyes of each dog. "What's in it for me, you guys?"

They had no suggestions. A crash sounded from above us, followed by some loud swearing. "Oh no," I said. "That doesn't sound good."

Camilla stared up at the ceiling, as if trying to see through it. "I hope no one is hurt."

"I hope the air conditioners are still intact," I said, perhaps selfishly. Camilla had central air, but somehow it only cooled the ground floor of her big old house. When the heat wave began, Adam Rayburn, Camilla's steady boyfriend, enlisted the help of a group he called "The Three Amigos," namely Doug Heller, Sam West, and Cliff Blake, to install window units in the bedrooms upstairs. The younger men had spent a great deal of time together since the spring, and they did in fact seem to function well as a group of three—at least when they were doing "guy" things. At other times they invited me to join them, along with Doug's girlfriend, Belinda.

"It will be nice to have those window units," Camilla said. "They should make for better sleeping. Adam assured me that they are not loud."

"It will be wonderful. Up until this last week I never had a problem with the temperature. I slept with the window open and always had a nice breeze. But now the air is just—stagnant. I thought it was always cooler by the lake."

Camilla nodded. "We mostly have mild summers, but we've always been prone to heat waves in July. I know you're more of a fall person, aren't you? And you do look a bit like a wilted flower there on the floor."

"I'll perk up now that I'm in here. But walking to town this morning wasn't a good idea. It's incredibly humid out there."

We heard loud footsteps descending the stairs, and Doug's blond head poked into the room. "Camilla, where might I find a tool box?"

Camilla pointed. "The closet in the kitchen hallway. Bottom shelf."

"Great, thanks!" he said, darting into the next room.

"Everything okay up there?" Camilla asked.

"Fine," Doug said. "A minor emergency, but we handled it."

"You taught me some new swear words," I called to him, winking at Camilla.

Doug appeared in the doorway with a guilty expression. "You heard that? It wasn't me, anyway, it was Cliff. Something fell on his toe."

"Oh my gosh! Is he okay?" I asked. The dogs became alert at my tone; their ears stood at attention.

"He's fine. He's looking forward to the cold beer Camilla promised."

"I'm chilling the glasses as we speak," Camilla said. She stood up behind her desk and moved toward the kitchen. She wore a light summer dress of pale pink and a pair of white sandals. "Let me go check on them."

Doug went in with her, and I was left alone with the dogs. "I mean it, you guys, that's enough petting. I'm too hot to be surrounded by fur." I gave them each one last pat and then pushed slightly on their flanks. They got the message and ambled over to Camilla's desk, under which they liked to sleep during the day.

The doorbell rang. I managed to pull myself upright, feeling languid still, and walked to the entrance hall. I peered through the window to see an elderly woman on the steps, looking like a mirage in the hazy heat; I did not recognize her.

I opened the door. "Hello."

She studied me for a moment. She was tall and thin, with a halo of white hair, and she wore a black cotton dress that draped down to her ankles; it looked severe in the heat, almost punishing. Her hazel eyes were narrowed in a quizzical expression. "I'm here to see Camilla," she said.

"May I ask your name?" I said. I had no idea if this woman was a friend or a determined fan—Camilla did get unwelcome visitors now and again.

She jutted out her chin. "Tell her it's Jane Wyland. She knows who I am," she said. "But it's been a long, long time." She didn't smile when she said this.

I knew it would be polite to invite her in, but I didn't want to admit anyone to Camilla's house unless I knew Camilla wanted them there. "Excuse me for just a moment," I said. I left the door slightly ajar, so it didn't seem as if I were closing it in her face, and then I jogged to the kitchen.

Camilla was peering into the freezer, where the glasses were nicely chilled and waiting to be filled with beer. "Lena, can you call up to the boys and ask when they think they'll be down?"

The boys. This made me smile, but something about the woman at the door distracted me from my amusement. "Yes, in just a moment. I don't know if you heard the doorbell, but there's a woman here to see you."

She closed the freezer and looked at me, brows raised. "Oh? Who is it?"

"I don't know her. She said her name is Jane Wyland."

Camilla blinked at me. "Jane *Wyland*? I—my goodness. I haven't seen that woman in more than forty years."

"Should I—?"

"I'll talk to her. Thank you, Lena."

I lingered near the doorway and heard Camilla greet the woman in a rather stiff voice. The woman said something, and Camilla said, "Why don't you come in? We can talk in my study." And then, in response to a question, she said, "That was Lena. She is my friend and writing collaborator. She lives here with me, actually."

They were closer now, and I heard Jane Wyland say, "You probably didn't think you'd ever hear from me again, did you, Camilla?"

Camilla's voice was smooth, unruffled, when she said, "I confess I didn't imagine our paths would cross, but then again I encounter very few people these days."

They went into Camilla's office, and Camilla closed the door.

A shadow moved on the wall, and I jumped when a pair of hands touched my shoulders. "Hey," said Sam West.

I turned and whispered, "Hey."

He leaned in to give me a warm kiss. "Hey," I said again, appreciatively.

"Why are you whispering?" he asked, smiling at me.

I spoke a bit louder, though still quietly. "Camilla has some woman in there. She hasn't seen her in decades, and they went in the office and closed the door."

"Do you think we should call the police?"

I poked him in the chest. "Very funny. But I've got a weird vibe. And it's not like ominous things haven't happened around here before."

"That's for sure." He looked around the kitchen. "I'm supposed to make sure that beer is in the offing."

"Oh, right. I'll help you pour." We retrieved the chilled glasses from the freezer and I pulled three bottles of Corona from the fridge. As we worked, I asked, "Everything okay up there?"

He was pouring carefully, trying to avoid too much foam. "Your chamber shall be cool and pleasant, my queen."

"Oh, thank goodness. I just cannot sleep when it's this hot."

He took a sip of his drink. "If you were awake, you should have walked down the hill to your boyfriend's house and told him you couldn't sleep. He has all sorts of ideas for night activities."

I laughed. Doug and Cliff came in and practically dove on the refreshments. Sam said, "Do you guys have time to sit for a while?" They nodded, and our group of four moved to Camilla's sunroom.

I flopped into a chair near the window. "Thank you so much to all of you. I am not a creature who thrives in the heat. Camilla said I looked like a wilted flower, and I felt like one this past week."

"You need to go down and jump in the lake when it gets this hot," Doug said, shrugging. "Belinda and I have been in the water constantly."

"You just want to see her in a bathing suit," I joked.

Doug grinned. "She has some great bathing suits, but we've also opted for the au naturel experience. She rocks that, too."

Sam's eyes met mine. "We should swim more, Lena."

Cliff sighed. "Have a heart. Some people at this table have no significant other."

I touched his arm. "Why is that? How does a handsome guy like you end up coming to Blue Lake all alone?"

Cliff took a swig of beer and sighed. "Sam has already heard this whole story. There was someone. Beth. We lived together for several years. It didn't work out, but we parted on good terms. I think she's married now." He looked out the window at the lake, which was still as glass on this windless day.

"Maybe she just wasn't the right one for you," I said.

Cliff shrugged. "I've always been a little too devoted to the job. And I was—kind of obsessing over Sam West in those years. Following up on every little thing I could learn about my little brother here. Beth told me to just contact him, but I was stubborn."

We thought about that for a while. Cliff had finally taken a job in Blue Lake just to be closer to Sam, who hadn't known he had a half brother in the world.

Doug pointed at his fellow cop. "We've got to get this guy back into the dating pool. Lots of attractive women in this town."

I studied Cliff and had a sudden inspiration. "You know what, Cliff? I know someone I think you would really enjoy meeting. And I know she would like you. You meet several of her criteria for what makes a good man."

Sam laughed. "And how do you know this woman's criteria?"

"She went to high school with Allison and me. She graduated a couple years before we did; she pursued law school, and she got a job at a law firm in Chicago, but they ended up cutting her loose because the firm was downsizing. Allison's been trying to get her to Blue Lake—you know Allison. She wants all her friends to come here."

"It worked with you," Doug said. We exchanged a smile, both recalling the day that I came to town, lured by a phone call from Allison Branch.

"Allison's been sending her clippings of job openings at law firms in this area. Allie is hilarious in her enthusiasm, as always. But Isabelle really is considering coming out for some interviews."

"Isabelle," said Cliff appreciatively. "That's a pretty name."

"Yes." I studied him. "Isabelle's the whole package: smart, pretty, fun. Like you, she was with someone, but he ended up revealing his true character, and Isabelle dumped him."

"Good for her," Sam said.

Cliff shrugged. "Well, if she ever comes to town, I'd be happy to meet her. Meanwhile, I'm on duty in about an hour and I need to get home and put on the uniform."

Doug's face changed; he always looked serious when he thought about cop things. "I'm off today, and I have plans to take Belinda to Warrenville for a movie and dinner. But if you hear any more about our vandal, let me know."

"Blue Lake has a vandal?" I asked.

Doug and Cliff both took on that shuttered look that law enforcement people get when they can't share information. "Don't we always?" Doug said lightly. He stood up, and so did Cliff.

I turned to Sam. "I think your playmates are leaving."

Sam stood, too, and joined the other two as they walked to the kitchen door. The men exchanged some of those hearty man-hugs and thumped each other loudly on the back. I darted in and hugged them all, too. "I appreciate your help, and I always love your company. Come back soon, and we'll play a board game in Camilla's nice cool house."

"Invite Isabelle, too," Cliff joked.

Doug put a hand on my shoulder. "Belinda wants to have a little get-together at her place soon. She'll be contacting you."

"Okay! Sounds fun," I said.

I waved and watched from the kitchen doorway as Sam walked them to the front door and saw them out. He turned to say something to me but was interrupted by a loud voice.

"Of course you would protect him! You were in *love* with him!"

Camilla's study door flew open and the woman named Jane Wyland came stalking out, her fists clenched at her sides. Camilla emerged as well, her face paler than I had ever seen it, her eyes desolate.

The Wyland woman moved to the front door without saying a word, but when she reached the place where Sam stood, she pointed at him and said, "The notorious Sam West. It figures *he* would be your friend. That says a lot about your family, doesn't it? The whole *Graham* family. I'll be back tomorrow, Camilla. So make your decision."

She scowled at me, and then at Sam, and then she swept out of the door.

Shocked, I turned to Camilla, who seemed on the verge of tears. "Camilla? What in the world—?"

She held up a hand. "Lena, would you call Adam and cancel my lunch date with him?"

"Yes, if you want, but Camilla, are you all right? That woman—"

She covered her face with her hands for a moment, and then moved swiftly to the stairs. She spared me one quick glance; her eyes were full of tears. "I can't talk about this right now," she said, and she ran up the stairs toward her room.

Sam and I stared at each other across the space of the foyer, our mouths open in disbelief.

Finally he said, "Who was that woman?"

I narrowed my eyes. In the ten months I had known her,

Camilla had never lost her composure in any situation. And no one had ever dared to speak to her in that tone. Now this Wyland woman, this stranger, in her grim black attire, had waltzed in and upset my mentor, my friend—my family. "I don't know," I said. "But I'm going to find out."

I ran out the front door and saw that she was just reaching her car—a long dark vehicle that seemed to emanate heat. I tore down the steps and met her as she was unlocking the door. "Miss Wyland," I said. "I think there's been a misunderstanding. Camilla is very upset . . . "

If I thought that confronting her would make her back down, I thought wrong. Her face looked almost triumphant when she heard about Camilla's distress. "Oh, did I upset her? Well, that is a shame, isn't it? For forty years this family hasn't faced justice, and now that I try to hold them accountable, you take her side. They'll *all* be on her side! That's why I am taking a different route. She'll want to keep the family pride intact, won't she? So now I have my chance. Now I can stand up for *my* family, and for once, people will listen. You can count on it." She climbed into her car and slammed the door.

I was too shocked to do anything but watch her drive away.

ADAM WAS CONCERNED when I called but promised to wait until he heard from Camilla before he came over.

Sam went home, promising to check in on me later. "Give her some space," he advised. "She'll open up eventually."

I did just that. I cleaned up the beer glasses and recycled the bottles; I went to the store and bought some ingredients for dinner salads (Camilla's chef, Rhonda, was in Italy for two weeks with her family, so we were in charge of our meals); I walked the dogs briefly, until I couldn't stand the heat anymore; I took a brief, cooling shower and donned a T-shirt and some shorts; and I ruffled the fur of my cat, Lestrade, who lay stretched out to his full length on my bed, letting the new stream of chilled air cool his belly.

Then I went to see Camilla. Her room was a space I did not normally enter, although I'd ventured in once or twice if called there. It was a wide airy room that looked down on the driveway, the start of the path down the bluff, and the forest vista behind it. Camilla's bedspread was a lovely European-looking blend of garden colors, and above it hung a framed reproduction of Pierre Bonard's *Woman Writing*, given to her as a gift by her late husband, James. He told Camilla that it reminded him of her when they first met. On a table near the window sat a vase of flowers and an antique typewriter that had belonged to Camilla's grandmother. There was a blotter there, too, so that Camilla could write her correspondence or jot ideas for books if they came to her while she lounged.

She sat at this table now, looking out the two panes of the window that didn't hold the new air conditioner. I had already opened the door to peer in at her, but I knocked on it. "Camilla? I waited a few hours, but I wanted to check on you."

"Come in, Lena," she said.

I moved into the room, which felt cool and smelled subtly like Camilla's perfume. "Are you all right?" I asked, sitting on the edge of her bed.

"I'm better now, thank you."

"I—I don't understand what that woman wanted."

She turned to face me for the first time. Her eyes were dry now, and her color looked better, but she still looked distressed. "I don't understand, either. I confess I am at a loss. I need to ask for your help."

"Of course! Anything, Camilla. You know that."

She nodded. "You are such a sweet girl." She got up and came to sit next to me. I put an arm around her.

"Tell me," I said.

"I only met Jane Wyland a few times, when James and I were first married. He was working near Blue Lake, and we came to live here for a time. His mother had died, and his father was ailing, so James and I essentially ran the house. He had a brother, Allan, but he had moved to Philadelphia."

"You've mentioned Allan," I said, my tone encouraging.

"William Graham was an influential man here in Blue Lake. His family, for generations, had owned businesses in the town. James's great-grandfather ran the sawmill, and his uncle had a stake in what is now Schuler's ice cream. His father was on the School Board and had his own law practice in Blue Lake. It no longer exists."

"Ah."

"Back to Jane," she said. "When James and I first arrived, he gave me a tour of the town. He was a proud local boy; he loved Blue Lake and was happy to have me here. We ran across Jane at a pub in town called The Lumberjack. It's no longer there, either, but it was a favorite haunt of the locals. James introduced me to Jane, and everyone was very polite, but there was palpable tension. Jane taught at the local grade school—"

"She taught children?"

"She was very good, and very popular. The parents and children loved her, from what I heard. I thought, at the time, that my children might one day end up in her class, and I said something of the sort to her."

This made me sad. I knew that Camilla found, not long after arriving in Blue Lake, that she could not have children. "So you were all—friends?"

She shook her head. "No—Jane was friendly, or at least polite. But there was something stiff about her even then. Something felt off with the encounter, and when I mentioned that she might one day teach my children, she stood up quite abruptly, although she'd been there dining with some friends, and said she had to go. And she left, to the surprise of her friends and the consternation of James. He was quite upset about the scene, as I recall."

"That must have been, what, 1970?"

"1971. Just after our wedding, when we came to Blue Lake for the first time."

"What did James say after that?"

She shrugged. "I asked him about it when we returned home. Here," she said, gesturing around us. "He said he didn't know what would have caused her to react that way, but that he felt badly about it. He said she was a nice woman, and that they had always gotten on well. He had gone to school with her."

"How strange—the whole encounter."

"Yes. After that I saw her now and again in town, and she was polite, but rather—cold. Then a couple years later she moved out of Blue Lake, although I think she still taught at the grade school. I never ran across her again. Until today."

I squeezed her shoulder. "What did she want?"

"She said she wanted to 'finally make things right.' I had no idea what she meant, and told her so. She said she felt sorry for me, because I was ignorant of the Graham family's biggest secret."

"Maybe she just always resented them. They were

powerful, and rather wealthy, right? Living in this big house on the bluff. Maybe life disappointed her, and . . ."

"I don't think so. The Wylands were a nice family. Well respected, well educated, although James did say they had some unlucky investments and were always at a loss for money. In fact, Jane had a sister who once worked for James's family. James said she was very sweet, and did a good job. She came every day to clean and cook; it was especially helpful because his father needed looking after, which took James's time when he wasn't working. He really didn't have anything bad to say about the Wylands."

"But this Jane is insisting that the family has a secret?"

Camilla nodded. "Yes. And normally I would dismiss it as nonsense, but she's given me a bit of an ultimatum."

"She *what*?"

"Yes. She said that I should tell the truth to the press about my husband James, or she will."

"What truth is she referring to?"

Camilla looked into my eyes, and I saw the worry in hers. "I have no idea," she said.

Ready to find
your next great read?

Let us help.

Visit prh.com/nextread